HOKUS
POKUS

FERN MICHAELS

HOKUS POKUS

Doubleday Large Print
Home Library Edition

ZEBRA BOOKS
KENSINGTON PUBLISHING CORP.

ZEBRA BOOKS are published by

Kensington Publishing Corp.
850 Third Avenue
New York, NY 10022

ISBN-13: 978-0-7394-9073-0

Printed in the United States of America

**This Large Print Book carries the
Seal of Approval of N.A.V.H.**

HOKUS POKUS

Prologue

McLean, Virginia

When Judge Cornelia Easter looked up at the monitor outside her security gate, she gasped so loud that the two cats she was holding leaped to the ground. She heaved herself out of her recliner and hobbled over to the security system to press a button. "Pearl, is that you?"

"Does it look like me, Nellie? Will you open this damn gate and let me in before someone sees me out here? Hurry up, Nellie."

Her mind racing, Nellie Easter pressed the remote that would open the huge iron gates (compliments of the federal government). The moment the gates opened, a battered black pickup truck barreled through.

Nellie winced at the sound of the truck's grinding gears when it screeched to a stop outside her kitchen door. She held the door open for her old friend. "Pearl, it's after midnight. What in the name of God are you doing out here? What's wrong?"

"Everything's wrong, that's what's wrong. God, Nellie, I didn't know where else to go except here. You have to help me."

"Do you want a drink? Whose truck is that?"

"Hell yes, I want a drink and the truck belongs to the gardener. I stole it. How else do you think I got away from my security detail? Being the chief justice of the United States Supreme Court isn't easy these days with all those nutcases out there ready to bump us off. You had your share of that when you were on the bench so you know what I'm talking about. It must be wonderful not to have all those people crawling all over you. You said something about a drink. Make it a triple, straight up, no ice. How's your arthritis?"

"Worse than ever," Nellie said as she poured a good four ounces of 100 proof bourbon into a squat glass that almost overflowed. She blinked as she watched her longtime friend down the contents in three long gulps and then hold the glass out for a refill. Nellie poured with a steady hand. Whatever brought Pearl Barnes out here had to be serious. Pearl would sip at sherry on occasion. Nellie found herself wondering if her old friend was a closet drinker.

Who was this wild-looking woman drinking 100 proof bourbon in her kitchen? Where was the impeccably coiffed, Chanel-wearing Pearl Barnes who had come to her retirement party just months ago? The same Pearl Barnes who had whispered in her ear, "Now you can really go for the gusto, Nellie." And then Pearl had winked at her and Nellie felt her blood run cold. She didn't sleep well for weeks afterward, wondering if somehow the chief justice knew about her role in the Sisterhood.

"I think that will do it for now, but don't put the bottle away. Is this house secure? Is it monitored in any way since you retired?"

"It's safe. They sweep it twice a week.

I like your outfit," Nellie said, tongue in cheek.

Pearl Barnes looked down at the dirty bib overall she was wearing. "It belongs to the gardener. I stole it when I stole his truck." She reached up to remove the baseball cap she'd scrunched down over her gray hair. "Do I smell? I seem to smell manure."

"I wasn't going to say anything," Nellie grinned, "but, yes, you smell. How about if I make some coffee? Are you hungry?"

"Yes to the coffee and no to the food. I'll probably never eat again. I need your help, Nellie. And it goes without saying, I was never here. Are we straight on that?"

Nellie nodded as she spooned coffee into a cone-shaped filter. She pressed the coffeemaker's red button, then took her seat across the table from her old friend. "Spit it out, Pearl."

"I need you to get in touch with the Sisterhood. Yes, I know all about it. I want you to tell Myra I need her help and don't pretend you don't know what I'm talking about. I know you're involved up to your ears with those women. I watched you that day in court. You were so slick you made me proud of you. I cheered you all on. But I *know,* Nellie, so don't insult me by playing games. In case you haven't noticed, I'm desperate or I wouldn't be here."

"Pearl, what's wrong?" Nellie wasn't about to give up anything until she knew what was troubling one of the most powerful women in the nation.

Both women waited silently for the coffee to finish dripping. The moment the cup was in Pearl Barnes's hand she gulped at the coffee, her gaze raking the modern kitchen. "I like this kitchen. I like to cook, but then you know that, right? What do you do about the yellow leaves on the plants?"

"I throw them out. I'm going to throttle you if you don't tell me why you're here. I've never seen you frightened before, Pearl. Is it your daughter or did something happen to Grant?"

"It's me, Nellie. And, yes, Beka. And my granddaughter, Mandy, too. Grant is... Grant is just Grant. That doesn't seem to be working out these days, either."

Nellie clenched her teeth as she played with the fringe on the placemat in front of her. With all the patience she could muster, she said, "Tell me everything."

Pearl gulped more coffee. "Myra isn't the only one who broke the law, not to mention all those other women. You, too, Nellie. I... Well, what I do is... Oh, God, I don't know if I can say this out loud."

"Well, you damn well better and you better do it quick." Nellie sloshed bourbon into Pearl's coffee cup.

"Fine! Fine! I'll tell you. I operate an underground railroad for... for... women with kids—mothers whose husbands, fathers and boyfriends abuse them and get away with it. Grant and I have been doing it for years. We've saved thousands of women and children. There, I said it. Beka's ex-husband, that Tyler, is threatening to blow the whistle on me. I have no idea how he found out. He's an arrogant bastard. Now do you see why I need the Sisterhood?"

Nellie stared across the room at a stained glass panel hanging over her kitchen window. It was her pride and joy. She tried to contain her astonishment. Whatever she had thought Pearl was going to tell her, this wasn't it. She tried desperately to wrap her mind around the words she'd just heard.

"Say something, for God's sake! Can't you see I need help? I'm a sister under the skin. This is not a trap, if that's what you're thinking. Nellie, I need you to say something right now."

"How long have you been...uh...doing this?" Nellie managed to choke out.

"Since before I was nominated. I couldn't turn my back on those women any more than you and the Sisterhood could. I lied to everyone, even Grant in the beginning, and then when he started to get suspicious, I had to tell him. He's into it just as much as I am but I think his interest is waning. Will you please fill this cup up again?"

"Do you have a window of time here? Did something specific happen that brought you here? Are you sure no one knows you came out here?"

"No one knows I came out here. If there's one thing I've learned, it's how to watch my back. Grant doesn't even know I'm here. And, I never told him my suspicions about you, Myra and the others. As to the window of time, I don't know. A week maybe, possibly a little longer would be my guess, unless I can stall Tyler Hughes.

He's trying to blackmail me. He wants me to vote...a certain way on...something. I can't go into that with you, Nellie."

"What is it you want?" Nellie asked in a shaky voice. She stuck her old, gnarled hand into the pocket of her sweater to touch the special phone Charles Martin had given her.

"Oh, God, Nellie, I don't know. For Tyler to be...taken care of, I guess. The problem is I don't know who else he might have told. I don't know if I should take Beka and Mandy and get the hell out of Dodge or not. I suspect that isn't a good idea right at this moment. Blackmailers never give up, they just keep coming back for more and more. I can't go to the authorities. My people need me, they depend on me and, most important, they trust me with their lives. God dammit, Nellie, are you going to help me or not?"

"Have you considered going to the FBI? The new director, Elias Cummings, is a good man."

"Cut the crap, Nellie. If you were me would you go to Elias Cummings?"

"Probably not. Listen to me. Go home and stall for time. Let me see what I can do.

Pearl, I can't promise anything. Make sure you understand that."

Pearl Barnes stood up and stared down at her friend. "Oh, I understand all right. Now it's your turn to understand. Either you help me or I blow the whistle on you and Jack Emery and that kickboxing guy. If I go down, so do you. On that note, I think I'll leave you now. Don't worry, I'm sober as a judge. No pun intended."

Nellie's jaw dropped as she watched the kitchen door open and close. She knew she was going to get sick. Should she wait for her stomach to erupt until after she called Charles Martin or should she just get it over with?

The special encrypted phone in her hand, Nellie took a moment to think about her retirement and all the things she'd planned on doing. She shuddered as a vision of a six-by-nine-foot prison cell appeared behind her closed eyelids. A mighty sigh escaped her lips as she pressed the numbers on the special phone. With the time difference between Virginia and Spain, the members of the Sisterhood would probably be having breakfast right this minute.

Chapter 1

Barcelona, Spain

Charles Martin stood in the middle of his command center, a setup that would have been the envy of the CIA or the White House if they knew about it. He stared at the wraparound television monitors that displayed the 24-hour news channels and what was going on in the world in real time, but right now he wasn't interested in the news. He was trying to come to terms with Judge Nellie Easter's excited voice on the satellite encrypted phone at his ear.

"Slow down, Nellie. Tell me again, word for word, what Justice Barnes said to you." The voice on the other end rose shrilly

and Charles could hear the fright in the retired judge's voice. "All right, all right, I'm
getting the picture. I'll call Jack as soon as
I hang up. Try and get some sleep. I'll get
back to you in a bit." The squawking on the
other end of the line forced Charles to hold
the cell phone away from his ear. "That's
an order, Nellie."

Charles walked over to the round table
in the middle of the underground room.
He sat down, his mind going in all directions. If Nellie was right—and he had no
reason to believe she wasn't—he had to
take seriously the threat to his beloved
Sisterhood and Nellie herself, not to mention Jack Emery, Harry Wong, Lizzie Fox
and Maggie Spritzer.

He wondered why he was having so
much trouble comprehending Chief Justice
Barnes's extracurricular activities. After all,
he and the Sisterhood were doing the
same thing—breaking the law and serving
justice their way. He realized suddenly it
wasn't Pearl Barnes's activities that trou-
bled him but the threat she'd made to the
Sisterhood. Blackmail was something he
absolutely would not deal with. But, he
asked himself, was it his decision to make?

Charles looked down at the Patek Philippe chronometer on his wrist and then up at the row of clocks hanging between the plasma monitors. His girls were still sleeping since it was Sunday morning. Jack Emery would also be sleeping but he had no qualms about waking up the district attorney back in Washington. Before he could change his mind he pressed the buttons that would allow him to have a private conversation with Jack.

The groggy voice on the other end of the phone mumbled something that sounded like, *"This better be good."*

"I don't know about good, Jack, but it is important. Wake up and get some coffee and call me right back." Charles broke the connection before Jack could protest.

Charles Martin, aka Malcolm Sutcliff, aka *Sir* Malcolm Sutcliff, thanks to his friend Lizzie, also known as Queen Elizabeth II of England, leaned back and closed his eyes. He let his mind travel back in time to when he was a young man in Her Majesty's Secret Service. He'd met a very young Myra Rutledge and fallen in love but Myra's parents had whisked her back to America and he hadn't seen her again until his cover was blown as an MI6 special agent. With his government's help he'd been relocated to America to protect his life and the secrets he carried in his head. His new job was head of security for Myra's Fortune 500 candy company. He smiled when he recalled how they'd fallen in love all over again.

If he ever had any second thoughts about his situation, all he had to do was look at Myra and he knew this was where he belonged.

He continued to smile when he thought about how Myra had asked him to help her break the law. Not that she had to twist his arm. He was so glad to be back in the field he would have begged her to allow him to orchestrate the game she and her adopted daughter had come up with. And while it was dangerous, he had enough contacts all over the world to pull it all together.

Charles was jarred from his reminiscences when the encrypted phone rang. "Good morning, Jack."

"Charles, do you know what time it is? Of course you do, you take perverse pleasure in waking me from a deep sleep. What's up?"

Charles told him. From time to time he could hear Jack's intake of breath and a few mutterings. "That's where it is at the moment, Jack. I want you to gather the others and meet at the farm. I'll arrange things on this end and we'll have a conference via satellite."

"Wait just a damn minute, Charles. Tell me you aren't thinking what I think you're thinking."

"What would that be, Jack?"

"I'm not snatching the chief justice of the United States Supreme Court. Do you have any idea how much security those people have? No. You have to be crazy to even think...No! The others aren't ready for something like this. No. No, no, no! Even with Nikki and the others who are more seasoned, I'd still say no. Do you hear me, Charles? *I said no.* The old judge . . . Nellie . . . is so nervous she can't speak a clear sentence these days. Lizzie Fox and Maggie Spritzer are in no way ready for a mission of that magnitude. Even Harry will tell you to go pound salt. No! You are out of your frigging mind, Charles, if you think this is doable. It's beyond impossible. One more time, *no!*"

"What time can you get everyone together? Today is Sunday so it shouldn't be a problem. I don't need to remind you, you are all on call 24/7. I'm going to hang up now and make breakfast for my ladies. In the interests of normalcy, life goes on. Call me as soon as you have things set up."

"What are you making for breakfast, Charles?" Jack asked in a resigned voice.

"It's Sunday. Eggs Benedict. I'm waiting for the chickens to lay the eggs, which should be momentarily. What are you having?"

"A Pop-Tart."

Charles laughed. But his laughter died in his throat the moment he broke the connection. Jack was right. Nellie's little group was in no way ready for such a mission. His heart heavy, he made his way up the steep stone steps to the main part of the house on the mountaintop.

"There you are, my darling. I missed you," Myra Rutledge said as Charles entered the kitchen.

Charles stared at the love of his life. He smiled the way he always smiled at the first sight of his beloved in the morning. "Did you sleep well?" he asked as he gathered her in his arms. Myra always smelled so wonderful.

Charles held her a few moments longer than usual, just enough time for Myra to worry. She stepped backward and asked, "What is it, Charles? Did something happen during the night?"

How well she knew him. He must be losing his edge. There was no point in trying to hedge with Myra. "Yes, my dear, something happened. I thought I would wait and tell all of you at the same time. I promised Eggs Benedict this morning."

"Oh, dear, I don't like the sound of that at all. Of course, wait and tell us all together. I gathered the eggs as soon as I came downstairs. Can I help, darling?" Offering to help Charles in the kitchen wasn't something Charles appreciated. It was more a standing joke than anything else because Myra was a terrible cook.

"Are we eating on the terrace? If so, you can set the table. Do you know if the girls are up?"

"Yes, we're eating on the terrace. I heard the showers running when I came downstairs. The girls will be down soon. How bad is it, Charles?"

"It's not good, Myra."

Myra didn't press the subject. Charles would talk only when he was ready to talk.

Outside in the brisk mountain air, Myra stretched and looked out at her surroundings. It was breathtakingly beautiful. Beautiful but confining. She as well as the others still hadn't gotten used to the idea that they were prisoners of a sort. How she missed her farm back in the States. Still, she was lucky she wasn't in prison and she did have Charles with her. Home was wherever Charles was. The girls missed home, too, especially Nikki, her adopted daughter. Still, if Jack Emery was here, Nikki wouldn't care if she ever left the mountain.

In some ways this was paradise and in other ways it was hell on Earth because to leave this beautiful mountaintop in Spain meant a life in prison.

And to think this all began when her daughter Barbara was killed by a hit-and-run motorist who was untouchable because of his diplomatic immunity. She and her little band of ladies had taken care of the killer vigilante style, and avenged her daughter's death. It seemed like a life-time ago.

Myra's gaze went from the colorful flowers on the terrace to the sparkling blue Mediterranean below the mountain and then to the kitchen window where Charles was preparing breakfast for his flock. None of this could have been accomplished without Charles's expertise and the contacts he had in the covert world. Charles was her protector, her savior. God alone knew how much she loved that man.

Myra tilted her head to the side when she thought she heard a phone ringing in the kitchen, something that rarely happened. When Charles's special phone rang it usually meant trouble was brewing somewhere. She turned away to pluck a yellow leaf off one of the plants. When she turned around, Anna de Silva, childhood friend, one of the richest women in the world, and owner of this mountain retreat, greeted her with a huge smile.

"Another golden day in our lives, right, Myra? I don't think there's a spot in the whole world that can compare to this," Annie said, waving her arms about.

"Something is going on," Myra whispered. "Trouble," she clarified.

Annie's eyes popped wide. "When you say trouble, do you mean trouble or do you mean *trouble?* I didn't hear the bell ring at the base of the mountain. The cable car is still here. The padre said he would alert us if any strangers appeared in the village so the trouble isn't coming from there." She raced to the far side of the terrace to get a better view of the ocean below. "There aren't any boats down there except for two sailboats. That has to mean the trouble is back home."

"Exactly," Myra said softly.

"Do you think it has anything to do with our...our little ancillary group?" Annie clapped her hands in glee, her eyes alight with expectation. "A mission! Oh, I can hardly wait!"

"And to think not too long ago you were vegetating on this mountain and I almost pushed you off it. Now you've turned into this...this gung ho, bloodthirsty person."

"I prefer ass-kicking vigilante fighting crime the way only a woman can do it," Annie said, grinning from ear to ear. "I just love, *just love* getting the bad guys and making them pay. Our way. Oh, Myra, admit it, you love the action, too."

Myra laughed. "If I was thirty years younger I might just love, love all that action," she said, mimicking Annie.

"Age is merely a number. Most young people think people our age don't have sex, too. Look at you and Charles!"

Myra looked around, her face pink. "Annie, for God's sake, keep your voice down."

Annie lowered her voice. "Well, I'm not afraid to admit I could handle sex a couple of times a week. As you can see, there are no prospects up here on this mountain. I'm thinking of venturing forth in my quest for..."

"For heaven's sake, Annie, will you be quiet? I don't need to hear—"

"Stop being such a prude, Myra. Sex makes the world go round. Just ask the girls. They aren't *getting any,* either. We need to do something about that. We aren't nuns, you know."

"I knew I should have pushed you over that mountain that day. Enough!" Myra hissed as the girls descended on the terrace.

"Good morning, everyone," Annie chirped. "Isn't it a gorgeous day? I can't wait to take a walk and a swim. Charles said he's going to have a barbecue this evening. Weenies, burgers and ribs." She babbled on as the others listened indulgently. It was hard not to get caught up in Annie's enthusiasm. "If Charles allows it, let's take a sail this afternoon."

"Well, scratch that idea, as wonderful as it sounds. Charles is not going to allow it," the ever-verbal Kathryn Lucas shot back. "I say we gang up on him, head down the mountain and head out to open water and never ever come back."

The others gaped at Kathryn as they grappled with the scenario she had just presented.

Annie looked around the table. "Myra said Charles's phone rang. That means there is trouble somewhere. I think, girls, we're about to go on high alert. Code red."

"Damn, Annie, how many times did you watch that last espionage movie?" Alexis asked.

"A lot. I needed to get the verbiage down pat. Lingo is all important in this business. You have to be able to converse with your adversary in a language so he or she understands how serious you are so you get your point across before you belt him in his Adam's apple therefore rendering him speechless so you can then speak in your own refined lingo. Any questions?" Annie asked breezily.

Myra sighed. She'd created a monster. "No questions. Just shut up, Annie. Please," she pleaded as an afterthought.

"For you, Myra, anything." Annie shook out her linen napkin with a loud snap.

Charles opened the back door that led to the terrace. He held it open with his back as he slid a serving cart out onto the flagstone terrace. He tried for a cheerful note but knew he'd failed when the girls stared at him with unblinking intensity. He shifted into a neutral zone and said, "First we have breakfast, then we can talk."

The rule of thumb at mealtime at the monastery on the mountain was that no business was discussed until coffee was served.

"Darling, it all looks wonderful," Myra said. "Whatever would we do without you?" She busied herself pouring their usual Sunday-morning Mimosas.

"Well, I for one never want to find that out," Annie said as she dug into her Eggs Benedict. Low-voiced murmurings echoed her delight as Charles poured coffee from an heirloom coffee server.

Anyone observing the scene would have thought the breakfast meeting was a happy occasion, what with the women making small talk, occasionally laughing at something one of the others said.

As Charles sipped and munched and tried to keep up his end of the conversation, his mind raced with what and how he was going to tell the women when they retired to the command center. His latest phone call had disturbed him more than he cared to admit.

He looked up, aware of the sudden silence at the table. "Yes, my mind is somewhere else. I wasn't expecting... Well, let's just say few things in this life can surprise me. This morning I was surprised. So, clean up, ladies, since I did the cooking, and then join me in the command center where I will inform you of some very startling events that have just transpired on the other side of the pond."

Nikki Quinn's eyes challenged Charles, as did Yoko's.

"Both of your gentlemen friends are fine, ladies," Charles said, getting up from the table. "It really is a beautiful day. Did I tell you I plan to barbecue this evening?"

"Yeah, you said you were going to roast a whole steer," Kathryn mumbled.

"Hmmm," Charles said as he left the terrace.

"See, see, he didn't even hear what I said. I've never seen Charles so..." Kathryn paused, suddenly at a loss for words.

"'Distracted' is the word you're looking for. Charles has always been unflappable. He's the glue that holds us together. I for one find this new Charles a little scary," Isabelle said.

"At least we know Harry and Jack are okay. Whatever it is, the problem is back in the States. Maybe we can go home again," Yoko said wistfully. "I would like to drive by my old flower shop to see what it looks like. Of course I want to see Harry, too. If we go back to the States I might decide to marry him."

Alexis hooted with laughter. "How will that work, Yoko, with you living here on top of a mountain in Spain and Harry Wong back in the United States? I seem to recall you saying the same thing the last time we were in the States."

The diminutive Yoko fixed her gaze on Alexis. She spoke slowly and deliberately. "Maybe I won't come back. Assuming, of course, that we even go back to the States."

"Then you'll go to prison," Kathryn Lucas said coldly. "This is our life now, so get used to it, kiddo."

Sensing a mini rebellion Myra slid her chair back from the table. "Girls, let's all calm down and wait to see what Charles has to say. I'll take Murphy and Grady for a short walk around the compound. It will be good exercise for the dogs and for me, too."

"Knock yourself out," Kathryn said.

"What's bothering you, Kathryn?" Nikki asked.

"Nothing. Everything. I got up early this morning and went for a walk. While this mountain paradise is all rather wonderful, I don't know if I can stay here. I know, I know, prison is not an alluring alternative. My clock is ticking, Nikki. I can't even believe I'm saying this because when my husband died, I swore I would never look at another man, nor would I ever get married. Now, because I can't have that, I want it more than anything in the world. I don't know how you do it, Nik. Jack is back in the States, you're here, you're engaged. You're in love. Just tell me how you do it."

Nikki gathered up a stack of plates and loaded them onto the serving cart. "Take a good look at me, Kathryn. Do I look like I'm handling it very well? I don't want to go to prison, that's my bottom line. I cry myself to sleep at night. I live for Jack's phone calls just the way Yoko lives for Harry to call her. My only consolation is that we have made a difference. I also tell myself if we didn't do what we've been doing, someone else would. At least we're in control of our lives. There are people all over the world who know about us, who want our help. I have to be satisfied with that. By the way, my clock is ticking, too."

Kathryn licked at her dry lips as she stacked up the coffee cups next to the plates. She nodded. "Maybe I just need to kick someone's ass."

Nikki brushed at her short blond hair. "I don't know why I say this but I think you just might get a chance to do that. Come on, I'll hold the door and you push the cart. Alexis and Isabelle can load the dishwasher."

The screen door slammed shut with a loud bang. The women in the kitchen whirled around. "Alexis thinks the FBI or maybe the CIA has a lead on us and that's what has Charles worried. There's no place to go from here," Annie said. "I happen to love it here and I have no intention of letting a bunch of people who talk into their sleeves, wear sunglasses even in the dark and are only known by the initials of their organizations take us out of here."

"Well, damn, when did you turn into such a scrapper, Annie?" Kathryn demanded.

"I'm a late bloomer." Annie looked around to make sure the kitchen was neat and tidy. The dishwasher whirred to life just as Myra entered the kitchen. Both dogs walked around the table before they lay down to take a nap.

The others looked at Myra as she squared her shoulders for the trip down the steps to the catacombs where, thanks to Isabelle's architectural expertise, there was an exact replica of the command center back at Myra's farmhouse in McLean, Virginia.

The first thing the women noticed was that all the plasma television screens were blank except the one that showed Lady Justice balancing a set of scales.

Nikki, typical lawyer, correctly interpreted the blank plasma screens: whatever was going on in the world that was newsworthy wasn't as important as what was going to be said in this room. She leaned back and waited for Charles to speak. She wished her heart wasn't fluttering so madly in her chest. She didn't have to look at the others to know they were feeling the same way. *Get on with it, Charles,* her mind shrieked.

Charles walked over to stand under the plasma screen showing Lady Justice. He cleared his throat. When he was sure he had their attention he said, "It seems that the chief justice of the United States Supreme Court, Pearl Barnes, sought out

Judge Easter and threatened to blow us and, of course, Nellie and the others, out of the water unless we help her. It appears that for the past twenty or so years, Justice Barnes has been doing much the same thing we've been doing—breaking the law. To be specific, she's been running an underground railroad leading women and children to safety. Her ex–son-in-law has threatened to expose her and she needs our help. Neither Nellie nor I know if Justice Barnes was making an idle threat to expose all of us—Nellie and her new recruits in particular—or if she is scared out of her wits.

"That information was in my first call from Nellie. Nellie then made a second phone call to me. Justice Barnes left a note in her mailbox that said seventeen women and children are stranded at the second-to-last stop on her underground railroad somewhere in Oregon. There is no way for Justice Barnes to move them out to the next leg of the journey since she is under such scrutiny. The evil ex–son-in-law, Tyler Hughes, works for a very prestigious think tank in Washington. His threat to Justice Barnes concerns a vote in a very important decision. It is not known how many people besides Hughes know about the underground railroad.

"In a few minutes we'll be having a conference meeting via satellite with Nellie and the others. Now you can talk, ladies."

Chapter 2

The moment the words were out of Charles's mouth, Nikki Quinn spoke up. "Does this mean we're going back across the pond?" Oh, let it be so, she prayed silently. If that was what Charles had in mind, she would see Jack again.

"We need to discuss the matter in great detail, ladies. We threw caution to the winds once since arriving here when we went back to take on the director of the FBI. Yes, you were successful in outing him, but that doesn't mean your luck will hold a second time. However, I'm open to any and all suggestions as long as you understand I have the final word."

Myra leaned forward. "I don't understand, Charles. How did Pearl manage to keep that kind of secret? When she was nominated to the Court the vetting process was so intense I cried for her. They dissected her to the bone and laid her bare. I know for a fact she wanted to throw in the towel but her daughter and Grant Conlon talked her out of it. It's a lifetime position. I guess she lied and got away with it," she finished sadly.

"She'll have to resign," Isabelle said. "Being vetted and being subjected to the media circus will be more than most people can tolerate. We're the living proof. And, she'll be looking at prison time. I just don't understand how she figured us out. Or, is she shooting blanks in the hope we respond? How could she possibly *know?*" she repeated. "I was there in court, as you all were. Jack, Lizzie and Nellie gave the performance of their lives in their quest to save us from prison. Something isn't right."

"Trust me, she knows," Myra said quietly. "Annie, Nellie and I have known Pearl since we were six years old. We went to the same schools, the same dance classes. We came out together. There was a time when we were fast friends but life has a habit of getting in the way. I still consider us friends. Pearl never issued a statement when we were caught. The press hounded her and all she would say was we grew up together and she had no comment. She was closer to Nellie than to Annie and me because they both worked in the District. I like her. In her position, I'd threaten us, too."

"Pearl is a 'what you see is what you get' kind of person," Annie said in defense of her old friend.

Charles cleared his throat. "Justice Barnes told Nellie that she watched the court proceedings and she silently cheered you all on. I imagine, knowing Nellie as well as she does, she saw something no one else saw. In the end it doesn't matter. She knows. We're the deer in the headlights, ladies."

"It is not a good place to be," Yoko said so quietly it sounded as though she were whispering.

"What can we do?" Alexis asked.

"Well, if my vote counts, I say we find a way to help Pearl," Annie said.

"We all need to understand one thing here," Nikki said. "This won't just be helping Justice Barnes. The women and children in the underground have to be helped. Something will have to be done with the ex–son-in-law and anyone else he might have told about Pearl. A trifecta, girls. I agree Justice Barnes needs help."

The others murmured their agreement. Even Myra, who was obviously worried by Nikki's words.

Charles moved quickly when he heard a pinging sound announcing an email. "This might be Jack. We're about to have a video conference if he can work it out from his end. You'll all have a voice in whatever decision we come up with."

The only sounds to be heard in the underground room were the soft whirring of the ventilating system and the tapping of computer keys. Suddenly the tapping stopped and Lady Justice disappeared from the overhead screen. The women seated at the round table ooohed and aaahed as they saw their counterparts seated at an identical table back in Virginia. The second string, so to speak. Jack stood at the step-up railing next to the plasma screen. Maggie, Lizzie and Nellie looked cranky and half-asleep at the round table. Harry Wong looked alert. Jack looked angry.

How wonderful Jack looks, Nikki thought. Out of the corner of her eye she could see Yoko wave to Harry. He smiled in return and wiggled his fingers.

Jack *was* angry. The women could hear it in his voice. "So, what's it to be, Charles?" he demanded. "You sending your posse over here or are we on our own?"

"Can you handle it, Jack?" Charles asked evenly.

"It depends on the time constraints and the game plan. Do you have a game plan, Charles?" He spoke in a voice Nikki had never heard before. She shivered at what she thought it could mean.

"Not at the moment, Jack. I need a few hours. Nellie, you spoke to Justice Barnes. Did she give you any idea how terminal her situation is? With all her security, how are you to get in touch with her?"

"She wants it all yesterday. She was scared out of her wits, Charles. For her to come out to the farm in the middle of the night proved it. She didn't say how we

were to get in touch. I would think anything and everything would be suspect.
Perhaps we could get in touch through
her daughter, Beka. Or I could call her
and arrange a lunch date with Grant. Jack
and Harry could be dining at the same
restaurant. Or maybe Maggie could offer
to do a piece on her for the *Post*. Lizzie
could go to the art gallery where Beka
works. We have avenues to explore but I
don't think we have much time. A week,
possibly a few days longer, according to
Pearl."

"I don't know if I need to remind any of
you of this," Jack said, "but Grant Conlon,
Justice Barnes's longtime significant
other, is the brother-in-law of Elias Cummings, the new director of the FBI."

"Grant is as committed as Pearl is to
her . . . her cause," Nellie said.

"What exactly does Pearl want or expect us to do?" Myra asked. "Does she
want us to spirit her away? Does she want
us to kidnap her or the ex–son-in-law,
Hughes? Then the jig is up and the world
knows what she's done. Or does she want
us to . . . uh . . . take care of Hughes so she
can go back to her life without fear and

worry? We need more to go on, Nellie. What about the women and children stranded in Oregon?"

Lizzie Fox made her presence known. "How many people know what Hughes knows? Do we know what it is he wants her to vote on? I can have a profile of him within an hour. I'm willing to put my ass on the line to get to him if you think that's what's needed. Plus, I know the guy. He's an egotistical son of a bitch. He's also very smart. The crafty conniving kind of smart. I heard, but I don't know if it's true or not, that Justice Barnes paid through the nose to get him out of Beka's life. Seven figures," she said sourly. "High seven figures. Guess he went through it all already. He's a high-dollar spender. There are also whispers that he's a gambler. He's the type that likes to be seen and talked about. A mover and a shaker. Most people think he's a bit of a joke."

Maggie Spritzer raised her hand. "How about if I interview him? I can say I'm doing a profile, talking to *everyone* in Justice Barnes's life, and that includes an ex–son-in-law."

"Well, it appears we have options,"

Charles said. "We need a time frame. How soon can we get that? Nellie?"

"It's five o'clock in the morning here. At seven o'clock I can call and invite Pearl and Grant to brunch in town. But inviting Grant might be a mistake since Pearl said he doesn't know about Hughes's threat. As you know, brunch is big in this town on Sunday. Jack and Harry can be there. Everyone goes to brunch on Sunday so I don't think it will throw up any red flags. What that means is if Lizzie and Maggie want to go, I don't think it will cause a stir of any kind. The big question is, what do I tell Pearl and what do I promise her?"

Nikki spoke for the first time, her eyes on Jack. "If you do that, Nellie, it's an admission of guilt and we're caving in to her threat. I don't think we want to do that, do we? We all know you can never get out from under a blackmailer. We could, however, work undercover and try to stay out of sight. It's just a thought," she said.

Jack smiled for Nikki's benefit. "Nik's right. We need to kick this around a bit more. Worst case scenario, I'm sure Harry and I can figure out a way to snatch the justice. We'll need a little backup but I think we can pull it off. That will halt any threat to us by Justice Barnes, at which point we'll put all our efforts into Hughes and the people he's working for."

"I like that idea," Annie said, excitement ringing in her voice. She turned around and fixed Myra with a wide grin. "I'd gladly pay money to see the expression on Pearl's face when we pull her bacon out of the fire. She always thought she was smarter than we were. In a nice way, of course. Ha!"

"We also need to find out if the women and children at the underground stop in Oregon are in any kind of danger," Charles said. "We'll shut down for now and reconvene in three hours. With the time difference it will still give you time to do a brunch if you think it's a viable plan."

Before anyone could say good-bye the plasma screen went dark. Lady Justice once more looked down on the women. Nikki bit down on her lower lip. She felt like crying. She risked a glance at Yoko, who had tears in her eyes.

"Well, this is certainly something to chew on," Kathryn said. "Let's run this up the flagpole and see if anyone salutes.

I say we head home to help out. Our little group back in Virginia is top-notch but I don't think they're up to a gig like this one. Alexis, shift gears and tell us how you can get us back to the States with the aid of your Red Bag of magic tricks. This might be a good time for you, Annie, to haul out that spiffy yacht you have in dry dock and make it work for us."

"You're a thinker, Kathryn. I like that. So while you're thinking, try to come up with a crew for my spiffy yacht that won't draw attention to us," Annie said smartly. "A yacht is not the way to go if one is in a hurry."

"Annie's yacht, the *Moonraker,* is being readied as we speak," Charles said quietly. Myra smiled. Why had she doubted even for a moment that Charles would have things under control?

Back in Virginia, Maggie Spritzer and Lizzie Fox were now wide-awake as they waited for Nellie or Jack to speak. Nellie leaned forward and started to speak as Jack flopped down in his chair next to Harry Wong, the number two martial arts expert in the world.

"In my opinion it's dangerous for the others to cross the pond," Nellie said. "I do admit I would feel better if they were here, but if there is any way we can do this on our own, I don't think we should jeopardize the others. If they get caught again there's no one left to help them. They'll go to prison and there won't be a thing we can do. Do any of you have any suggestions?"

"I say you go the brunch route," Jack said. "We'll all be there as lookouts. Justice Barnes will have security. I think we need to get as much information as possible about Hughes, so, Lizzie, dig up all the info you can on the guy. Maggie, see if you can get in touch with Justice Barnes's daughter. I know it's Sunday, but try to make an appointment to speak with her tomorrow at the art gallery where she works. If she agrees, make it as early as possible."

"I guess this means we're the first string this time out. Are we up to it, Jack?" Harry asked. "Does that mean the second string is on the bench warming up in case they have to pull our fat out of the fire? I like things like that explained to me."

"Yeah, that's what it means, Harry."

"Second string? I don't *think* so!" Lizzie stood up and glared at the others around the table. "I resent the implication, gentlemen. Now you've pissed me off. You don't ever want to piss me off, Jack."

Jack thought the lawyer was one of the most beautiful women he'd ever seen. Delectable eye candy. She was probably also one of the smartest. He shuddered when he remembered all the sleepless nights and nightmares he'd had in the past when he had to go up against the Silver Fox, as Lizzie Fox was referred to by her colleagues in the courtroom.

"Resent it all you want, counselor. This isn't a courtroom where you can bewitch the jury and the judges, not to mention the media, with your short skirts, cleavage and all that sex appeal you toss out there."

"Gee, Jack, I didn't think you noticed. Just for the record, I resent that, too," Lizzie snapped.

"This isn't a game, Lizzie. We could all go to prison if we make a wrong move. We're being watched 24/7. One false move and it's all over. Think of this as our maiden voyage and then remember Murphy's

Law. What *can* go wrong, *will* go wrong. The others are seasoned. I don't think we qualify as the second string, but we're up to bat. Now, if you don't have anything constructive to offer, sit down and shut the hell up. You aren't in charge here. In fact, you're low gal on the totem pole."

"I second that, Goldilocks. I'm not real anxious to go to prison so let's proceed in an orderly manner or I'll personally slice your tits off. Are we clear?" Harry snarled.

"I always do what I'm told," Maggie dithered in case a preemptive strike was going to be delivered in her direction. "Hey, I'm okay with all this...this spook stuff. So is Lizzie. In case you hadn't noticed, we haven't had any sleep and we're cranky so let's just start over."

Lizzie was magnanimous in her apology. "You're right, Jack. I'm sorry. It won't happen again. How's this for starting fresh: what do you want me to do?"

"Be a team player," Nellie said.

"You got it, Judge," Lizzie said quietly.

Nellie looked around for her gavel and seemed surprised that it wasn't on the table. She grinned sheepishly. "I think we need to be open and up front with each other. I admit to some misgivings. Prior to . . . to all this," she said, waving her hand, "I just helped out. Myra was in much the same position I find myself in right now. She used me as a sounding board and I was only too glad to help. This situation is quite different. Having said that, I will now call Pearl to see about a brunch date. Jack and Harry, you will be in the restaurant with me watching and observing. The moment Pearl leaves, join me for coffee. Lizzie and Maggie, if you can join us, please do. We're adjourned for now."

When no one moved, Nellie snapped, "What? Adjourned means the meeting is over. What?" she repeated.

"We have to call Charles with our decision. He wants us on video, doesn't he?" Harry asked.

"Yep. I'll do it, Judge. Twenty minutes and we're out of here."

Ten minutes later, Jack said, "You're on, Judge!"

Nellie cleared her throat and spoke forcefully, so forcefully the others looked at one another. This was a new Nellie. One they hadn't seen in action.

"Charles, my little group has decided, since we're the first string, we're going to act like it and go for the gusto. I'll check back in later today after our brunch. At the moment I see no reason for the others to risk a prison sentence to come here. We have excellent backup with Harry's friends."

Charles listened attentively before he spoke. "I'm glad to hear that. In the meantime we're having Annie's yacht readied. Just in case, Nellie."

"That's ridiculous, Charles. If I need you I don't plan to sit around sucking my thumb while you sail the high seas. Do you know how long it will take you to get here? Thank you for the offer but I'll manage with my people, thank you very much."

"Atta girl, Nellie," Annie could be heard chortling in the background.

The moment the plasma screens turned black, Jack said, "Well, damn, Judge! I bet that's the first time anyone has stood up to Charles Martin. I liked the way you referred to us as your 'people.' Now, if we screw up, and there's no reason to think we will, we'll have no one to blame but ourselves. So, let's get this show on the road."

Nellie was the last to leave the command center. She was almost to the door when she turned around and walked back to the table. She sat down and dropped her head into her hands. Who was she kidding? There was no way in hell she could ever fill Charles Martin's shoes. Talking up a plan of action and carrying it through were two decidedly different animals. Well, she'd give it her best shot and hope for the best.

Swiping at her damp eyes, Nellie struggled to get out of her chair. When she felt a pair of strong arms lift her, she whirled around. "Jack!"

"If it's any consolation, Judge, I pretty much felt the same way you're probably feeling right now my first time out. I didn't know if I was going to wet my pants, faint or drop dead on the spot. Somehow or other, instinct takes over and you know it's survival of the fittest. You got it going on, lady, so settle in and take the ride. If one of us goes down we all go down and I'm not going to let that happen. Trust me, okay, Judge?"

The relief on the retired judge's face

brought a smile to Jack's face. "Okay, Jack. I really need a cigarette."

Jack laughed, a genuine sound of mirth. "Me, too. Let's go, boss."

In spite of herself, Nellie laughed. She linked her arm with Jack's and followed him up the steps into the main part of the house.

"Where's brunch?" Jack asked as he slipped into his windbreaker.

"Wintergreen's," Nellie said. "I'll call you if Pearl turns me down, which I don't think will happen."

The phone was in Nellie's hand the moment the kitchen door closed behind Jack Emery.

Chapter 3

The women settled themselves on the terrace with the last of the coffee. The day was beautiful, the kind of day resorts tout in their high-dollar glossy brochures to entice guests. Clear blue sky, cotton-candy clouds, golden sunshine. The slight breeze whispered among the trees as birds rustled and foraged for food. The scene all looks so peaceful, Myra thought, but she knew the girls were feeling anything but peaceful. Out of the corner of her eye she watched the younger women as they fidgeted and squirmed in the colorful Adirondack chairs.

Myra brought her coffee cup to her lips as she continued to watch her five chicks. That's how she thought of Isabelle, Alexis, Kathryn, Yoko and Nikki. They were unhappy, but she'd known that for a long time. She wasn't at all surprised when Nikki bounded out of her chair and announced that she was going for a run to work off the bountiful breakfast she'd consumed. Within seconds the others joined her.

"Something's going on," Annie said quietly.

"A revolt is imminent would be my guess. You notice they didn't ask us if we wanted to go for a run," Myra said quietly.

Annie gasped in horror. "Dear, dear Myra, surely you don't think we could keep up with them, do you?"

"No, but it is nice to be asked. They could have said they were going for a walk and invited us along. We *can* walk, Annie. Sometimes I think they think we're not . . . What's that term I'm looking for?" Myra asked fretfully.

"Kathryn would say we aren't cutting it. Holding up our end. If that's what you think, you're wrong. If you and I disappeared from this little group, they'd be lost without us. They look to us for direction. Not all the time, but we are the glue that holds us all together. Listen to me, Myra, getting caught has had a psychological effect on all of us. We've been forced to give up our lives as we knew them. We say we're adjusting but we're not. We just keep repeating the lie over and over and sooner or later we'll begin to believe it."

Myra shrugged as she fingered the pearls at her neck. As she stared off into space she said softly, "I'm so glad you agreed to join us, Annie. I feel I have an ally in you. Why do I feel like I need an ally? Us against them in a manner of speaking. I don't understand where these feelings are coming from. I don't like feeling like this and it's starting to worry me."

Annie, her eyes downcast, contemplated the crimson polish on her toenails. "I'm new to all of this, Myra, but I have to admit, I love it. I'm having the time of my life. The isolation up here on the mountain doesn't bother me at all. I've lived here a long time so it's home to me. It's different these days but it is still home. However, I understand what you're saying. Let's face it, my friend, we're old. The girls are young.

When you're young you think you're infallible. You and I have lost children and we'll never be the same again. We both know that, so it has to be factored into our feelings. Did any of that make sense, Myra?" she asked anxiously.

"Yes," Myra said, patting her old friend's hand. "Now, what do you think they're up to?"

"This is just my humble opinion . . ."

"Just stop it right now, Annie, you don't have a humble bone in your body."

"That's true," Annie responded airily. "So, it is my opinion the girls are scheming and plotting to find a way to go Stateside and *not* on my yacht. For the life of me I do not understand why Charles wants to take that boat to sea. It takes forever to cross the Atlantic. We might as well swim. At the risk of repeating myself, the girls want some action, sexual and otherwise, and don't look at me like that, Myra. You really have to stop being such a prude."

Myra got up and started to pace the confines of the terrace, all the while fingering the pearls at her neck. "I'm afraid for Nellie and Pearl. For all of them, actually. Backup is all-important. We were so

cocky early on. We thought we were infallible. We weren't, Annie. Our backup was
Jack and Harry. Nikki knew it but the rest of
us didn't. You also have to factor in all of
Charles's old friends from his spy days.
We're half a world away from Nellie and
the others. I guess what I'm trying to say
is I want to be there doing whatever I can
to help. Backup support is crucial."

Annie joined Myra at the railing of the
terrace. She propped her elbows on it and
looked down the mountain, then her gaze
went to the sparkling blue ocean. She
whirled around and said, "Then let's do it,
old girl!"

"Just like that!" Myra gasped.

"Yes, just like that. You're the boss,
Myra. Act like it. The girls will love you for
stepping up to the plate for them. Me, too."

Nellie looked around the restaurant.
She'd been given an excellent table at the
back of the dining room that afforded her
a view of the bar and the other diners,
something she'd requested. With the new
smoking laws in effect she couldn't
smoke. She knew she couldn't doodle on
the fine linen tablecloth so what was she

going to do until Pearl arrived? Drink, of course. Hopefully she wouldn't be snookered by the time Justice Barnes arrived.

Pictures and caricatures of past US presidents lined the burgundy walls. Nellie stared at them as she mentally calculated how many of them she'd seen come and go. Which one was her favorite? Harry Truman, of course. Good old "the buck stops here" Harry. When she'd committed the pictures and the presidents' attire to memory, Nellie looked around. She saw Jack and Harry Wong a few tables away, perusing menus. Across the room, toward the front, Lizzie Fox and Maggie Spritzer were sipping on what looked like Bellinis. Where in the hell was the guest of honor? Five more minutes and she'd have to go outside and walk twenty-five feet from the building to have a cigarette or she'd have a nicotine fit. Five more minutes. If Pearl was a no-show five minutes *after* she had her cigarette, she was leaving. Let Justice Barnes get her bloomers in a knot.

Nellie was shaken out of her reverie when she heard her name. She looked up to see Justice Barnes in the process of seating herself. "You're late, Pearl. I was going to give you five more minutes and then I was going to leave."

The only sounds to be heard in the restaurant were tinkling glass and clinking silverware.

Justice Barnes brushed at her steel-gray hair. "I couldn't decide what to wear. I'm sorry."

Nellie looked at the shabby outfit the Justice was wearing. Her hair hadn't been styled, either, and there was a clump of mascara at the corner of one of her eyes. "You should have taken more time, Pearl. You look like a bag lady instead of the impeccably dressed Pearl I've known all my life."

"Cut the crap, Nellie. I'm in no mood for levity of any kind. I'm late. The world didn't come to an end, this restaurant is still serving food. Did you do as I asked?"

Nellie leaned back in her chair. Suddenly she felt all powerful. Here she was, seated with a Supreme Court justice who looked like a bag lady and was scared out of her wits. A Supreme Court justice who needed her help, a Supreme Court justice who had threatened her. "I wasexpecting you to bring Grant for support,"she said.

"Grant golfs on Sunday. Well?" She looked over her shoulder at the waiter and said, "Scotch, straight up. Make it a double."

The moment the waiter was out of earshot, Nellie said, "I'm here but that doesn't mean you should take that as an admission that you were right about the vigilantes and me. Threats mean nothing to me. I saw how much distress you were in the other night and I want to help you. Tell me what I can do." She gulped at her gin and tonic, aware that Jack Emery was on his way to the men's room, which meant he had to pass their table. For one brief second their eyes locked. She was to tug on her earlobe if she wanted him to stop at the table. Not yet, she decided.

"I don't need your help, Nellie. I need the help of those women. Are you going to sit there and lie to my face? I *know,* Nellie. I swear to God, I'll tell everyone who will listen if you don't promise me the vigilantes' help," she hissed.

"Pearl, this might be a really silly question but I'm going to ask it anyway. What do you think I'll be doing if you even try to spread that lie?"

Pearl Barnes drained her glass. "What

do you mean?" She brushed again at the gray locks of hair that kept falling over her forehead.

"Look alive here, Pearl. I will retaliate by telling everyone the story you told me the other night. Your son-in-law, since he seems to be at the crux of your angst, will back me up, I'm sure. Blackmailers have no backbone."

Pearl looked around and snapped her fingers to gain their waiter's attention. She held up her glass to indicate she wanted a refill.

"Well, that was certainly ladylike, Pearl. You really must be upset. Now, tell me what I can *personally* do to help you."

"You would jeopardize the lives of all those women and children I've been helping?" Pearl asked, anger ringing in her voice.

"Well, hell yes, Pearl. Do you think I'm going to let you blackmail me and ruin my life? I don't think so. Survival of the fittest is the name of the game. You know how it is in this crazy town."

"Oh, God! Oh, God! I'm being watched and I don't mean by my own security detail. Grant said he thought there were people watching him also. Please, Nellie, help me. Call Myra or Annie and explain my situation. And stop lying to me. I can't tolerate a liar."

"Guess what, Pearl, I can't tolerate someone who tries to blackmail me. I think what we have here is a Mexican standoff. One more time, how can I help you?"

"You can kill that son of a bitch Hughes who is blackmailing me, that's what you can do. What if he goes after my daughter and granddaughter? I'm afraid that if I don't do what he wants, they're his next target. I'll be in prison and won't be able to help them. Please, Nellie. I didn't mean to threaten you. No, no, that's a lie, I did mean it because I was so desperate." Suddenly Justice Barnes deflated like a pricked balloon. Her eyes filled with tears. "I wouldn't have said a word, Nellie. I thought if I . . . Oh, hell, I don't know what I thought. I'm sorry. Tell the others, Myra and Annie, I didn't mean it. I was so sure . . . so sure, almost positive you . . . It doesn't matter anymore. I'll take care of that bastard myself. Did we order, Nellie?" She looked around and seemed startled that she was sitting in a restaurant.

Nellie watched as Pearl let her gaze rake the room. When she turned back to face Nellie, her expression was set, her eyes cold and hard. "You set me up! Damn you, Nellie, how could you do that to me? Don't tell me you don't know what I'm talking about. There's District Attorney Emery, and that jujitsu expert, and look over there, that's Lizzie Fox and wonder of wonders, she's lunching with a *Post* reporter. Isn't that another *Post* reporter sitting at the bar? Looks like old-home week. Damn you, Nellie. I thought we were friends." A lone tear rolled down Justice Barnes's wrinkled cheek.

Alarmed, Nellie leaned forward. The only thing she heard was "a *Post* reporter sitting at the bar." Ted Robinson. In a frenzy, she started to tug at her ear. When Jack remained seated, she started to tug on both ears, hoping Harry Wong would notice. He did. Within minutes, Jack was making his third trip to the men's room.

"Judge Easter, fancy meeting you here," he said cheerfully. "I miss your slap downs. Court isn't the same without you. How have you been? Are you enjoying retirement?"

"Jack! Nice to see you. Allow me to introduce Justice Pearl Barnes. We're old friends. Pearl, this good-looking young man is District Attorney Jack Emery."

Justice Barnes held out her hand. Jack shook it and said something that sounded like, *"It's a pleasure to meet you, Justice Barnes."*

"Would you care to join us, Jack?"

"Thanks for asking, Judge, but I'm lunching with someone. Wintergreen's is a nice place, this is only the second time I've been here."

"I come here all the time. So does Justice Barnes. I think I know everyone in the room. Even the ones at the bar," she said, emphasizing the word "bar."

Jack nodded, smiled, said it was a pleasure to meet Justice Barnes, and continued his trek to the men's room.

"Now what?" Pearl asked.

"What is your window of time?"

"What does that mean, Nellie, my window of time?"

"When are you supposed to give your ex–son-in-law your answer?"

"He said he'd be in touch with me by the end of this week."

"Can you stall him?"

"God, Nellie, I don't know. I suppose I could say it's taking longer than I thought to liquidate my holdings to meet his demand. He wants...so much money...On top of...changing my vote. He's such a bastard. My...My...What I do is not like what you and the others do. I don't know how to...I can try. How much time do you need?"

"I don't know, Pearl. I have to talk to some people. How do you want me to get in touch with you?"

"I'll get word to you somehow. Just be on the lookout. I meant it, Nellie, I wouldn't have blown the whistle on you."

"I know that now, Pearl. That's why I'm going to do my best to help you. By the way, I wouldn't have turned you in, either. We're on the same team, so to speak."

"I wonder where our food is," Pearl said vaguely.

"This might come as a surprise to you, dear lady, but we haven't ordered. You need to get it together, Pearl or you're going to blow yourself out of the water. Now, what about Grant?"

Pearl straightened in her chair, looked

around and snapped her fingers for the waiter again, who appeared almost immediately. "French toast, one sunny-side up egg on the side, more coffee and a bowl of whipped cream," she said.

"I'll have the same thing," Nellie said, even though she hated French toast.

Pearl looked down at her glass, surprised that it was empty. She picked up her water glass and took a big gulp. "Like I said, Grant is Grant. Lately it doesn't seem to be working as well as it has in the past. I cannot ignore the fact that the current director of the FBI is Grant's brother-in-law. You know what they say about family and how blood is thicker than water. Grant adores his sister and Elias. Really adores them. I can't risk telling him. If the time comes when I have to tell him . . . Well then, that's when I'll tell him but not before. I can walk away, Nellie, if I have to. I can make myself disappear, the way I make all those women and their children disappear, but I don't want to have to do that unless there is no other way. Do you understand what I'm saying, Nellie?"

"I do, Pearl. It might come down to that."

"I know. I've been preparing myself. If

Myra and Annie can do it, then so can I. What does Emery have to do with all this? God, he's a shill, too, right? Tell me more, Nellie."

"I'd rather not, Pearl."

Justice Barnes pursed her lips. "Emery, the jujitsu guy, the hottest reporters in town and that sex-bomb lawyer, all in the same room." She laughed as she held up her water glass to clink it against Nellie's. "To sex, lies and audiotapes," she said, slapping a small mini recorder down in the middle of the table. Nellie was no slouch. She yanked at her pocket and pulled out a matching recorder.

"Trust is such a wonderful thing," Nellie said.

"Isn't it, though?" Justice Barnes responded.

Chapter 4

Post reporter Ted Robinson finished the last of his hashbrowns and slid his plate across the bar where he was sitting. Wintergreen's asked all single diners to eat at the bar instead of taking up a table for two or four in the dining room. Ted was comfortable eating at the bar so he didn't mind. He ate here only on rare occasions because he thought it a little too pricey for his wallet. He was on his third cup of coffee. If he drank any more he would have to weave his way through the huge dining room to the restrooms at the back of the restaurant, something he didn't want to do.

He hated Sundays. Really hated Sundays. Lately, he hated them more than usual because his live-in significant other, Maggie Spritzer, always had something to do on Sundays that didn't include him. Maybe he needed to think about kicking good old Maggie to the curb and going it alone. But if he did that, he'd have to give up the spectacular sex they enjoyed together.

As Ted sipped at his final cup of coffee, he stared into the huge mirror behind the mahogany bar. It always amazed him how the bartenders knew exactly where to reach for the liquor they needed. No wasted motions whatsoever. The bar mirror afforded him an excellent view of the Sunday diners. Who's Who at Sunday brunch in the nation's capital. Everyone in Alphabet City came to Wintergreen's for their hashbrowns and Scotch Eggs. That's what they said, but reporter that he was, Ted knew they came to be seen. Everyone knew Scotch Eggs and hashbrowns played hell with your arteries and cholesterol.

Whoa! Whoa! Whoa! Was that Jack Emery and that pipsqueak Harry Wong scoffing down Scotch Eggs? Yes, it was.

And was that Maggie at the front of the restaurant, brunching with Lizzie Fox, jurisprudence's answer to sex in the courtroom? Well, bless my soul, it certainly was. Ted's gaze continued to scan the bar mirror. Well, well, well, was that Judge Easter in the far back of the restaurant? His keen reporter's instinct said she was hiding. He did a double take when he recognized Easter's dining partner. Justice Pearl Barnes of the United States Supreme Court. Yep, they were hiding. From the looks of things they weren't eating Scotch Eggs. In fact they didn't appear to be eating at all, even though there was food in front of them. Robinson's mind raced. What were the odds of these six people dining at the same place on a Sunday morning? Somewhere over the rainbow, that's where.

Ted pulled out his wallet and paid his tab. What to do now? A trip to the men's room was definitely called for. He could try to make eye contact with Judge Easter just so she would know he'd seen her. Then, on his way out, a stop at Emery's table. Last but not least, he would creep up on Maggie and scare the shit out of her. All doable. Definitely doable.

Ted was glad he'd worn his good creased khakis and his tweed jacket with the leather elbow patches, he thought as he made his way to the men's room, because he was going to *be seen*. He dodged waiters with huge trays being carried at shoulder height. He wondered what would happen if he accidentally on purpose bumped into one of the waiters. Everyone would look at him. He would definitely be *seen.* Nah, it wasn't worth the mess, and the three cups of coffee demanded he move right along.

Judge Easter saw the reporter approaching and did her best to fix a smile on her face. She wondered if he would notice that she hadn't eaten any of her lunch. Of course he would. Reporters were trained to pay attention to insignificant details. More important, would he recognize Pearl Barnes and observe her full plate? Without a doubt. He was almost to their table. Nellie inclined her head and offered up a sickly smile. So far so good, she thought when Ted acknowledged her presence with a nod of his own. On his way out, he'd see Pearl full face. That's when he would start to wonder what was going on. He would also see Jack, Harry, Lizzie and his girlfriend, at which point his reporter's nosy instincts would go into overdrive.

Play it cool, Robinson, he told himself. Just get the hell out of here but let the others know you've seen them. No conversation, just keep walking. He could figure it all out later, whatever *it* turned out to be.

Since Jack Emery was number one on his personal shit list, he strode past his table with a scowl on his face. By the time he reached Maggie's table he was in rare form, the scowl still intact. He shot himself in the foot and said, "I'd appreciate it if you move your shit out of my digs this afternoon. Find your own damn apartment." Without another word, he stalked out of the restaurant. He had to take deep breaths to calm himself down. He kept walking even though he could hear Maggie calling his name. His feet picked up speed and then at the first break in traffic, crossed the road. He knew Maggie wouldn't follow him because she was wearing high heels.

He was piss-ass mad now. Breathe in, breathe out. He stopped at the first deli he came to and bought the Sunday paper and a cup of coffee to go. Outside he hailed a cab and told the driver to take him to Rock Creek Park. He needed to get himself under control. His cell phone rang continuously and was still ringing when he paid the driver. Paper under his arm, coffee in hand, Ted looked for a vacant picnic table. He finally found one but had to shoo three squirrels to another nearby location.

Ted waited for his cell phone to stop ringing before he clicked it on and called a friend and fellow reporter on the *Post*. "It's Ted, Espinosa. Look, how about doing me a favor? Yeah, I know it's Sunday but I think I might be onto something. C'mon, Joe, the only thing you do on Sunday is drink beer and watch ball games. If it works out we share the byline. See what you can find out about Justice Pearl Barnes besides the obvious stuff. The first thing that's going to jump out at you is her boyfriend of long-standing is the brother-in-law of the new director of the FBI. You might want to work on that, too. What do you mean what am I doing? I'm doing stuff. Important stuff. I'll call you later this afternoon. Don't drag your ass on this, Espinosa."

The moment he clicked off the call,

Ted's cell rang again. He looked down at the number, saw it was Maggie. He turned off his cell. "Screw you, Maggie Spritzer, and the horse you rode in on," he mumbled to the three squirrels at the next table who were watching him with sharp-eyed interest.

Maggie walked back to the restaurant wringing her hands. At the door she backed out when she saw Lizzie, Jack and Harry about to walk through the revolving door. She waited to see who would speak first.

"What the hell was that all about, Maggie?" Lizzie demanded.

"Ted's in one of his moods. He gets like that from time to time. He wanted me to go to brunch with him today but because I'd committed to you guys, I had to say no. He's no fool, he saw everyone in there. Right now he's trying to figure out what's going on. I called him fifty times but he isn't answering his cell phone. He won't answer it if he sees my name on the caller ID. Look, let me take on Tyler Hughes, you do the daughter. I can get stuff from the archives at the paper. Will that work for you?"

"Sure, no problem. Was Ted serious about kicking you out?" Lizzie asked. "That would be the day I'd let some guy dictate to me. Do you have a place to stay? I have a spare bedroom if you want to bunk in with me."

"I might have to take you up on that. I better get going. If any of you need me, call." The others watched as Maggie hailed a cab and stepped into it.

Jack walked the requisite twenty-five feet from the restaurant and fired up a cigarette. Out of the corner of his eye he could see Nellie and Justice Barnes walking to the curb. Two black Crown Victorias slid alongside. Nellie got in one and Justice Barnes got in the other. Jack puffed furiously as he tried to figure out his next move. Since Robinson hated his guts, he needed to do something preemptive to throw him off whatever he thought might be going on. But what?

"I guess I'll leave you, too," Lizzie said quietly. "Jack, should we be worried?"

"Oh, yeah, Lizzie, we definitely need to worry," Jack drawled before he dropped his cigarette to the curb. He ground his heel into it and then picked it up to stick it in his pocket. "Smokers have no rights these days," he grumbled. The others ignored him.

Quiet up to this point, Harry spoke up. "That's because those things will kill you and if you're too stupid to recognize the surgeon general's warnings, then other people have to take your best interests to heart. How about if I just take Robinson out? That will solve everything."

Jack snorted. "It might come to that, Harry. For your information I only smoke seven cigarettes a week."

"That's seven too many. See ya," Harry said, striding off toward his *dojo*.

"Guess it's just me and you, Jack," Lizzie said.

"I don't think it's a good idea for us to be seen together. Where are you headed?"

"You're right. Home. Where else on a Sunday afternoon? Should we pick a fight and I bop you for some alleged obscene comment in case anyone is watching?"

"You're really full of yourself, you know that, right?"

Lizzie held his gaze for a long time before she turned and walked off without saying a word.

Jack walked in the opposite direction. The rest of the day loomed ahead of him. He hated Sundays. Everybody he knew hated Sundays. One time, back when he and Ted Robinson were friends, they'd had an hour conversation about why they each hated Sundays. Why was that? he wondered. When no earth-shattering answer entered his thoughts, Jack stepped to the curb and hailed a cab to take him to Georgetown where he lived in Nikki Quinn's house.

In the cab, he leaned back and closed his eyes. He could do his laundry. Get his dry cleaning ready to drop off in the morning. He could stop and buy some groceries. The sheets on the bed needed to be changed. Hell, he could clean the windows if he was desperate to do something. What he really should do was balance his checkbook. One of these days he was going to do his banking online. Except he'd probably never do that because he hated everything online as much as he hated Sundays.

Screw it, he'd go home and take a nap.

Fifteen minutes later, Jack stepped out of the cab at his front door. The cell phone in his pocket started to vibrate. He fished it out and looked down at the caller ID. His blood ran cold. "Why are you calling me, asshole?"

"To get a comment, asshole," Ted Robinson responded.

"To think you and I used to be buddies, not to mention friends. I have no comment other than to say the Scotch Eggs aren't what they're cracked up to be. Didja get it, Ted? Eggs not being what they're cracked up to be. Forget it, you always were slow on the uptake."

"What's up with Justice Barnes, Jack?"

"How the hell should I know? I don't travel in those circles. Why don't you call her and ask her? By the way, asshole, that was a shitty thing you did to Maggie. I have no love for either one of you, but guys don't air their dirty linen in places like Wintergreen's. The whole damn place heard you. All you did was make an ass of yourself. And you made Maggie cry. What that means to you, Teddy boy, is I have absolutely no respect for any man who makes a woman cry. Now, I'm going to hang up so you can go back under that rock where you live."

Livid with the phone call, Jack stormed his way into the house and headed to the kitchen where he popped two Budweisers and gulped them both down at the speed of light. He popped two more. When he finished them he dug around for his special phone and punched in Charles's number.

The first words out of his mouth after Charles said hello were, "I think we just ran into our first problem."

Chapter 5

It was midafternoon on the mountain in Barcelona when Charles escorted the girls down to the command center. They were meeting in work mode for the second time that day. All were curious and a little nervous. Charles looked more than serious, he looked worried. Normally the women were not allowed to see Charles worry.

"It's time to bring you all up to speed since we met earlier this morning. Things seem to be happening rather quickly. But before I get to that, I want to ask, have any of you ever heard of a mountaintop, quite similar to this one, in North Carolina, called Big Pine Mountain? There is also a third mountain operation, owned and operated by the United States government, and it's called NORAD."

The women, more curious than ever, shook their heads.

"The one in North Carolina works, or I should say worked, much the way we do. Privately funded by a consortium. The mountain itself is owned by two Greek men, a father and son. The operation is run by the son, anex-covert operator who was compromised much the way I was. He, too, had to get out of the game. I met him several times, and he was the best of the best. Every special op in the business knew Kollar Havapopulas was born to that life. But, as we all know, nothing lasts forever. When things went south, with the help of some very important people, Kollar moved to the mountain that he and his father own. He's been a virtual prisoner there ever since. He does, however, run a top-notch operation for the consortium, supported much the way Myra and Annie fund our operation.

"I'm sure you're probably wondering why I'm telling you all this. I'm telling you because I think—and we need to take a vote on it—that we should relocate to Big Pine Mountain for a period of time. I've been in touch with Kollar and we've agreed to trade mountains, so to speak. That will put you Stateside and Kollar and his family—he's married now—over here where his family can enjoy our village life. The padre and the villagers will take care of them the same way they've taken care of us. Before I finalize things I want to be sure you're all in agreement."

"Does the United States government know about...what went on up there?" Nikki asked. Stateside meant seeing Jack. She crossed her fingers under the table hoping the answer was no.

"Absolutely no one knows about it except the people on the inside—the consortium members, of course, me and a few others like me, and the people involved in the missions they brought to conclusion. The consortium is made up of wealthy, powerful older men in our government. They will never blow the whistle on themselves. They're also afraid of Kollar, who still has contacts all over the world, much the way I do. Rest assured, their silence is golden."

"If we agree to go there, will we be prisoners like we are here?" Alexis asked.

"More or less. The only access to the mountain is by cable car, as it is here. You all need to understand there is no village at the base of Big Pine Mountain. There will be no padre or villagers watching our backs. It could be very dangerous. I want you all to think about this very carefully. Yes, we'll all be back in the States. Yes, Nikki and Yoko, you will be able to see Jack and Harry, perhaps more than you would see them here. That, too, will be dangerous. You must first and foremost think about your own safety."

"What happened to all the offers, invitations, if you will, from other agencies to help out?" Isabelle asked. "It was our understanding we'd be hired guns on this side of the world."

Charles turned his back to reach for a thick folder. "The invitations are all right here in this folder. Notice how thick it is. I didn't say anything earlier because I needed to check out their bona-fides. Actually, an invitation came in late last night. These people want to know if you're paratrooper trained. If so, the job is yours. What say you? In addition it's a name-your-own-fee offer. I take that to mean the sky is the limit."

"I don't think so!" Annie said. "I have to take Fosamax as it is. Unless, of course, you can guarantee a soft landing. It's the impact that will break your bones. I saw that on the Discovery Channel. Floating until your parachute opens must be a heavenly feeling, but the impact of the chute opening would probably pull our bones out of the sockets. I vote no," Annie said breathlessly.

Charles tried to hide his grin. "Girls?"

Six verbal dissents rang in the air.

"Then I guess that takes care of that particular invitation. I'll decline with good grace. The other invitations are more or less the same. Terrorist/mercenary projects. I'm still weighing them. There are several possibilities and the money appears to be unlimited. You can name your own price if you decide to accept any of the invitations. I would be remiss if I didn't tell you the agencies are getting impatient waiting for your response."

As one, the women shrugged.

"Dear, when do we have to make the

decision to transfer to North Carolina?" Myra asked. "How would we get there?"

Before Charles could respond, Alexis asked how dangerous it would be to relocate.

"Time is of the essence. Possibly we can figure out a way to fly commercial or I can commandeer a private jet since Myra and Annie's planes come under scrutiny. I'm thinking of a turnaround with Kollar's private Gulfstream but only if you all agree. At this stage, it's just a thought. I've got a lot of work to do to... Well, let's just say I have a lot of work to do, so I suggest you go outdoors, discuss it among yourselves, and think this through very carefully. I'll abide with whatever decision you come up with. You also need to know that while our own people were having brunch at a place called Wintergreen's, Ted Robinson was sitting at the bar having his own lunch. He saw everyone. He told Maggie to get all her stuff out of his apartment by late afternoon. That is a glitch you also have to consider."

Myra, the last one to leave the command center, turned back and winked at Charles. "Darling, I can almost guarantee the girls will vote to go Stateside. So do what you have to do. If I'm wrong, you can rub my feet tonight."

Charles threw his head back and laughed. "That's cheeky of you, my dear. If *you're* wrong you can rub *my* feet this evening."

"And anything else that needs rubbing. Get on it, darling. Tallyho and all that good stuff," Myra said breezily as she wiggled her hips. She laughed outright when she heard Charles groan.

Charles watched as the love of his life sashayed out of the command center before he burst out laughing. A second later he was back at work, all thoughts of getting rubbed forgotten.

"It looks like rain," Yoko said as she fell in line with the other girls for a walk around the compound. "An hour ago there wasn't a cloud in the sky. I think I want to go to North Carolina."

"What's NORAD, does anyone know?" Kathryn asked.

"North American Aerospace Defense Command," Annie said. "Didn't you watch that movie the other night when all those fighter planes left from there? They defend the security of North America. At least that's what I got out of it. NORAD is in Colorado."

"Living on top of mysterious mountains must be the in thing this year," Kathryn grumbled. "I don't know if I want to go back or not. Charles didn't say anything about coming back here after we deal with Justice Barnes and her problem. I want some kind of guarantee."

"Guarantee of what?" Yoko asked.

Kathryn shrugged. She bent down to pick up a stick and threw it for Murphy. The big shepherd bounded off, Alexis's dog, Grady, hot on his heels. "Like how long are we going to stay in North Carolina? This," she said, waving her arms about, "is home. We're safe here. We are not going to be safe back in the States. I think we all know that. I suspect there was something else Charles didn't tell us. It's just a feeling. I think something happened back home, something that will probably make the situation even more dangerous. I could be wrong but I don't think so.

"And, another thing. Why didn't Justice

Barnes get in touch with Nellie in the beginning instead of paying off that crud her daughter was married to? She bought him off. Right off the bat, that alone spells trouble. Is the woman stupid? The timing on this isn't good. Charles hasn't had time to do all the things he usually does to make sure we're as safe as can be. The window of time is way too short in my opinion. Where's our backup? Yeah, right, Jack and the others, but what can they do if we get caught this time? So, I'm voting no."

Murphy bounded back with his stick for Kathryn to throw again. She did and then sat down on a rotted log. The others stopped and looked at her. This was one of those rare times since forming the Sisterhood that they were out of sync.

Alexis sat down next to Kathryn and put her arm around her shoulder. "Having been in prison myself, I have to agree with Kathryn. I do not ever want to go back there. Going Stateside is like we're taunting them, offering ourselves up to get caught. I don't think Justice Barnes will blow the whistle on us. To do so means she'd be blowing it on herself and I don't see someone of her stature doing that. I vote no."

Myra stepped forward. "I'm not trying to change your mind, girls, but I would like you to ask yourselves what we would have done without Nellie, Jack, Harry and Lizzie's help. Even Maggie Spritzer when we were caught. They all stepped up to the plate, as you would say, Kathryn. We're safe because of them."

Annie looked overhead as the sky turned darker. The first fat rain drops fell through the dense foliage overhead. "Pearl doesn't have the kind of backup we have. What she's done, she's pretty much done on her own. I don't think I would have the guts to do what she's been doing, considering who she is. They'll crucify her."

Kathryn jumped to her feet. "And what in the hell do you think they'll do to *us* if we get caught? *AGAIN!*" she screamed at the top of her lungs, the sound ricocheting off the mountain.

Murphy growled deep in his throat, the hair on the back of his neck standing on end. Grady followed suit.

Isabelle started to wring her hands. "I don't like where this is going. We need to sit down and talk it all out. We all have our opinions and deserve to be heard. Right now, right this moment, I'm inclined to go along with Kathryn and Alexis, but I'm open to listening to reason. We all understand Justice Barnes is a friend of Myra and Annie and of course they want to help her. We all understand that Yoko and Nikki want to see their lovers, but all of that can't be at our risk. The reason we've been successful in our missions is because we were always on the same page. Right now we aren't even in the same book, never mind the same page. That's all I have to say."

"It's raining. We should go back," Nikki said.

Myra looked at her sharply as she imagined what was going through her adopted daughter's mind.

Annie and Myra were the last in line as they trudged back to the old monastery, the others sprinting ahead. They linked arms as they walked along, the warm rain drenching them to the skin.

"This is not good, Annie. A rebellion is imminent. Isabelle was spot-on so how can we argue with how the others feel?"

"What does it mean, Myra? I used to like to run naked in the rain. Of course, that was a lifetime ago."

"It means we're a team divided. A lot of things happened a lifetime ago, my friend."

"I know, Myra. I know. I can see all sides of this problem. Let's just hope for the best. I think our barbecue is going to be called off. Maybe we should do Charles a favor and prepare something for dinner."

"Oh, let's not. Charles gets...Well, he gets..."

"Pissy?" Annie laughed.

"That pretty much sums it up, my friend."

"Alexis told me one evening what it was like in prison. I cried for her and what she went through, and she was innocent, framed by those awful people. She can never get those years back, Myra. You and I would probably die in prison, considering our age. It is something we need to think about."

"Yes, Annie, it is definitely something we have to think about."

Chapter 6

Maggie Spritzer looked around the spartan corporate apartment the *Post* maintained for interviewees who were nervous about staying in hotels when they were about to spill their guts to a reporter. Her boss had okayed a temporary arrangement until she could find a suitable apartment of her own. She looked down at her two large suitcases and her laptop, and knew she would have to unpack sooner rather than later.

Tears dripped down her cheeks. She'd been so certain Ted would come back to the apartment, if only to rail at her, at which point they'd kiss and make up. When it didn't happen, she knew he was seriously pissed off at her and there was no going back. Her relationship with Ted was now a thing of the past. She was going to miss Mickey and Minnie, Ted's two cats, as much as she was going to miss Ted. Why did he have to be such an ass? Because he is *a man,* she answered herself.

Crying wasn't going to get her anywhere. She might as well unpack and get on with this new life that had suddenly been thrust on her.

An hour later, Maggie had her laptop propped up on the kitchen countertop. She pulled the counter stool toward her with her foot and plopped down to log on. Thirty minutes later she had a two-inch stack of printouts of one Tyler Hughes, Justice Barnes's ex–son-in-law. She read every word, hoping something would jump out at her to make things easier. Nothing did. He seemed ordinary enough. Born and raised on the Chesapeake, liked the water, had a catamaran. He was a Yalie, graduating summa cum laude. Captain on the crew team. Popular. Good-looking. Worked for two years as Senator

Hawthorne's top aide until the senator's retirement. Then did three years as a high-powered lobbyist, socking away money by the pound before going to work for a prestigious think tank in the District—his version of giving back and helping the little people, according to the fifth article she read.

By all indications, a mover and a shaker with the wardrobe to match.

Married Rebecca Barnes. Classy wedding. Five hundred guests. Champagne fountain. Truffles. Tons of wedding presents. Honeymooned in Hawaii for a month. A child born of the union nine months later named Amanda who was now six years old. The marriage ended three years ago, an amiable parting, according to the press. He moved into the Watergate Apartments. The wife, Beka, stayed in the family home with the daughter. The home being a wedding present from Justice Barnes.

Maggie scribbled a note to herself to ask Judge Easter if the couple had a prenuptial agreement. While Tyler Hughes came from a good family—father a surgeon, mother a principal in a high school—there wasn't an unlimited supply of money the way there was with Beka Barnes. Even if Tyler made some really serious money during his lobbying days, it wouldn't last forever with his lifestyle. Where did Justice Barnes's payoff money go? Exactly how much was it? More than a million? Two or three, perhaps? Which was another way of saying he'd be ripe to engage in a little blackmail scheme if he had already spent the big buy-off and the lobbying money was dwindling.

Maggie scribbled another note to herself. Does he pay alimony and child support? With his high salary, she suspected he'd be paying through the nose. That would also hurt his bank account.

Maggie reached for her cell phone to call one of her favorite snitches, Abner Tookus, who also happened to be one of the best computer hackers in the business. For a price, he'd get you anything you needed. Well, almost anything.

"Abner," Maggie said when the snitch picked up after the fourth ring. "I need a favor."

The voice on the other end of the phone was high-pitched, almost a squeal. Maggie knew for a fact that Abner hated to talk, preferring to send messages. "The kind that pays or doesn't pay? You get what you pay for, Miss Reporter."

"How about an IOU?"

Abner scoffed.

"Okay, how about if I sleep with you at some point?"

Abner scoffed again.

"Okay, how much?" It was Maggie's turn to scoff when she heard the amount. "Let's do this, a quarter of the amount and I sleep with you next month after I wind this down. Yeah, of course I'll put it in writing. So, is it a deal?"

"What do you need?"

"The financials on Tyler Hughes. Works at some think tank in the District. He was married to the chief justice's kid, Rebecca Barnes by name. Lives at the Watergate. Get me his credit report, too. Any and all clubs he belongs to. Who he associates with on a regular basis. I don't know why I say this, but I think the guy might gamble. In other words, I want everything."

"Not for one sleepover you don't. We need to renegotiate. Every other weekend for two months."

"You're nuts. I don't even sleep with my

boyfriend that much. Two sleepovers and a hundred bucks. That's my final offer," Maggie said, knowing full well she wouldn't hold up her end of the bargain. Abner was just jerking her chain. Abner always settled for a nice dinner at some secluded place that had real tablecloths and candles on the table. Abner was a true friend.

"When do you need this?"

"An hour ago. ASAP. Give me a time, Abby."

"Oooh, I love it when you call me Abby. Gives me goose bumps and I can feel my eyelashes curling upward as I speak. So how come you and that boyfriend of yours don't have much sex? Can't he get it up? Are you still with that guy who has the cats?"

"None of your damn business, Abner." Then Maggie broke the connection to stare down at the stack of papers on the kitchen table. She couldn't help but wonder if she was missing something.

A minute later she was back online searching out case histories of women and children who had made use-of-the-secret underground railroad that had taken so many to safety over the years. While she couldn't find those who were spirited away, she did find histories of those who had come back and ended up in jail, put there by their spouses. To their credit, none of the women spilled their guts. Two of them were still in jail because they wouldn't talk. That had to say a lot for Justice Barnes and her operation. Maggie could now see why everything was so secretive, why one leg of the journey was just that, with the person in charge not knowing anything about the next stop or the one that came before. Nameless people dedicated to a cause, out-of-the-way safe houses volunteered by other dedicated people in their quest to keep the underground running smoothly.

This story, if it ever got written, Maggie knew, would make a hell of a Pulitzer Prize. But, since she wasn't really working that side of the fence any longer, she tossed the thought out of her mind.

It was early evening before Maggie found a way to contact Tyler Hughes via email. Everyone at the think tank had a private email account. She typed out several messages, then deleted them before she finally came up with one she liked. How long would it be before he responded, if he responded? Probably at least a day.

Maggie blinked when she sat back to look out the window. She blinked again; it was totally dark outside. She could see the lights on Connecticut Avenue through the kitchen window. She closed up her laptop, wondering what she was going to do with the rest of the evening. She'd seen a deli around the corner so she might as well head out to stock up on a few provisions. She'd go ballistic if she didn't have coffee in the morning.

Maggie checked out the refrigerator. A bottle of ketchup. Ice cubes in the freezer. She'd starve unless she developed a love of ketchup.

Maggie debated a moment, wondering if she should take her heavy backpack or just her wallet. She finally opted for her wallet and left the apartment, careful to lock the door behind her. She wouldn't be gone more than an hour, so there was no sense in lugging the heavy bag, plus she would be carrying groceries on her return trip.

Her mind racing in all directions, Maggie rode the elevator to the ground floor without seeing a soul. She walked out into the warm, dark night to head for the corner. She spotted a neon sign—Jade Pagoda—so she stopped to order a full dinner she would pick up on the way back from the deli.

The hour she'd anticipated turned out to be closer to two because the Jade Pagoda was jammed to the rafters with people waiting to be seated. She sighed as she sat back on a padded chair to wait for her take-out.

It had been a hell of a day. And it still wasn't over and she wanted to cry so bad she had to squeeze her eyes shut to stop the flow of tears.

Ted Robinson kicked the door shut behind him and whistled for Minnie and Mickey. When they didn't appear as they usually did he ran through the apartment. It would be just like Maggie to steal his cats. He kept whistling and from somewhere he heard a sharp hiss and then both cats started to snarl as they bounded out from under the bed. Their food was late, something Maggie usually took care of. "Get used to it, she's gone," he grumbled as he made his way to the kitchen where he scooped out hard food into the cats' bowls. The cats watched from the doorway before they turned and left. "Don't eat, see if I care!" Ted shouted at them.

In the bedroom, Ted did his best not to look at the queen size bed. Out of the corner of his eye he could see that it was neatly made. There was nothing out of place. Even the bathroom was neat and tidy. How empty it all looked, how unlived in. He further tormented himself by looking in the closet.

Did he make a mistake by booting Maggie out? Was Jack Emery right? Where did she go? What the hell was he supposed to do? Let her make a fool out of him? Betray him? She had secrets, he'd always known that, just the way he had secrets, but he never let his secrets interfere with their relationship. He wasn't sure about Maggie. He'd always shared. Maggie did not like to share. It was more than that, though, he could feel it in his gut. Where the hell did she go? He shouldn't care but he did care.

In the kitchen Ted opened a Diet Pepsi and swigged from the can. He hated Diet Pepsi but Maggie drank it by the gallon. Did she go to a hotel or to a friend's house? Maybe she was bunking with her brunch partner, Lizzie Fox. The name alone left a bad taste in his mouth. It really rankled him that Maggie would rather have lunch with the glamorous attorney than with him. Especially since they usually spent Sundays together unless Maggie had plans. Lately, she always seemed to have plans, now that he thought about it.

Where the hell was she? Ted sat down on one of the kitchen chairs as he tried to figure out where Maggie might have gone. For the most part, she guarded her personal privacy. He knew he had embarrassed her at Wintergreen's, which didn't say much for the kind of person he was. No, Maggie wouldn't go to Lizzie, she'd be too humiliated. Maggie was thrifty, she wouldn't want to spring for a hotel room unless she could put it on her expense account.

Suddenly, Ted's eyes narrowed. Expense account. The *Post*. The corporate apartment. Yeah, yeah, that's the way she would have gone. Every reporter at the paper had a key. Hell, he even had one. Where was it? The kitchen drawer. He yanked at the drawer, found the key on a red string. Well, so what?

If he went to the apartment Maggie would probably kill him or at the very least, cripple him. Assuming he was right and that's where she'd gone. Well, there was only one way to find out.

Ted was out the door in minutes and in a cab. "Dupont Circle. I'll let you know where to let me out. Just drive."

He needed a plan. Jack Emery always said a guy needed a plan when it came to women. Like he was going to believe anything that asshole said. Everyone knew plans never worked.

Fifteen minutes later, Ted tapped the driver on the shoulder. "Let me off at the corner."

Ted's heart thumped in his chest as he tried to convince himself he just wanted to make sure Maggie was okay. And maybe to apologize. He walked along, barely noticing the warm spring evening. Not many people were out and about, probably because everyone was home getting ready for the workday tomorrow. Normally he and Maggie watched old movies on Sunday night just like an old married couple.

He stopped in front of the building, hesitated for a bare moment, and then went indoors and rode the elevator to the sixth floor. He found the apartment, knocked loudly three times. When there was no response, he pulled the red string from his pocket and fit the key in the lock. He called Maggie's name several times as he made his way around the small apartment. He saw her suitcases in the bedroom and her backpack in the kitchen. He told himself she probably just stepped out to get something to eat because she never, as in never, went anywhere without her backpack. Which begged the question, should he look inside it?

Ted fought with himself as he weighed the consequences if he did just that. Well, he was a reporter, it was his job to investigate such things. Without a moment's hesitation, he opened the backpack and pulled out the thick wad of papers. He whirled around to look for a printer. There it was on the kitchen counter. An old one that could have passed for a breadbox. He blinked when he saw the name on the stack of printouts. Tyler Hughes, Justice Barnes's ex–son-in-law. So his instinct was right. He folded the papers and jammed them into the back of his pants under his windbreaker.

Ted continued to paw through Maggie's belongings. He pulled out a cell phone and looked at it. He had noticed a cell phone next to the laptop. Why the hell did she need two cell phones? Well damn, this was like no other cell phone he'd ever seen...

The fine hairs on the back of Ted's neck stirred. Instinct warned him to get out of the apartment. He dropped the mysterious-looking cell phone into the pocket of his Windbreaker before racing to the front door. He opened the door a crack to peer up and down the hallway, he closed and locked the door, and ran to the EXIT sign to take the stairs to the lobby. When he reached the door that led to the lobby he opted to take the stairs to the basement level. All thoughts of apologizing to Maggie for his behavior in Wintergreen's were forgotten. Now all he wanted was to get back to his own apartment to go over what he'd just stolen.

"Now, Jack, *that's* a plan," Ted chortled as he made his way down the street, his head down, a grim smile on his face.

Chapter 7

Jack Emery clicked the remote control to change television channels. He'd already gone through all the cable shows and there wasnothing of interest, so now all he had left were the three prime networks. Another reason to hate Sundays. Maybe he should have another beer and pack it in for the day. He looked down at the coffee table in front of him where the special phone rested—when it was out of his pocket, it was never out of sight. When it rang, which wasn't all that often, it was usually Nikki. She hadn't called yet today, so maybe he shouldn't go to bed just yet. The beer, though, was definitely needed. He got up, gave his pajama bottoms a hitch as he trotted out to the kitchen.

It was times like this, when he was alone with his thoughts, that the enormity of his situation and his commitment to Nikki and the others hit him like a sledge-hammer. He was a district attorney for Christ's sake, sworn to uphold the law, and he had tossed all that aside and went at it full bore. What was that saying, fools go where angels fear to tread? Well, he was no fool and he sure as hell was no angel, so what the hell was he? A stupid, dumb schmuck seemed an appropriate title.

Jack was twisting the cap off a long-neck when the front doorbell shrilled to life. He looked over at the clock on the stove. Nine o'clock. No one came here on a Sunday night at nine o'clock. Harry was the only one, aside from Mark Lane, who ever visited him at Nikki's house, and he knew for a fact that Mark was in New York. He'd spoken to Harry a half hour ago and he said he was going home to bed. For sure Ted Robinson wouldn't be visiting. Then who? Go to the door, stupid, and see who it is.

Jack looked through the peephole just as the bell shrilled again. He blinked. Maggie Spritzer! And she was dancing from one foot to the other. She probably had to go to the bathroom. He opened the door and stared at her. "The bathroom is at the end of the hall."

"Huh? What? Why should I care where your bathroom is?" Maggie brushed past him. Even from where he was standing he could tell the reporter was twitching from head to toe.

"The way you were jiggling around out there I thought you had to use the facility. What the hell are you doing here, Maggie? Reporters visiting district attorneys is not a good thing. I hope you're here to tell me your boyfriend got hit by a *Post* delivery truck and has amnesia. Tell me that's why you're here. Want a beer?"

"No. Yeah, yeah, give me a beer. No such luck on Ted getting hit by a *Post* truck and getting amnesia. If I thought that would work, I'd give it a shot myself."

Jack handed over a long-neck and waited until Maggie took a healthy swig before he asked again why she was visiting.

Maggie squared her shoulders and

took a deep breath. "I moved into the *Post* condo that they keep for VIP interviews. While I was out to get some dinner someone broke in and took all my printouts on Tyler Hughes. And...And they stole the encrypted phone. I almost had a heart attack. I didn't know where else to go. I thought about going to Lizzie but figured you were the best person. I'm sorry, Jack."

"Son of a bitch! Who knew you were staying there?"

"No one. Well, my boss, he gave me the key. The lock wasn't tampered with so it had to be someone who had a key. I was only gone about two hours."

Jack's brain sizzled. "Does Ted have a key?"

Maggie swigged again as she danced from one foot to the other. "I knew you were going to ask me that. Not to my knowledge. My boss, Liam Sullivan, wouldn't have told him I was there, even if he asked. I asked him not to. Liam thinks we had a lover's quarrel, that kind of thing. I know I wasn't followed. I made sure of that. I suppose it could have been a random break-in, but then why didn't they take my little pouch of jewelry I keep in my backpack? Maybe it was someone on Justice Barnes's side. It doesn't have to be Ted."

"If you believe that for even one nanosecond, I have a couple of bridges I can sell you on the cheap. It was Ted all right and we both know it. Now he's got his nose into it and he will play it out to the end. Plus he's pissed at you big-time."

"Well, whose fault is that? Not mine. I told you when you ordered me to go to Wintergreen's, and you did order me, Jack, that I always try to spend Sundays with Ted. He had a right to be pissed to find me having lunch with Lizzie Fox. What he saw in Wintergreen's was Reporting 101. Every damn red flag in the world went up for Ted to see. I would have done the same thing he did. Tough if you don't like hearing that, Mr. Big Shot! Right now I need your help and we need to go into damage control."

"Wrong! The first thing we have to do is call Charles. I bet you never saw that cranky Brit with his knickers in a knot, did you? It ain't pretty, Maggie."

Maggie squared her shoulders. "Oh, boo hoo, too bad, too sad. I can always quit if you or Charles think I'm at fault here. I'm a victim! What part of that don't you see?"

"No, he won't fault you, he's going to want you killed. Rubbed out—86'd, fitted with concrete boots and dumped in the Potomac. What part of that don't *you* understand?" Jack asked as he tried to imagine Charles's reaction to Maggie's tale of woe.

Maggie gulped but she held Jack's gaze, her eyes defiant. "Well, what are you waiting for?" Maggie demanded. *"Call him."*

"I'm going to call him when I'm damn good and ready and not one minute before. Why didn't you go to Judge Easter? Why me? You need to pick your friends more carefully, Maggie. Ted's got you in a whole shitload of trouble."

Maggie struggled to drag up all the disgust she could muster into her voice. "Yeah, like you pick your friends. I'm talking about Nikki here. Look at yourself before you start judging me. I heard the stories about the lengths you went to way back when you were trying to nail Nikki and the others. You're no better than I am, so get off your high horse, Jack Emery."

She was right and Jack knew it. "You're supposed to keep the phone on your person," he said. "I thought you understood that."

"I did. I do. I keep it in my backpack. I don't always have a pocket in what I'm wearing. Look, it happened, Jack. I can't undo what happened, so just make the damn call already."

Jack made his way to the living room to get his encrypted phone. He drew a deep breath, pressed buttons and then put the phone to his ear. He couldn't resist the impulse to say something witty so he ran with it. "Spain, we have a problem." Rather than wait for King Charles—that's how he thought of him—to speak, he said, "Someone heisted Maggie's encrypted phone and some printouts on Tyler Hughes. Maggie is here right now. I think it was Ted Robinson. Maggie will have to tell you herself who she thinks it was. She moved into a condo the *Post* maintains for VIP interviews. Ted kicked her out when he spotted her having lunch with Lizzie today at Wintergreen's. He could be our worst nightmare, Charles."

When there was no response, Jack removed the special appliance from his ear, shook it, and then placed it back at his ear just in time to hear Charles say, "I'll get back to you on this, Jack."

Jack clicked off the phone and looked over at Maggie, who was wringing her hands. He shrugged.

"Wha'd he say, wha'd he say, Jack?"

"He said he'd get back to me."

"What the hell does that mean?" Maggie flopped down onto the long couch. "You need a dog or a cat," she said inanely. She bounced up immediately and started to pace the exquisitely decorated living room. "Nice digs. Nikki has good taste. In furnishings, not men. Don't people wonder about you living here in her house?"

"Let's not get personal here and invade each other's space. That's another way of saying it's none of your business."

"No, I guess it isn't. I'll leave now," she said, heading for the front door.

Jack was tempted to ask her to stay but couldn't get his mouth to work. He followed her. Neither said a word. When the door closed behind her, Jack threw the security bolt and turned on the alarm system. Before heading to the second floor and bed, he gathered up the empty beer bottles for the recycling bin. He turned off all the lights, checked the back and side doors. Safe and snug.

Upstairs, Jack brushed his teeth before climbing into bed. Once, a long time ago, these sheets had smelled like Nikki. He'd loved getting into bed with her, savoring the feel of her, loving the scent of the bed where they made such glorious love. He knew in his heart of hearts that he was never, ever going to get that time back again.

Screw you, King Charles.

Maggie was right. He needed to get a dog or a cat.

Tomorrow.

Charles Martin held up his hand. "Before you all say whatever it is you want to say, let me tell you there has been a new development back in the States. It seems that Ted Robinson saw Maggie lunching with Lizzie Fox and he also saw all the others. In a fit of pique, Ted got cheeky and told Maggie she had to move out of his domicile, which she did. I believe I told you all that earlier. She relocated to a condominium owned by her newspaper that is used for visiting VIPs. When she went out to get something to eat, someone entered that condo and stole her encrypted phone and some printouts about Hughes.

"Maggie went over to Jack's and apprised him of what happened and he just called me. I think that updates our situation for the moment. Now, ladies, since you asked to gather here at our command center, tell me what's on your minds."

Nikki took the initiative and spoke first. "Before we get to that, does this mean our counterparts back in the States are in danger?"

"Yes, I believe so. I don't think I need to refresh any of your memories where Mr. Robinson's bulldog tendencies lie. Is it serious? Very much so. Jack and Harry are the only two we can count on. I'm not saying Nellie or Lizzie can't...uh...cut the mustard, as Kathryn would say. Maggie is going to be under a microscope. She's not going to be much help this time around. This could all fall apart, ladies."

"Well, we can't let that happen, now can we?" Annie asked as she looked from one to the other of the women. "Let's get this show on the road. I'm ready to go right now."

"I am, too," Myra said. "Poor Maggie. All she wanted to do was help us. I'm ready to leave right now, too, Charles." She purposely didn't look at the others so as not to influence any of their decisions.

Charles waited, unaware that he'd been holding his breath when he noticed the others nod their heads in agreement after a slight nod of Kathryn's head. He felt light-headed when the long-held breath exploded from his body. "Does that make it unanimous, then?" he asked calmly.

"It's unanimous, Charles," Alexis said.

"Then I had better get to work. Pack lightly, ladies. Alexis, work quickly with your Red Bag of magic tricks. It will be wheels up in exactly twenty-four hours. You will be returning to the States right out in the open by a private tour jet, compliments of . . . a friend."

The women stared at Charles with their jaws dropping. "How did you know we would agree? What if we had said no?" Nikki asked.

"Let's just say I had a small wager going on. Maggie is one of ours now. We have to help, it's that simple."

"What exactly do you mean by being 'out in the open'?" Alexis asked in a jittery-sounding voice.

Charles chuckled. "You're going to be rock stars from Cape Town, South Africa. That will be the originating takeoff for the private tour jet, in case anyone checks. No one will ever think you'd all be brazen enough to return in such a manner."

"Rock stars!" the women squealed like teenagers.

"Yes, from here on in you will be known as the G-String Girls. You will hit the ground running and no one will ever look at the Dixie Chicks again. I hope you are all impressed with my abilities."

The women just stared at him. Annie was the first to untangle her tongue. "I suppose you had...uh...help with this, too."

"Let's just say my royal friend Liz is a big fan. Yes, I had tons of help. Now, no more questions. Alexis, I'm printing out a picture of the realG-String Girls. Work quick and fast."

Still speechless, the women left the

command center muttering about rock stars and talent and skimpy outfits with knee-high boots and belly piercings.

Annie could barely contain herself as she made her way up the stone steps to the main part of the monastery that was now their home. "I'm so glad you girls agreed to go with Myra and me. We'll be fine if we work together in sync. I trust each of you with my life. I know Myra feels the same way, don't you, dear heart? Ooh, I can't wait to get my belly button pierced. Will it hurt? I heard somewhere you have to put the hot needle in a raw potato. This is beyond exciting. Aren't you girls excited? My goodness we might pick up a whole new fan base for the G-String Girls."

"Annie, shut *UP!*" Myra said through clenched teeth.

Myra saw the worried looks on the other faces. "Not to worry, we'll be fine, girls. Annie and I talked about this earlier. As you can see, neither of us is young so if things go...badly, we'll stay and take our punishment. It goes without saying we will never divulge your whereabouts. Now, doesn't that make you feel better?"

In spite of herself, Kathryn laughed. "Myra, you're turning into an Annie clone."

"I'm going to take that as a compliment, dear. Now, Alexis, tell us what we're going to look like when we set foot on American soil."

Alexis pretended to think. "Just like this picture! Not that this will mean anything to all of you, but I think we're going to have to take a crash course in guitar playing on the trip to the States."

Within minutes, the women were jabbering a hundred miles a minute. Their excitement was contagious.

"Oh, Myra, when was the last time we performed on a stage? Back in dance class when we were seven years old, that's when. Do you think they'll want us to sing or dance? I think I might be a little rusty," Annie gushed. "That's all we can do unless we *pretend* to play a guitar. We'll have to clip our nails. This is just too much. Way too much."

Her eyes as big as saucers, Myra looked up at her friend. "Annie, I can't quite picture either one of us in any kind of skimpy attire cavorting around on a stage. No one is going to pierce my belly button. I think the girls will relegate us to stagehands. We'll be carrying clipboards." Her voice sharpened. "They're just talking about dressing us up for the trip. No one is actually going to perform. At least I don't think so. God, I hope that's what it means. I don't even know who the Dixie Chicks are."

Annie deflated. "Oh, poop."

Chapter 8

Charles Martin sucked in his breath before he pressed in the numbers to a very special telephone in England. He hated that he had to make the call, much less ask for help from the woman he loved almost as much as he did Myra. He knew his favor would be granted, that wasn't the point. The point was that he was *asking,* something he had promised himself he would never do. He was going to have to explain the why of it all to his special friend. He knew she would do all in her power to do whatever he asked without asking questions, aware that she was his last resort. He pressed the numbers before he could change his mind.

The voice on the other end of the phone was friendly, calm and curious. "Sir Malcolm calling," Charles said quietly. A smile tugged at the corners of his mouth as the queen queried him on personal issues. There was a smile in the voice. He answered the questions, asked about her dogs and grandchildren. He laughed aloud as she regaled him with some of their antics. And the world thought she was a stiff, unfeeling woman out of touch with the world. He knew better.

And then as if by some invisible signal, it was down to business. Charles spoke quickly, outlining his needs and apologizing again for asking for help. It took only another moment for the voice on the other end of the phone to agree to lend her support in whatever way that was needed.

A promise to stay in touch ended the phone call but not before the quiet voice said, "Promise me, Sir Malcolm, to send a video in a plain brown wrapper."

Laughter rippled from Charles's lips and his step was lighter when he mounted the two steps that led to the bank of computers where he worked like a wizard for the benefit of the Sisterhood. He flexed his fingers before he lowered them to the keyboard. The result was a blizzard of outgoing emails. Fifteen minutes later a return blizzard of emails came through. He shifted and collated the emails before he began to speed-read them. A second later his fist shot in the air.

Upstairs, the women were laughing hysterically at the pictures Alexis was passing around showing the glorious bodies of the real G-String Girls.

Annie clutched Myra's arm. "Myra," she whispered, "when I was nineteen I never looked like that. Those young women don't have sagging breasts or cellulite." Myra didn't bother to respond, she simply clutched her grandmother's pearls that she was never without. Recognizing the panic in her old friend's eyes, Annie nearly swooned.

"Easy does it, Mom. It's all going to work out."

Myra whirled around. "Oh, darling girl, if I ever needed you it is right now. I don't think...Oh, dear, I had no idea...Dear girl, we're *old.*"

There was a hint of laughter in her spirit daughter's voice when she responded.

"Mom, you always said age is just a number. Run with it, have some fun for a change. Trust Charles. Trust the girls. Mom, just go with the flow. Don't frighten the others, okay?"

"Is it going to be all right, darling girl?" Myra whispered.

"Mom, trust me, okay?"

"I do, darling. I do. I really do. Trust you, that is. I don't even know what a G-string looks like."

"Turn around and you'll see." The laughter was back in Barbara's voice.

Myra whirled around, her eyes big as saucers as Nikki held up a glittering G-string. "Are those diamonds?" she asked in a strangled voice.

"Nope. Zircons, I'm thinking," Nikki said, peering closely at the G-string. "Or rhine-stones. What are the pasties made of?" she asked Alexis.

Myra knew it was Annie's voice when she squeaked, *"Pasties?"* because she was looking at her. "Didn't you hear me when I said our boobs sag? And, don't forget the wrinkles. We look like weathered road maps."

"Not to worry, Annie. I can hike your boobs up to your ears if you want me to. Relax," Alexis grinned. "I can work miracles with latex." The others laughed when Nikki passed the G-string around the circle. Then it was like old times, when they'd planned a mission back in the States. Their adrenalin was pumping as they high-fived each other. "And, girls, we have *VIDEO!*" Alexis said, her eyes sparkling with laughter.

Annie looked around at the others, her eyes bigger than saucers. Her shoulders squared and she waved her arms wildly when she said, "I think, girls, we're in business. Now, let's get to it. Alexis, show me how you can hike my...uh...breasts up to my ears. And while you're at it, tell me how you're going to hike up our rear ends? In precise detail, dear."

Jack Emery clicked on his email and read his most recent message. In the Subject line the word "URGENT" glared up at him. He clicked on READ and then cringed again. His boss was asking for volunteers to help the District police cover the Russian delegation that was to arrive sometime within the next thirty-six hours. Like that was going to happen. Working twelve hours a day as it was, he needed to get his sleep sometime. He kept reading and then whistled. Well, he might seriously consider moonlighting to protect the G-String Girls, who were due around the same time as the Russians were. Interesting detail, and time and a half wasn't bad, either. What the hell, every cop worth his salt would be volunteering for that particular detail. He could hardly wait to call Harry to see if he was interested in partnering up.

Jack read the rest of his emails and then went back to the first one from his boss. Then he called Harry.

"You just trying to yank my chain, Jack? No. No! And No! Those girls are obscene! What the hell are they doing coming to the States, anyway? I read an article where they said they would never come Stateside because distance adds to their allure. Soon as you can't book a group, they become so in demand they start throwing money at you. So much money you can't be true to yourself. It's all about money, Jack. One more time, no! That goes for the Russians, too."

"I suppose you're going to tell me you don't own any of their albums or CDs, too!"

"So I own one. I wanted to see what they were all about. Yoko likes their music. How many do you own?" Harry asked slyly.

"None," Jack lied.

"Yeah, right."

"Have you heard from Yoko?"

"Three days ago for five minutes. Nikki call?"

"Yesterday morning. Like you, five minutes. The shit hit the fan with Maggie." Jack quickly brought Harry up-to-date. Harry whistled in surprise. "I'm waiting to hear back from Charles. I'm going to call Maggie when I hang up from you. I know in my gut Ted is responsible for her break-in. We just might have to flatten his ass, Harry."

"Say the word and it's done. Of course if we make an issue of it he'll know it's us."

Jack snorted. "And we should worry about *that?* I-don't-think-so. Stay tuned and I'll get back to you."

Jack stared down at the open email,

knowing he had to respond to his boss sooner rather than later. He typed in a carefully worded response that thanked him for the opportunity of overtime but he regretfully had to decline. He pressed SEND and then sighed so loud he startled himself. He was about to log off when the envelope on his email started to jiggle. "Ah, shit!" Jack read the email and uttered another "Ah, shit."

I think you misunderstood, Emery, my email wasn't a request, it was an order. That goes for Wong, too. Pick up your schedule from the duty officer. Court is dark on Wednesday, so you can give this your full attention.

"Ah, shit!" Jack said again. He called Harry on his speed dial.

"I'm taking my name off your shitty payroll, Jack. I don't need this crap. In addition, I have more work than I can handle. Tell your boss to stuff it. I'm not guarding a bunch of naked females. Yoko will pitch a fit!"

"Too late, Harry. You're still on the payroll. Listen, I have to head to court. I'll pick up the assignment sheet after court. I want you to track down Ted Robinson and put the fear of God in him. We're probably too late already, but I sure as hell don't want him showing that encrypted phone to anyone, especially the FBI. See if you can get hold of Bert Navarro. He might be able to help. Call me if things get sticky. You're up, Harry!"

"Why don't you just come out and say I'm going to be doing your dirty work instead of saying 'you're up, Harry'?"

"Because it sounds better, that's why. Put some grease on those sandals of yours and make me proud!"

"Screw you, Jack!"

Jack laughed. "See, see, you're ungrateful. It's going to be a cold day in hell when I invite you to my ranch in Montana to fly fish if you continue to be so negative."

"Be still my heart. Promise me you'll never make me go to Montana again. I hate Montana. I hate you! I hate Charles Martin. I hate all this bullshit."

"I hear you, Harry. I hear you," Jack said, breaking the connection.

Jack waited until he hit the ground floor before he pulled out his cell phone to call Maggie Spritzer. "I'm just calling to tell you I have nothing to tell you. I'm still waiting to hear back from Charles. Stay loose, Maggie. I'll be in court till four so if anything goes down, call Harry or wait till four and meet me outside the courthouse. By the way, where are you?"

"Okay, Jack. I'm at the paper. I'm waiting for Ted so I can kill him. No one seems to know where he is. It's bad, Jack, when no one knows where Ted is. That means I'm limited as to where I can go because he'll be following me, or one of his buddies will be. Listen, I hate to cut you short but I gotta go, my boss is summoning me."

"We'll catch up later, Maggie."

Jack looked around and noticed for the first time what a nice spring day it was. There was a time, and it wasn't too long ago, when he was aware of everything around him—his surroundings, people, traffic, animals, the world. These days he was lucky if he knew what day it was and never mind the time. He was capable of losing *hours* at a stretch. He choked up as he loped along to the courthouse.

Childishly he crossed his fingers as he wished for yesterday. It wasn't going to happen and he knew it. He'd made his decision to join forces with Nikki and the Sisterhood because he loved her with all his heart. He took a deep breath as he mounted the steps to the courthouse. Life was going to go on no matter what he did or didn't do.

When Jack Emery settled himself behind the old, scarred courthouse desk he had a moment of panic as he tried to recall who he was prosecuting and the why of it. His mind a blank, he had to open his briefcase for the legal papers and the list that outlined what he had to do for the next three hours. Like Harry Wong, right now he hated everyone.

Just as Jack got to his feet to acknowledge the Honorable Adam Wright, Maggie Spritzer was entering her boss's office.

"What's up? You hear from Ted today?"

"Your boyfriend seems to think I work for him, not the other way around. That means, no, I haven't heard from him. Espinosa, his shadow, said Ted was hot on some big political story and would call in from time to time. Look, with Ted out doing his own thing I'm going to need you to work some overtime. I know you hate covering the doings at the White House so I'm giving you a pass on covering the Russians' arrival. Instead you're going to be covering the arrival of the...the...some...what they are is a musical group out of South Africa called..."

Maggie let out a whoop of pleasure. "TheG-String Girls! I have every CD and album they ever made. Ted loves them more than I do. Sometimes," Maggie said happily, "there is a silver lining. When do they arrive?"

Liam Sullivan tossed a thick blue folder in Maggie's direction. She caught it in midair, two of the glossy pictures falling to the floor. She offered up a wicked grin as Sullivan turned beet red. A devil perched itself on her shoulder. "Guitars...strings . . . G-strings. Get it?"

"I get it. Now get out of here and make sure your readers get a good human-interest story. I don't see any need to play up all that...skin."

"That's what it's all about, Chief—skin,

long legs, bosoms and a little music and lots of sparkle and lust."

Sullivan grumbled something that sounded like, *"It's a damn sick society where women have to cover their naked bodies with guitars and the damn music sounds like a bunch of sick cats squalling their heads off."*

Maggie shrugged. Liam was old, at least fifty, what did he know about good music? She clicked on her computer, swivelled her chair a little to the right so she could see Ted's desk if he decided to grace the *Post* with his presence. *Political story slash scoop, my ass.*

Before Maggie could work herself into a frenzy over what she considered Ted's thievery, she logged onto the think tank where Tyler Hughes worked. She fired off an email and wrote the word "URGENT" in the Subject line. All she could do now was wait for a reply.

The newsroom was quiet. Maggie looked around. Half the desks were empty, the computer screens blank. Obviously nothing newsworthy was going on in the nation's capital. When that happened the bosses told the reporters to get creative. In other words, make up something but make sure you have two sources. Not that Liam Sullivan ever said anything like that. All that would change in a matter of hours when the Russian delegation appeared. Maggie knew in her gut that no one was interested in the Russians but would be incredibly interested in the G-String Girls. Maybe interested was too mild a term. She liked the word "obsessed." Just in case the G-String Girls didn't generate enough interest mediawise, she knew how to be creative.

Maggie leafed through the glossy publicity pictures. It wasn't fair that these women were so gorgeous, so long limbed and she was soordinary-looking. With freckles and flyaway hair to compound the problem. They were satiny and sexy-looking. So visual. Even the damn guitars looked sensual.

Maggie blinked when out of the corner of her eye she saw her intrepid colleague approaching his desk just as she received an email alert. She quickly shuffled the photos of the G-String Girls back into the blue folder. Within seconds she changed her password again and then clicked off the computer before Ted could see what she was doing. She'd pull up her email on her laptop the minute she left the building.

"Maggie, wait," Ted said, trying to grab her arm.

Maggie swung the backpack at the same moment her foot lashed out. The backpack caught Ted square on the side of the head, her foot making impact with his groin. An evil grin spread across her face when he howled with pain. "I hope they have to amputate," she bellowed as she raced from the newsroom and headed for the elevator.

Chapter 9

Charles Martin, ever methodical, even anal at times, according to Myra, stared down at his cryptic notes. In a matter of hours with all the high-tech knowledge at his fingertips he now had a plan. It always amazed him that things could come together so quickly when the right people were in place to carry out one's plan. He was confident now that he could get his girls in and out of the nation's capital with ease. The only negative he could see was the human element. Things could go wrong when a person trampled on concrete plans, as he'd found out. But potential snafus were something he tried not to worry about.

He let his mind wander as he packed up his notes and files. How would the girls like living on Big Pine Mountain? Being back in the States would definitely be a plus, that much he was sure of. But...Being so close to their old homes and haunts, not to mention Jack Emery and Harry Wong, might be a problem...

Only in moments like this did Charles allow his deepest fear to surface. No one was around to see his shoulders slump. No one could see the worry in his eyes. It was the human element that bothered him. Yes, they'd made a getaway and lived to fight another day, but others had picked up the gauntlet. No matter what they did, no matter how prepared a plan was, things could go wrong. The thought of a second possible capture made his blood run cold, keeping him awake at night.

Charles sighed. He had to clear his thoughts and prepare for this new mission. He had no time to worry about what *might* or might not happen. He was about to leave to join the others for lunch when his encrypted cell phone beeped. His eye-

brows shot upward. "Good morning, uh…
afternoon, Jack."

There were no greetings, no pleas-
antries on the other end. "Charles, Mark
Lane, my contact who is a programmer,
and used to be with the FBI, just contacted me. I think I told you he knows
what's going on in the Hoover Building before the occupants know. Justice Barnes
is off the grid. It seems her live-in significant other, Grant Conlon, who is also the
brother-in-law of Elias Cummings the current director of the FBI, has asked for discreet help. If you're going to ask me if she
was snatched or she walked away on her
own, I can't tell you. She has some serious security so I don't know how she'd
pull off a disappearance. As we speak,
Maggie Spritzer is meeting up with Tyler
Hughes. What, if anything, do you want
me to do, Charles?"

"Sit tight, I'll get back to you. For now,
stay in touch with Maggie."

Charles broke the connection and retraced his steps to his bank of computers.
His fingers flew over the keys as he
chewed on his lower lip. *That* he was not
expecting. The human element rearing its

ugly head even before the mission got off the ground was not a good thing. His right foot tapped impatiently as he waited for responses to his various emails to pepper his computer screen.

Did Pearl Barnes simply walk away or was she abducted? He discounted the latter as soon as the thought popped into his head. He told himself she'd panicked and left without thinking things through. Right now, if Jack was right, the worst possible thing that could happen had just happened. If Grant Conlon alerted the FBI, Elias Cummings would be on it like, as Alexis would say, white on rice, whatever that meant. The agency sorely needed some good press after the last fiasco with the vigilantes. That would be a terrible mistake on Conlon's part, one that would make his own and the girls' jobs much harder.

Charles's foot tapped faster. For some reason he thought Nellie Easter was behind Justice Barnes's disappearance. His anxiety lessened with the thought. He snatched the printed incoming email before it was all the way out of the printer. For the second time in less than an hour his clenched fist shot in the air.

* * *

It was a relaxed luncheon as Isabelle brought out the salmon soufflé, an early garden salad and fresh yeast rolls with soft, golden butter. A pitcher of ice tea sat in the middle of the table. Yoko poured the amber liquid into frosted glasses that Alexis handed her on a silver tray.

They chatted like the old and good friends they were as they served themselves and sipped the freshly brewed tea.

Sensing food, a bevy of small birds settled themselves on the railing that surrounded the terrace, their anticipation obvious, their eyes bright. A brilliant golden-yellow butterfly flirted with the colorful blooms that lined the entire terrace. Within seconds a swarm settled down in the various clay pots. Murphy and Grady watched, their gaze keen, but they didn't bark or attempt to chase the winged visitors away.

The moment the golden sun was overhead, Charles got up to press the button that would roll out the retractable awning. The birds watched but didn't move. Charles thought it remarkable that such small creatures trusted him.

Thirty minutes later it seemed to Charles that he heard a collective sigh of relief when Annie entered the house to wheel out a serving cart with a silver coffee urn.

In unison the women started to talk. "What? Tell us. Details, Charles."

Charles allowed himself a small smile. "For starters, Justice Barnes has disappeared. Her partner, Grant Conlon, contacted the FBI. We know this because Jack's friend, who is privy to details at the Hoover Building, informed him of this less than an hour ago. My personal opinion is that Justice Barnes panicked and Nellie helped her escape. But, it's just my feeling. Intuition, if you will.

"Now, having said that, let's get down to the details of your trip to the States. The padre will have someone take you to the airport in Barcelona. There you will board a private jet that belongs to the G-String Girls. It's winging its way to Barcelona as we speak. The real G-String Girls are in, uh...concert, for lack of a better word, in Germany. Another concert has been scheduled five days from now in Washington, DC. It's a benefit, with all proceeds going to AIDS Relief. It's a sold-out performance. I'm told that the moment the news went out that the G-String Girls were willing to go Stateside the tickets sold out in three hours. You are the advance team, so to speak. Your trip, your arrival, your stint at the hotel have been choreographed down to the smallest detail. To add to your mysterious arrival there will be a cordon of security with you at all times, headed up by one Jack Emery and Harry Wong." When Yoko squealed her pleasure and Nikki nearly swooned Charles allowed himself a big grin. "Neither Jack nor Harry know you are impersonating the real G-String Girls. If you can fool them, you can fool everyone.

"You will be giving no newspaper interviews unless it's by phone. Television is definitely out. You are going to be in seclusion until the night of the concert when the real stars will perform and you will all be on your way to Big Pine Mountain in North Carolina. At best you will have ninety-six hours to accomplish your mission. I'm holding an extra day in case something goes wrong and we have to fall back and regroup. Any questions?"

"Tell us the downside," Kathryn said.

"You might get caught! Jack thinks Ted Robinson has Maggie's encrypted phone and Maggie says Ted is on her tail. By the way, she will be covering your arrival for the *Post*."

"What about Ted? Where is he going to be? Do you know?" Nikki asked.

"Covering the Russian delegation's arrival. A job it seems no one wants," Charles said. "Think about it. It's the perfect cover for all of you. All of the agencies in Washington will be concentrating on the Russians. Rock stars won't be on their radar screen."

Kathryn posed a second question. "Clarify our mission again, Charles. Is it protecting Justice Barnes and her secret or is it snatching Tyler Hughes and finding out to whom he's told his mother-in-law's secret? What? If Justice Barnes is gone, how do we find the last stop in the underground where those women and children are stranded? You just said her life partner contacted the FBI. That sure as hell can't be good for Justice Barnes or us."

Charles leaned in closer to the table. "If we're successful in getting that location, you, Kathryn, will be driving a big yellow bus from Oregon to Jack's cabin in Montana until other arrangements can be made. You'll be back on the road, Kathryn, with Murphy riding shotgun."

"I guess a bus is almost as good as an eighteen-wheeler. I want to assure you that Murphy will know the difference," Kathryn said. She sighed, remembering the time in her life when she was a long-distance truck driver with her dog by her side.

Charles addressed Alexis. "Is your Red Bag of magic tricks filled to the brim? Is there anything you need?"

Alexis dug into the pocket of her shorts. She slid a long, detailed list across the table. Charles looked at it. He nodded. "Everything will be on the plane when you board. It goes without saying you will be working your magic onboard before you land." Charles, as well as the others, considered Alexis a genius.

"Any other questions?"

"Where will we be staying?" Nikki asked.

"You'll be staying in the Embassy Suites. We've reserved the entire floor to ensure your privacy. These suites consist of bedrooms, sitting rooms and kitchenettes. In other words, you'll have walking-around room when you spend time there. For the most part, you'll be on the move. I have agents who will be on the floor as lookouts for inquisitive hotel staff.

"If there's nothing else, I have work to do. It was a wonderful lunch, Isabelle. Do I dare ask what's for dinner?"

"You dare but I'm not going to tell you," Annie said. "I'm cooking and it will be a surprise. We aren't coming back here, are we, Charles?"

Charles turned in the open doorway and looked from one to the other. "Not for a while. If Big Pine Mountain works for us, we may stay there. So, be sure you bring whatever you think you will miss when you leave here."

"Well, that's a no-brainer," Kathryn snapped, "since we arrived here with just the clothes on our backs."

Charles waved airily.

"I will clean up," Yoko said.

"Myra and I are going for a walk," Annie said as she nudged Myra, who gaped at her. "You said you wanted to get in shape for those G-strings."

"I did say that, didn't I? All right, Annie,

let me get my walking shoes. Just give me a few minutes."

Myra was as good as her word. She returned, walking briskly, not even bothering to stop. Annie had to jog to keep up with her.

The two walked along in silence, neither enjoying the gorgeous day, the pungent scent of the pine trees or the brilliant wildflowers dotting the path. Myra's arms were pumping furiously as she stomped down the path.

"Dammit, Myra, wait a minute. What's wrong?"

"You know damn well what's wrong. I am not going to wear a G-string and pasties. Did you hear me, Annie? I refuse!"

"But they said..."

"They said, they said...And you believe them? Six members make up the G-String Girls. All of them are white. That lets Alexis out, since she's black. You and I are needed to make up the number six. Read my lips, Annie, I am not wearing a G-string and pasties. I don't give a...a... damn what they say about hiking up our breasts and rear ends."

"But they said..."

"They're young, Annie. While they're taking this seriously it's still a lark for them. I repeat, they're young! My God, my pubic hair is gray and it does not match the color in my hair. I am not...I am not shaving... *down there.*"

Annie stopped in her tracks before she doubled over laughing. "Vanity, thy name is woman. I had no idea you were such a prude. Oh, Myra, who cares? I don't care if my toenails are yellow. That's why they make nail polish. Same thing," she said breezily.

Myra stared at her old friend. "You're an idiot, Annie. There is a big difference between gray pubic hair and yellow toenails."

"Okay, have it your way. I'm doing it. I'm viewing this as the ultimate challenge in my life. I'll leave it up to you to explain to Charles how you plan to compromise this mission even before it gets off the ground. I am not backing you up, either."

Myra, huffing and puffing, sat down on a rotted log, her legs straight out in front of her. She pointed to her wrinkled knees, at the liver spots on the calves of her legs.

She ignored her polished toenails. "Yours are no better, Annie."

"The nude nylon bodysuit will cover all those...those little flaws."

Myra picked up a stick, a wicked gleam in her eye. She waved it ominously. "What nylon bodysuit? I didn't hear anyone say anything about a nude nylon bodysuit."

"All right, all right, so I made that up. I'm sure it was an oversight by the girls in not mentioning it. They probably assumed since you and I are so worldly that it was understood."

"Do you want me to beat you to death now or later?" Myra asked, using the stick to get to her feet. Annie backed up warily.

"Myra, we are not going to be on a stage. It's all make-believe. We'll be playing a part. The real G-String Girls are the performers. Think of us as their stand-ins. We're just part of the package to make it all seem more real for the fans. Now, don't you feel better? You can apologize now."

"Not only are you an idiot, Annie, you're a fool. Nothing this little group has done has been easy. Each mission has its own set of problems and this one will be no different.

Remember, I'm the one who said it. Now, I'm going back to the monastery to take a nap."

"Only old people with . . . with gray pubic hair take naps," Annie shot back. "Go ahead, be an old poop, see if I care. I want my fifteen minutes of fame, even if it's anonymously."

Myra jittered and twitched all the way back to the monastery.

Chapter 10

Maggie headed for the nearest deli where she plopped down on a spindly chair at a high bar table. She placed her order and then opened up her laptop. She had one email from Tyler Hughes offering her his cell phone number with the words "Call me." Maggie closed her laptop, and plucked her cell phone out of her pocket. She identified herself and waited to see what kind of response Hughes would give her. She was more than surprised when he said, "I can meet you in fifteen minutes at the coffee shop in my building but I have to warn you, I don't have much time. Is that doable, Miss Spritzer?"

He sounded macho, arrogant and full of himself. Maggie said, "Yes, it's doable, Mr. Hughes. I'll see you in a bit." She slapped some bills on the table but not before she grabbed her toasted bagel and stuffed it in her pocket. If she ran all the way, she could just make the meeting. A taxi would take three times as long with all the traffic lights. Well, she was a runner, wasn't she?

Thirteen minutes later, at a dead run she sailed through the revolving door of the think tank and almost landed on her face. She got her wits together, tried to smooth down her wild bush of hair while she struggled to even out her breathing. A multitask person she wasn't. She was breathing like a long-distance runner when she introduced herself to Tyler Hughes, who looked so good she wanted to lather him with jelly and scarf him down. Talk about eye candy! She enjoyed watching him flinch when she stuck out her hand to offer up a bone-crunching handshake. She did love a good handshake.

"Coffee?" he asked as he held her chair in the small coffee shop. "They serve Kona coffee here. The owners fly in the coffee from Hawaii twice a week. Beats Starbucks any day of the week."

Well, that was more than she needed to know. Maggie looked around. It was a nice little shop, decorated with good taste. She wondered if she would have the guts to pull out her bagel and chomp down. No, she decided, not with this dude. She wondered if he had his very own silver spoon in his pocket to stir his coffee. In the end it didn't matter, he drank it black.

"I don't want to rush you, Miss Spritzer, but I don't have much time. Tell me what this is all about and how I can help you."

"Well, I've been assigned to do a human-interest story on Justice Barnes. I know she's your ex—mother-in-law but I do want to be fair when I write my story. Just anything you can tell me about your relationship. What kind of mother-in-law was she?"

"Distant. With my hours, her hours, we didn't see all that much of one another except for family functions. She was always polite and courteous to me. There were times when I felt I didn't measure up, but that could have been my own insecurities. I wasn't born a blue blood."

Maggie scribbled furiously for effect. Her recorder was whirring softly in the pocket of her jacket. No reason to spook him this early on. "Was she a good grandmother?"

"If spoiling my daughter Mandy constitutes being a good grandmother, then the answer is yes."

"Did you *like* her?"

"That's a very loaded question, Miss Spritzer. I always respected her abilities. Were we ever warm and fuzzy? The answer is no."

"Did she like you?"

"I don't think so. She thought I wasn't good enough for her daughter. That can play hell with a man's ego, you know. My wife had to juggle us. I didn't like that and Pearl didn't like it, either. Beka was caught in the middle. In the end the strain was simply too much and the marriage crumbled. I've moved on and so has Beka. I really don't follow Pearl's life these days."

Maggie continued to scribble. She stopped and looked up at the handsome man sitting across from her. She wondered how he was in bed. Would he be afraid to muss his carefully blow-dried hair? Was he the missionary type? She didn't know *how* she knew, but she suspected he was the type that would make an appointment with his wife to have sex and then choreograph the event right down to the cigarette afterward, when he would ask, *"Was it as good for you as it was for me?"*

"Were you ever involved in Justice Barnes's charitable activities? Not much is written about what she does in her private life. Can you shed any light on what she does outside of her professional life? I know you're removed from the family situation, but rumors spread like wildfire in this town."

Maggie could see the alarm in Hughes's eyes. She plunged ahead. "There are rumors circulating," she said vaguely. She watched the alarm spread across his face. His handsome features seemed to pull inward.

"I'm afraid I can't, Miss Spritzer," he said. "Rumors in this town are 99 percent fiction and 1 percent innuendo."

Maggie leaned across the small table. "Does that mean you have or you haven't heard any rumors?"

"I've had no contact with Pearl. I really

don't have contact with my ex-wife, either. On my visitation days the housekeeper meets me at the door with my daughter and opens the door for Mandy when I take her back. Other than that I have no knowledge of what goes on in that family. It works for all of us."

His voice had turned cool and his fingers were tapping on the table, a sign he was not liking the interview. Maggie had to wonder why he'd agreed to do it in the first place.

Maggie stopped writing long enough to look at him thoughtfully. She decided to go for the jugular. "How much truth is there to the rumor that Justice Barnes paid you in the high seven figures to get out of her daughter's life?"

"I thought you said you wanted to talk about Pearl. I've tried to answer your questions in a gentlemanly way. I have no ax to grind where Pearl is concerned. My divorce has nothing to do with her. I'm going to call your paper and lodge a complaint. I think this interview is over."

Maggie sighed. "If that's your final word, I guess I can quote you on it or say you refused to discuss the payoff to get you out of her daughter's life. You know that old saying, the paper trail or always follow the money. That's the way it went down, isn't it? And there are those out there who are saying you *do* have an ax to grind. Those same rumors are that you gambled the money away and are in dire straits. Do you care to comment on that even though it's a rumor?" Maggie was stretching the truth a tad.

Tyler Hughes wasn't so smoking hot now. Maggie thought he looked meaner than a snake at the moment when he flipped her the bird. The Devil goaded her on. "Be sure to spell my name right. It is S-p-r-i-t-z-e-r." She yanked the dried-out bagel from her pocket and bit into it. She sipped at the dark black coffee and grimaced. He was wrong. Starbucks was so much better.

As Maggie made her way on foot back to the *Post,* she tried to figure out what, if anything, she'd gotten out of the short interview with Tyler Hughes other than to piss him off. From a journalistic point of view she was back at square one.

Maggie was relieved forty minutes later when she entered the newsroom to see

Ted's empty chair. The first thing she did was call Jack Emery to tell him about the interview. She was prepared for his response.

"So you got squat. Now what?"

"You tell me. You seem to be the outside brains of this outfit. Tell me what you want me to do. By the way, when do I get my magic phone back?"

"Take it up with Charles. Justice Barnes has fallen off the grid. Vanished. You have any clues on that? I'll take a half-baked idea if you have one."

The reporter in Maggie kicked in. "How do you know that? Give me something with some meat to it and I'll run with it."

"It seems Justice Barnes's significant other went to the FBI on the QT to see his brother-in-law, Elias Cummings, and told him to check it out quietly. That's all we have on it. You can call Cummings and ask for a comment before you print it. I can't do it, Maggie. You have the credentials to pull it off."

"Okay, I'm on it. What do you think happened? Was she snatched or did she disappear on her own?"

"She's too smart to get snatched. I think

she left on her own but with Nellie's help. You have the credentials to check that out also. Why are you still on the phone with me, Maggie? It goes without saying you did not get this information from me. Time is of the essence."

"Eat shit, Jack," Maggie said, breaking the connection. She was getting sick and tired of Jack Emery. She knew he didn't trust her and she wasn't turning herself inside out again to try and convince him she was on his side. Today she hated men. All men.

Big decision: go to the FBI or call? Eyeball to eyeball was the way to go. You could see when someone was trying to snow you, even a director of the FBI. She was up and off her chair a moment later. Now she had a mission.

This time Maggie took a cab to the Hoover Building. God, how she hated this place. The memory of being grilled by the former director was still a sore point with her.

Maggie adjusted her backpack, tipped the cab driver and entered the Hoover Building. She spent another fifteen minutes with security, emptying her backpack and getting lots of reaction to the G-String Girls' publicity folder. Finally she was on the fourth floor talking to Cummings's secretary, an old bat who wore drugstore '50s Evening in Paris perfume and orthopedic shoes.

"You don't have an appointment, Miss Spritzer. Director Cummings does not see anyone without an appointment. Do you want me to make one for you?" She pursed her lips as if she'd just finished sucking on a lemon and waited for Maggie's response.

"No. I need to see him right now. It's an emergency. I thought he worked for the little people and wanted to hear from them. I distinctly heard him say that on a television interview. Well, I'm one of the little people, so chop-chop here. Tell the big man the *Post* waits for no man. If he doesn't want to talk to me I'll just talk to the little people and put my own spin on it. What's it going to be?"

"Just a minute." Maggie waited while the woman opened the door directly behind her. She was back within seconds. "The director can give you five minutes. Be quick."

Maggie grimaced as she hopped to it.

Director Elias Cummings looked like a nice grandfatherly man—gray hair, wire-rim glasses, shrewd gray eyes. Neatly dressed, spit shine on his shoes. He was holding out his hand. Maggie did her thing and smiled when he openly flinched.

"I'll get right to the point, Mr. Director. Your secretary said she would only give me five minutes."

The director grinned. "She thinks she's my personal dragon slayer. She says that to everyone. I'll tell you the same thing I tell everyone who comes into this office. You have as much time as you need. Now, what can I do for you?"

"You can tell me what happened to Justice Pearl Barnes. I hear she's disappeared and Grant Conlon came here to discreetly ask for your help. True or false? I know Conlon is your brother-in-law so it's understandable he would come to you."

Cummings's expression stayed exactly the same. He was good, Maggie had to give him that. Instead of answering the question, he asked one. "You know this how?"

"Sources. I don't have to tell you a reporter never divulges his snitches. It's been verified. I believe what Conlon said was, 'Pearl fell off the grid.' Do you care to comment?"

"No, Miss Spritzer, I don't care to comment."

"I can work with that, you know, put my own spin on it."

Cummings turned and walked back to his desk. He motioned for her to take a seat. Maggie sat and crossed her legs. She waited.

"I wouldn't do that if I were you."

"Why? Are you saying it isn't true? Surely it's not a threat. Can I quote you on that?"

Cummings waved his arm around. "This office is swept twice a day for bugs. There are no moles, so to speak, on my staff. That leads me to think you're fishing for information and we both know I can't help you."

"Then how is it I know what I know and so do two other sources? We can, of course, camp out around Justice Barnes's home and stake her out. Come on, Director Cummings, give me a break here. I know she's missing. What I want to know is if it's by choice or was Justice Barnes kidnapped?"

This time the director's expression did change with the use of the word "kidnapped." *Let's see how you weasel out of this, Mr. Director.* While she waited for him to respond, Maggie looked around. Nice digs. Quality paneling, Berber carpeting, Naugahyde chairs that were actually comfortable, a few lush plants, PR pictures with various presidents on the walls. A TV and DVD player along with a monstrous assortment of legal-looking books took up an entire wall. A nice enough place to spend eight to ten hours a day when you're trying to protect the good guys from the bad guys.

When there was no response, Maggie said, "I interviewed Justice Barnes's ex–son-in-law a short while ago. He met me in a small café in the lobby of the think tank where he works. He's not too fond of Justice Barnes. At least that's what I got out of it."

"That young man is a twit. He doesn't have a clue what it means to be a husband and a father."

Maggie chewed on her lower lip. Well, if

that's all she was going to get she might as well go back to the paper. She'd planted the seed Jack asked her to plant. If and when it would sprout would be anyone's guess. She stood up. "I think my five minutes are up. Thank you for talking with me, Director Cummings. I'll be sure to spell out your no comments properly."

The director got up, buttoned his jacket and walked Maggie to the door. In a low voice that was barely above a whisper, he said, "You're treading on dangerous ground, Miss Spritzer. I'll be speaking to your editor shortly."

"I'm sure you will, Mr. Director."

Maggie waved to the secretary and was gone a moment later. Downstairs in the lobby she called Jack Emery and reported the facts of her interview. "Is this what they call 'plausible deniability,' Jack?"

Jack said something she couldn't quite hear before the connection was broken.

Maggie walked to the curb to flag down a cab. While she waited, she looked to her left to see Ted Robinson staring at her. For the first time in a very long time, she felt her blood run cold.

Chapter 11

Charles stood by the cable car, his eyes moist. If he wasn't careful a tear was going to roll down his cheek. He brushed at the corner of his eye. His voice was gruff, unlike his normal upbeat British tone. "Ready, ladies?"

The women nodded as they looked around at what they were leaving, this beautiful mountain that was their sanctuary. Fortunately it was a bright sunny day and everything looked golden and lush. When the sun shone things didn't look so grim.

"Everything has been taken care of. I'll

be waiting for all of you at Big Pine Mountain when your mission is completed. I'll be leaving here the moment I welcome the new occupants to our mountain. We'll be in touch hourly. I wish you all luck. If you have any questions, now is the time to ask them." Charles waited and when no one spoke, he smiled.

Alexis whirled around, panic in her eyes. "Where's my Red Bag?"

"I sent all your gear down earlier. The padre has it and it's on the way to the plane as we speak." Charles pressed the button that opened the gate to the cable car. The girls filed in, Myra the last to enter. Her hands fingered the pearls at her neck. She made no move to swipe at the tears rolling down her cheeks.

Charles leaned forward to kiss Myra's cheek. "Stiff upper lip, old girl."

Myra did her best to smile but failed miserably. All she could do was nod before she stepped into the cable car.

Annie wrapped her arm around Myra's shoulders. "This is just a place, Myra. It worked for us when we needed it the most. Home from here on in will be wherever we all are. One mountain is pretty much the same as every other mountain, in my opinion. Charles did say Big Pine Mountain will put our little habitat here to shame so that has to be a good thing. We'll be home, dear, in the good old U.S. of A."

The others crowded around Myra, who until now had always been their rock. That she was crumbling was hard to take.

"Everyone is allowed a few moments of...of...self-pity. I don't want any of you worrying about me. I'm fine now and I won't let you down. I'm actually looking forward to...to...decking myself out in... in *costume.*"

Kathryn pummeled Myra on the back. "Atta girl, Myra. You have to think of this as just another road trip. Remember how antsy you were when you rode shotgun for me on that road trip in my eighteen-wheeler? In the end you had the time of your life. This will be no different. Trust me."

And then they were all talking at once. Excitement took over when the cable car came to a smooth stop. A small group of dark-skinned men, along with the padre, waited to greet them. Annie called each by name, asked after their families and then led the procession to an old white bus that would take them to the airport.

"Go with the angels, my children," the padre said, blessing each of them.

Nikki looked dubiously at the ancient bus. Annie leaned over and whispered, "It's the engine that counts, dear. And the tires. Look a little more closely and you'll see what I mean. There's brand-new horsepower under that hood. The tires are the best money can buy. And there are seat belts inside. Charles took care of all that. We elected to leave the chassis just the way it is for ... for security reasons."

Nikki grinned. "Now, why didn't I figure that out? Good old Charles."

"Yes, good old Charles. What would we do without him? Get on board, dear. It's going to start to rain any minute now."

Nikki looked startled. For the first time she noticed the sun was gone and the day had turned gray with a stiff wind blowing from all directions. Sea spray could be seen coming off the ocean in streams. Was this an omen of some kind? Better to keep her thoughts to herself and not worry the others. She let her mind wander to what it would be like to see Jack again. A warm feeling settled over her as her fingers played with her engagement ring that she wore on a chain around her neck. She closed her eyes and eventually dozed off as the old bus lumbered along the rutted road.

Three hours later, Kathryn shook Nikki's shoulder. "C'mon, sleepyhead, we have arrived. God, my kidneys are never going to be the same after that ride. Careful, everyone, I don't like the looks of that lightning."

"Where's the plane?" Alexis demanded.

"Somewhere," Isabelle grumbled, "but I can't see it in this heavy rain. I hope there is someone here to pick us up." She looked over at the driver of the old bus and asked in Spanish where their Limo was. The bus driver shrugged as he slumped behind the wheel.

"I guess that means we're supposed to wait for someone to show up. I don't see us getting off the ground on time," Isabelle said.

"If our flight is delayed it means we'll be arriving during daylight hours as opposed to midnight," Yoko said. "This is not good."

"No, dear, it is not good," Myra said. "I'm sure Charles is working on that little matter as we speak."

"Myra, it might not be raining and storming back on the mountain the way it is here. Perhaps you should call Charles and apprise him of our current situation."

Myra shook her head. "Charles knows everything. He'll be calling us any minute now." As if Charles could read her mind, Myra's special phone chirped to life.

"Hello, my darling. What news do you have for us?" She listened. "Yes, the rain is quite heavy. You can't see your hand in front of you. No, at the moment there is no fog." She listened again, aware that the others were tuned to her end of the conversation. "How much of a delay, Charles? What are the weather gurus saying?" She dropped into listening mode again. "Yes, yes, dear, we understand there is no controlling Mother Nature and the human element. I'll tell Alexis. Of course we can carry it off. We are not novices, dear heart."

Myra ended her conversation and then dropped her phone into the pocket of her jacket. "It's just this country's crazy spring weather. A band of storms is merging and that's the reason for the lightning and heavy rain. What that means to us is we're looking at a four- to five-hour delay getting airborne."

The women groaned.

"What did Charles want you to tell me?" Alexis asked.

Myra smiled. "Charles said you are to work your magic and make us up so when we deplane we look like the G-String Girls. He also said we are not to worry because there will be tons of security so no one will be able to get close to us."

Annie clapped her hands. "Ooh, ooh, I can hardly wait. Did Charles say anything about Pearl? Is there any news?"

"He didn't say, Annie, so I guess that means there is no news. I'm sure he would have mentioned it otherwise. We might as well settle down since we have to wait till the storm passes before we can be taken to the plane."

Nikki and Yoko sat down next to each other. They smiled, each knowing what the other's thoughts were. Nikki spoke first. "I had a dream before we arrived. Jack was handing me a small bouquet of violets. He was smiling and saying it wasn't much but he knew how much I loved violets so he ran all over town and had to go to twenty-two florists before he found them. It was so sweet. Don't you think it was sweet, Yoko?" But Yoko was sound asleep. A few seconds later, Nikki, too, was asleep.

It was late, almost midnight, when Jack Emery and Harry Wong parked their car at the side entrance to Judge Easter's farmhouse. Other cars were parked side by side, which meant Lizzie and Maggie were already inside.

His senses on high alert, Jack looked around trying to see in the dark. "I have this feeling I'm being watched. You picking up anything, Harry?"

"No one tailed us, Jack. I watched all the way. Or are you saying someone anticipated this little meeting and is already out there?" he asked, waving his arms about to indicate the dense stand of trees that surrounded the farmhouse.

"Yeah, I guess that's what I'm saying. Anyone could be out there. Remember, I lived in a tree for weeks at a time when I was trying to get the goods on the girls.

Ted Robinson will remember those days and try to pull off the same thing."

"So, do we go in or not?" Harry asked warily.

Jack shrugged. "Maggie and Lizzie are already in there. It could be classified as a hen party, you know, a girlie thing. Hey, we're here so what the hell, we might as well go for it. It will be up to Robinson to prove we're up to no good. You might have to go after him, Harry."

Harry mumbled something that sounded less than flattering to Jack's ears. "While I'm doing that, what are you going to be doing?"

"Guarding the G-String Girls."

"I hate you, Jack. When are they getting here?"

"The weekend, I think. Charles said he had details to work out. It's just a few days. The good side to all that is North Carolina isn't all that far from here. That's good for us, Harry. I love you, Harry, and don't you ever forget it. You saved my skin more times than I care to admit. I know you hate it when someone says nice things to you but I mean it. You're the brother I never had. Okay, enough bonding, let's get on with it."

Harry cuffed Jack on the side of the head. "I still hate you. Most of the time. Well, sometimes. Stop saying stuff like that to me or I'll deck you right here and now." He kicked at the kitchen door to alert the occupants.

Nellie opened the door and motioned both men inside. "You're late," she said.

"Jack thinks there's someone out in the woods watching the house," Harry said.

Nellie's round face lit up in alarm. "Should I call the police?"

"And have them see all our cars here? I don't think so, Judge. If there is someone out there, that someone is Ted Robinson. Harry and I will take care of him. Let's get to it. Any word from Charles or Justice Barnes?"

"Yes and yes. Come along, gentlemen. We're playing poker in the dining room. Refreshments are being served. That's in case anyone comes knocking on my door wanting to know what we're doing."

The greetings over, the cards dealt that no one looked at, the bourbon poured, Nellie took the floor. "Pearl is staying at Myra's house. Her housekeeper got her out of the house and took her there. She's probably climbing the walls as we speak. Lizzie is the one who arranged the escape. Successfully, I might add. Maggie had a meeting with Tyler Hughes that didn't go too well. None of us expected Pearl's partner to go right to the FBI but he did. So, we have to deal with that. Maggie went to the Hoover Building and Elias Cummings advised her not to print anything concerning Pearl or Grant. That's where we are at the moment. The floor is open for discussion."

"What does Justice Barnes want us to do?" Harry asked.

"Wait a minute. Just a damn minute!" Jack exploded. He fixed his gaze on Nellie and demanded to know if she'd told Justice Barnes about the vigilantes and his and Harry's part in it all.

"She already knew, Jack. To keep lying would just compound the problem. Charles said we're past the stage where we have to play games because time is of the essence. We need to get the people to safety that are stranded in Oregon. I'm waiting for Charles to get back to me on how we're to deal with Mr. Hughes and his blackmail scheme. I'm sure he can be convinced to *talk* to . . . one of us. Above all, we have to ensure that Pearl's secret remains secret. She's helped thousands of women and children over the years. We simply cannot throw that away and let her cover get blown."

"How long do you plan on stashing Justice Barnes at Myra's house?" Harry asked.

Nellie's arms flapped. "I don't know. She's on her way over here right now. She's coming through the tunnels."

Jack's eyes almost bugged out of his head. "If, and there is a strong possibility that it is possible, Ted Robinson is out there spying on us with some high-powered binoculars, and he sees Justice Barnes, what are we going to say? She's joining us for a little poker game? You better head her off at the pass and send her back."

"You don't know Robinson is out there," Lizzie said.

"He's out there," Maggie said. "If Jack says he is, then he is. Ted was trailing me all day. However, I'm positive he did not follow me out here tonight. Ted is very good at putting two and two together. He is, after all, a reporter and that's what reporters do."

"Well, that sure as hell doesn't make me feel better," Harry said. "I think you need to explain to all of us what Justice Barnes hopes to accomplish by coming out here and hiding. Won't that make her more suspect, bring the authorities to the surface?"

Nellie kept flapping her arms. She looked like a fat bird too heavy to lift off the ground. "She's panicking. Someone in her position simply cannot do the things she's been doing. Surely you all can understand that. Just think back to when the vigilantes were caught and the panic that ensued. I rest my case, no pun intended."

Jack's voice was ice-cold. "I'll meet her in the tunnels and send her back. She can't come into this house, that's the bottom line, Judge." A moment later he was gone.

The others looked at one another without saying anything. Lizzie chomped down on a pretzel. Maggie stuffed her mouth with a small cheese ball. Harry started to pace around the dining room table. The judge just rubbed her arthritic hands, wincing from time to time as she, along with the others, waited for Jack's return.

Twenty minutes later Jack took his place at the table. "She used some colorful language a few minutes ago. I think it's safe to say Justice Barnes is pissed to the teeth."

Nellie stopped rubbing her hands and said, "Pearl can be ... spirited at times."

Then two things happened. Nellie's special phone rang and there was a knock on the kitchen door.

"It's Charles," Nellie whispered looking down at the code on her phone.

"It's Ted at the door," Maggie said. "I know it's him. Who else would come all the way out here at this time of night? Your instincts were spot-on. You have to answer it, Jack."

Jack looked at Judge Easter. "Be quick, Judge. Answer it and tell Charles you'll call him back. I'll get the door."

Jack stomped his way to the kitchen. Fully expecting to see Ted Robinson on the other side of the door, he was stunned to see a tall older man he didn't recognize.

"Grant Conlon. I apologize for the late

hour but I'd like to speak to Judge Easter. It's important that I speak with her."

Not knowing if he should invite the man inside or not, he bellowed for the judge. If it was Ted out there, would he recognize the late-night caller?

Of course he would. Ted was a crackerjack reporter. Two plus two equaled four.

Chapter 12

Judge Easter did her best to hide the surprise she was feeling at the sight of Grant Conlon standing in her kitchen doorway. Never a serendipitous kind of person who adapted to the unexpected she barked, "What are you doing out here at this time of night, Grant?"

"I need to talk to you right now, in private, Nellie. I am well aware of the time and I wouldn't be here if it wasn't important."

"Well my poker game is important, too, and I was winning." She eyed the tall, good-looking man with the gray hair and matching eyes. His body language said he was nervous; the gunmetal gray eyes said something else. She couldn't fail to notice the creased khakis, the navy blue blazer and the white ribbed T-shirt underneath. He wore worn but polished Brooks Brothers loafers. With tassels. She looked down at his hands. She always thought it foolish of him to still be wearing his college ring. She didn't even know where hers was. She realized then that she had never really liked Grant Conlon.

"All right, all right, but I hope this isn't going to be a lengthy meeting, Grant." She turned to Jack and said, "There are sandwiches in the fridge. Do you mind serving them? I'm sure this will be a short break."

Jack moved off toward the refrigerator when he realized the judge wasn't going to introduce him to her late-night guest. He opened the door and removed a large serving platter wrapped in plastic, and then moved off.

Nellie waited until the swinging door closed behind Jack before she led Grant to the laundry room, well out of earshot of the others. "Why are you here? What's wrong, Grant?" Like she didn't know.

"I can't find Pearl."

The judge allowed a stupid look to cross her face. At least she hoped it was a stupid look. "You can't find Pearl! Well, she isn't here if that's what you're asking. Pearl is into bridge, not poker. Did you two have a disagreement?"

Conlon looked properly horrified. "Pearl and I do not have disagreements. She simply disappeared." He waved his arms about. "One minute she was there in the family room, listening to a book on tape and I was playing chess online with a friend, and when I got up to get a snack she was gone."

"Maybe she went to Beka's house."

"That's the first place I called. She isn't there. In fact Beka said she hadn't talked to her mother in three days. That's not unusual, they both lead busy lives. I called everyone I could think of. Her security detail said she did not leave the compound. I'm worried, Nellie."

It was Nellie's turn to flap her arms about. "I don't know what to tell you, Grant. Pearl is a big girl. Maybe she just wanted to get away and be by herself . . . to think about things."

Conlon pounced. "What kind of things? Do you know something?"

"No! Women need to think sometimes. Women like to go off by themselves from time to time. You play golf, don't you? You go to chess tournaments."

The gunmetal gray eyes narrowed slightly. "I have never *ever* gone anywhere without leaving a note or calling Pearl to tell her my whereabouts."

"Well, maybe that's your problem, Grant. Too much togetherness. How long has Pearl been gone?"

"Since last night." He frowned when he saw the judge take towels out of the dryer and start to fold them.

"I've learned how to multitask," Nellie said inanely as she folded a towel. When her housekeeper arrived in the morning she'd undoubtedly think some magic elves had invaded the laundry room. "Have you reported Pearl missing?" she asked.

"Do you think I'm crazy? Do you have any idea what kind of media storm that would cause?"

"Well, your brother-in-law *is* the director of the FBI. Perhaps he could make some discrete inquiries if you're that worried. Elias Cummings is a go-to kind of guy."

Conlon's head jerked upright, his eyes narrowing to slits. "Well, that isn't going to happen. Pearl would throttle me if I did that."

Liar, liar, pants on fire. Nellie folded the last towel and looked her late-night guest directly in the eye. "I can't help you, Grant. I don't know what else to say. I really have to get back to my guests."

"Who was that guy that opened the door? He looks familiar," Conlon asked.

"Not that my guests' names are any of your business, Grant, but his name is Jack Emery. He's a district attorney. Now, if there's nothing else, I really have to get back to my card game. As I said, I was winning when you arrived. By the way, did you query Tyler Hughes? I think I heard someone say not too long ago that you were seen having lunch with him," Nellie said craftily. She mentally gave herself a pat on the back. Maybe she was getting good at this spook stuff.

Conlon reared backward. "Whoever told you that erroneous information is dead wrong. This town never ceases to surprise me with the gossip content. That did *not* happen," he said vehemently.

"I'm only trying to help you, Grant. You said there was no reason for Pearl to take off and...uh...hide from you. Well, if Pearl heard that same story and, no, I did not repeat it, it would certainly be a good reason for her to be upset with you. Knowing Pearl as I do, I think she would view that as a betrayal on your part. Now, I really must get back to my card game. It was nice seeing you even under these conditions. Please let me know when Pearl returns."

Nellie brushed past him and in the process the pile of folded towels fell to the floor. "Screw it," she muttered under her breath. All she wanted was to get this man out of her house so she could lock the door.

At the door, Conlon turned. "I apologize again, Nellie. It's just that I am so worried about Pearl. It simply is not like her to disappear like this. Extend my apologies to your guests. Call me if you hear from Pearl."

"Yes, I will." Nellie thought she would explode as she made her way back to the dining room where her spook buddies waited for her. Well, damn!

Grant Conlon made his way to his car, a snappy bright-red 560 SEL. He stood for a good five minutes looking back at Nellie's house. Pearl never said where Nellie got the money to live in such a lavish farmhouse. He wondered how many acres came with the house. His eyes turned to slits. There was something off-kilter about Nellie this evening. He looked around as though he was looking for something before he lowered himself into the low-slung sports car.

"Atta boy! Whoever you are, smile pretty," Ted Robinson muttered to himself as he clicked and clicked the little night vision camera. He chortled in glee when he got a perfect shot of the driver's license plate. He was going to have a regular photo gallery before the night was done.

Judge Easter certainly had a wide range of friends. Who *was* that nifty-looking guy in the blue blazer and the pricey car? Why was he visiting at this time of night? What the hell were they all doing in there? Plotting and scheming, that's for sure. But why and for what?

Ted settled himself more comfortably in

the V of the tree. He took a moment to wonder if Jack Emery and his goons had sat in this same tree spying on the vigilantes during his hate-on for the women. Probably. He settled his backpack in the small of his back and proceeded to watch the farmhouse with his night vision goggles, thanks to a going-out-of-business sale at an army surplus store. He hoped he didn't fall asleep.

As Ted sat in the tree with his eyes glued to the farmhouse he let his mind wander to where and what the vigilantes were doing. This whole damn thing smacked of them and their shenanigans. He raised his head slightly and then leaned forward. He could see shapes moving in what he thought was the kitchen. It was hard to tell since everything was green with just dark shapes.

Forty minutes later he was rewarded with a mass exodus from the house. Ted watched as the judge's visitors got into their respective cars. Emery, that asshole Wong, his old love and Lizzie Fox. He had a bad moment wondering if he should follow the gaggle of visitors or stay in the tree and watch the judge and the house.

A no-brainer if ever there was one. The visitors were obviously going home. Where else would they go at two in the morning? He settled himself as comfortably as he could and watched the house. Nellie Easter was a night owl. He remembered Jack telling him that once. Something to do with painful arthritis. He made a deal with himself. If the lights went out, he'd go home.

At three o'clock the lights were still on in all parts of the farmhouse. At three thirty he saw movement in the kitchen. At four o'clock he saw two figures in the kitchen. At four fifteen, the kitchen door opened and both figures were outlined in the open doorway. He sucked in his breath when the light on the back porch was turned off. *Oh, be still my heart.* Who was the mystery guest? And where was the mystery guest going? And how was he or she going to get to wherever they were going, since there were no vehicles to be seen in the courtyard?

Ted strained to hear what was being said but he couldn't hear a thing. He turned slightly, the night vision binoculars trained on movement to the right. "Fuck!" A horse!

Why hadn't he seen the animal before? Jack Emery would have seen it and had a horse standing at the ready or whatever the hell horses did. He called himself every name in the book for his lack of foresight. There was no way he could get out of the tree and follow a damn horse.

Ted trained the binoculars on the two moving figures. He watched when one of the figures mounted the horse with ease. Obviously an accomplished horsewoman. A moment later the horse took off at a full gallop. He continued to berate himself as the fast-moving target fell off his radar screen. He went back to the heat-generated figure of Judge Easter, who was entering the house through the kitchen door. He watched as the lights went out one by one until the house was in total darkness.

"Well, shit!" Ted grumbled as he climbed down from the tree and made his way to his car that he'd parked over a mile away. If he burned rubber he could make it back to his apartment, feed Mickey and Minnie, take a shower and get ready to take on the Russian delegation if he wanted to keep his job.

Ted cursed all the way back to the District. He knew in his gut that something was going down and he also knew it involved those goddamn vigilantes. He knew it.

Chapter 13

Myra squirmed in her seat. She couldn't wait to get off the plane. An eight-hour delay had left them all cranky and out of sorts. The girls were snapping and snarling at one another and the words weren't pretty. Annie, on the other hand, thought it all a big lark and was marveling at the sparkling zircon embedded in her belly button.

"You don't think the glue will come off, do you, Myra? I am going to have a giant poster made up of me strutting my stuff. Not to worry, I'll hang it inside my closet door. Assuming at some point I'm going to even have a closet," she babbled. "Myra, did you notice not one of those...those strange people in the back of the plane has moved? I know they're the G-String Girls' people, but surely one of them has to pee."

"It might have something to do with the fact that they don't drink or eat. All they do is watch us. And yet they stare through us. I think maybe they're Charles's people," Myra whispered. "I certainly hope they aren't the type who will write tell-all books when this is all over."

"We only have an hour until we land at Dulles Airport. I do hope this all goes well. I have to admit, Myra, I'm nervous."

Myra rolled her eyes. "I know."

"What gave it away, Myra?" Annie asked. "Am I too hyper? Isn't this disguise fooling you? I haven't seen this much skin since...well, never. How do you think we'd do as pole dancers? I read somewhere that those...establishments that feature such things put oil on those poles. That would then require a great deal of skill and...*agility,* wouldn't you think? I think we need to get out and about a little more."

Myra played with the encrypted phone in her hand as she wondered why Charles wasn't checking in. With less than an hour to go till landing, she was starting to worry. "Now I know what I can get you for Christmas."

Annie ignored her when the girls marched to the front of the plane. Myra gasped. Annie's eyes almost popped out of her head when Alexis held up a large poster of the G-String Girls. "Tell me I don't do good work!"

Relieved that the snapping and snarling had come to an end, Myra nodded her head. "Absolutely perfect. I really didn't think it was possible but you made it happen, dear. Are you going to test out your appearance with the people in the back?"

"We already did, Myra," Nikki said. "They were stunned. They said they couldn't tell the difference between the real G-String Girls and us. They're going to get off the plane first. As far as the media is concerned, they are our bodyguards, and our hair, makeup, wardrobe, shoe and guitar people. There are a total of sixteen in our entourage. The trunks alone will cause a furor. It's working so far."

Isabelle held up a bundle of trench coats. "We deplane wearing these. We whip them open, give the press one shot of our glorious bodies, then we button up and head for the limos. I really think this is going to work. I really do. The truth is I'm a little excited," she gushed. The others agreed, even Kathryn, who was trying to examine her glittering pasties. "I can't believe I'm saying this but, girls, we're hot!"

"Smoking hot," Annie chirped.

"I feel so left out," Alexis groaned.

"Not to worry, dear," Annie assured her. "You are our backbone. Once you get into your disguise you will be one of us without...all your body showing. We're going to need you for patch-up work if...if something goes wrong. We can't do this without you."

"Can we cover up now?" Myra asked. The others laughed as they strutted back down the aisle to their seats. She had tied the belt so tight on her trench coat she was gasping for air. The encrypted cell phone that was still in her hand vibrated. Charles.

"Do not ask, Charles. Do not. Why are you calling?" Myra snapped.

"To tell you everything is in place. All our bases are covered with one change. You will be staying at the five-star Willard InterContinental, the crown jewel of Pennsylvania Avenue. I've engaged twenty suites and other assorted rooms for the entourage. As planned before, you won't be staying there that long. In fact, you will be leaving almost immediately even before the real G-String Girls arrive. Dear heart, you are all going to have one bloody reception committee when you land, so be prepared. Think of it as your fifteen minutes of fame."

"I already had my fifteen minutes of fame, Charles, the day we were arrested. I do not need any more fame." Myra could hear Charles laughing on the other end of the line. In spite of herself she felt a giggle erupting. "G-strings and pasties are not comfortable, my darling."

"But they look so good," Charles quipped.

This time Myra did laugh.

"Your welcoming committee is going to

be awesome. I think the entire male popu-
lation of Washington, DC, will be waiting
for your appearance. I understand almost
every male from Georgetown University
will be there. They chartered buses. In addition it seems hundreds of midshipmen
from Annapolis, not to be outdone, also
chartered buses. Every available law enforcement officer has been called in for
crowd control, even the special agents
from the FBI. The media coverage is going to be beyond belief. I'll make sure I get
all your press clippings."

"Oh, dear God!"

"Make me proud, Myra!" Charles said
before he broke the connection.

The tightly belted trench coat that was
choking Myra was forgotten as she got up
to run back to tell the girls what Charles
had just shared with her.

"Well, hot damn!" Kathryn said as she
high-fived the others.

Annie was so glassy-eyed, Myra had to
swat her on the back to bring her back to
reality. "This is not funny, Annie," she
hissed.

"Oh, yes it is, my friend. You really do
need to lighten up, and will you get rid of

the damn pearls already? The G-String Girls wear leather dog collars festooned with diamonds and nail studs. You need to get with the program or they'll spot you for a phony the minute we land."

Myra let loose with a string of colorful words that made Annie blush, but she undid her pearls and stuck them in the pocket of her trench coat. Alexis was at her side in a nanosecond to clip the dog collar around her neck. "Perfect!"

The pilot's voice pealed out of the intercom. "Ladies, buckle up, this plane is about to descend. We should be on the ground in seven minutes."

"I like it better when the stewardess makes the announcement," Annie grumbled. "He was way too flat sounding."

"Annie, shut the hell up or I will personally tighten that ridiculous collar around your neck until you scream for mercy," Myra said as she walked back to her seat to do the pilot's bidding.

It was one o'clock eastern standard time when the sleek silver bird hit the Dulles runway with a jolt.

"Showtime, girls!" Alexis shouted to be heard above the sound of the plane's engines. "You all know what to do, so let's show them our gusto!"

"Oh, God! Oh, God!" was all Myra could say.

"I'm ready! I am *soooo* ready!" Annie trilled.

"Myra, you screw this up and I will personally snatch those pearls out of your pocket and toss them to the four winds," Kathryn said. "You can do this. Charles is counting on you. You know damn well he's someplace watching us. More like leering, but it really doesn't make a difference. He *is* watching. C'mon now, give him the thrill of his life. Later, when all is said and done, you can make him eat shit if you want to punish him for making you go through this."

That was all Myra needed to hear. Her clenched fist shot in the air.

The plane door opened. The sounds from outside were deafening. Hoots, whistles, catcalls, shouts of "Bring it on, let's go, girls!"

The girls laughed, even Myra, as they formed a single line to deplane. The moment the moveable stairway was in place, the people from the back of the plane ran down the steps to form a tight cordon of security.

The pilot took a moment to stick his head out of the cockpit to say, "They closed all the runways for you, ladies. Dulles has never, as in *never,* done that. You're making history! Good luck!"

Alexis, who now looked like someone's old mother with kinky gray curls and a stoop to her shoulders, ushered the girls through the door, one at a time. "This is it, girls. The minute you hit the top step, throw open that coat and wave! I mean wave! When you get to the bottom, form a single line. Your space has been roped off. The security is manning the ropes. Give them a kiss. Give those guys something to have wet dreams about tonight."

Isabelle went first, followed by Nikki and then Annie. Kathryn followed Myra and Yoko was the last to hit the staircase.

The rope line and the yellow tape were straining as law enforcement struggled to hold back the throngs of young guys bent on snapping pictures. Offers of marriage were shouted among other things more lurid.

"I've never seen anything like this in my

whole life. I've never *read* about anything like this, either," Jack said to Harry Wong. "Jesus, did you see those bodies? Hey, Navarro, look alive here!"

Their trench coats swinging in the breeze, the G-String Girls strutted their stuff in their stiletto heels. As the guards ushered them along the rope line, Nikki spotted Jack and stepped over to the side to kiss him on the lips. "Hi there, big guy, I'm Mandy! You coming to my concert?" Nikki purred before she followed the beefy guard in front of her, all the while blowing kisses to the fans.

Jack reached out for the rope line to steady himself. "Son of a fucking bitch!"

Harry almost went down for the count when Yoko reached up and tickled his chin. "Oooh, I hope you have a front row seat, honey. I'm going to play just for you." In a daze, Harry reached for Jack's arm as Yoko stretched herself over the line to kiss a young kid with a Mohawk hairdo.

"We're stupid, Jack."

"Yeah," Jack said happily. "I knew I knew that body the moment I saw it on the stairway."

"Liar!" Harry said.

"Sounded good, didn't it? Hey, they fooled us. That was the test. We're good to go here!"

Kathryn had her lips locked on Bert Navarro's. "What's a great big guy like you doing out here? I'll leave a ticket for you at the door the night of the concert. You can come backstage if you want. Dream about me, okay?" For the crowd's benefit, she whipped off the trench coat and then strutted her way to the waiting limo.

"Get back!" Jack roared when it looked like the crowd was going to vault over the rope line. He pulled out his gun and yelled again, "GET BACK!"

Bert Navarro swung around, his gaze locking with Jack's. "Did...?"

"Hell no!"

The women standing next to the limos lined up again, blew kisses as they whipped off their trench coats. The crowd went wild. They all did a little dance, with the crowd begging for more. Annie obliged as she did her version of a bump and grind. Myra joined her, to the others' amazement. Myra pursed her lips, knowing some camera was focused on her, and mouthed the words, "Eat your heart out, sweetie!"

"Are we good or what?" Annie chortled as she turned her newly lifted backside to her adoring public. "I am loving this! How about you, Myra, are you loving this?"

"Damn straight," Myra said, borrowing Kathryn's favorite expression.

Inside the limos, the women collapsed amid groans and laughter. "We pulled it off, we really pulled it off. Charles is a pure genius," Nikki gasped. "Jack didn't recognize me."

"Neither did Harry," Yoko said, and laughed.

"And Bert's eyes might be back in their sockets by now. He sure can kiss," Kathryn said.

"Okay, fun's over. One more performance at the hotel and you can all go back to being who you were before we left the mountain," Alexis said. "We came here to do a job so let's not let our fame go to our heads."

"Oh, poop, I was just getting wound up. I have a lot more in me to show the world."

"Annie, I don't want to hear it," Myra said. "How far is it to the hotel? This latex is starting to itch."

"Thirty minutes tops but with traffic, it's anyone's guess," the driver said.

"I think we're on a roll, ladies," Kathryn said, a dreamy look on her face. "Yep, that guy is some kisser."

Chapter 14

Nellie Easter, flashlight in hand pointed at the floor and led her guest down a dark hallway to a bathroom bigger than most people's living rooms. She'd led Justice Barnes to this spot because this particular bathroom had no windows, but it did have exquisite lighting. She closed the door and then turned on the light.

"You're getting pretty good at this cloak and dagger stuff, Nellie," Pearl said in a jittery-sounding voice.

"Do you mean good the way you suddenly got good with your disappearing act? What the hell is going on, Pearl? And the reason for this cloak and dagger stuff, as you call it, is because there is probably someone outside watching the house. Someone who knows you're here. That means they're spying on me, you and the others. They also probably saw you riding my horse over here to Myra's house. I'm sorry you had to be alone here so long but there was nothing else I could do. I want to tell you right now, I do not like going through those tunnels. They spook me big-time. Enough said. Why are you here? Grant came looking for you tonight. He drove all the way out here to see if I knew where you were. Jack Emery opened the door to him. I had to think fast on my feet and I am the first to admit, I am not good at that. I like to ponder problems. I said we were playing poker. I have no idea if he believed me or not."

Pearl Barnes looked around the brightly lit bathroom. "This is very pretty. Myra always did have good taste. I really don't know where to start, Nellie."

"You've put me, the others and yourself in jeopardy by coming out here not once but twice. I will tell you this, I did not like the look on Grant's face tonight. I'm going to tell you something else and I don't care if it hurts your feelings or not. I don't like him, Pearl. I realized that tonight when I was talking to him. On top of that, he's a liar. He said he did not go to the FBI and he did. I'm really tired, Pearl, and I'd like to go to bed, so talk fast."

Pearl sat down on the edge of the bathtub. She clasped her hands in her lap as she looked around and then back at Nellie. "It all went wrong, Nellie. I think... I'm almost positive that Grant... that Grant and my ex–son-in-law are coconspirators. At first I didn't want to believe it, then I started watching and listening. All right, I spied on Grant. When I started the underground he was right there beside me. He broke the law right along with me. He never asked for anything. We both thought we were helping all those women and children get a better life. He never complained, did his share of the dirty work. We've been together almost twenty years, Nellie.

"A little over a year ago he started to change. It was subtle. He stopped being so attentive. He grew secretive. I was so busy with the underground and my work in court that I more or less chalked it up to plain old exhaustion on my part. As you know I can be cranky at times. I should tell you that there is a lot he *doesn't* know. Maybe in my heart of hearts I didn't trust him. All I know is he started pressuring me to tell him those things I didn't share with him, the things I won't share with you, either, for the safety of my people who are putting their asses on the line every day.

"One day Grant had to go to the hospital for some tests and his annual physical. I was home that day so I went at it. I went through his things. His portfolio is seriously depleted. He suffered some severe losses in the stock market. He has his pension and that's about it. Soon after that, he stopped giving me his share of the expenses. We stopped dining out. I let it go for a while and then I said something and he went ballistic. I stepped back, stopped including Grant in my . . . my mission. Of course he noticed.

"I digress here. Back to my spying. I looked through his day planner and I think he's meeting with Tyler, my ex–son-in-law. He just used intitials of the people he's meeting as opposed to spelling out a name on the days he has appointments.

Tyler's initials are the only ones that stood out to me. I might be wrong. Also, he's been taking cash advances on his credit cards. He's seriously in debt. He talks a lot on his cell phone. I'm sorry you don't like him, Nellie. Right now, I don't much like him, either."

Nellie reached out to take her old friend's hand in her own. "What I think of him doesn't matter. All I care about is protecting you. Do you have a game plan, Pearl? Is it your intention to . . . disappear?"

Pearl swiped at her wet eyes. "Damn it, Nellie, I've busted my ass all these years to save women and children. To give them a better life. I love my job. I worked hard to get there. If I'm meant to lose that, so be it, but I want it to be because of *me* not because someone blackmailed me. Do I want to go to jail? That's a stupid question, but it looks like that's exactly where I'm headed and there won't be anyone around to help me out. I might have to disappear. Do you have any idea what kind of circus that would be?" She closed her eyes and sighed heavily. "What should I do, Nellie?"

"Well, for starters I think you need to

call Grant and chop him off at the knees. As soon as it gets light out so he doesn't suspect I got in touch with you somehow. Then you need to call your daughter and tell her you'll be away for a while and not to worry. Tell her not to talk to anyone."

"They'll track my phone calls. I live under a microscope, Nellie, you know that."

Nellie held up her encrypted phone. "Untraceable. What about court?"

"I'll call in and say I have to take some emergency family time. It won't be a problem at first. In ten days it will become a big problem."

"Which brings me to my next question. What do you want us to do? Spell it out for me, Pearl."

"Stop Tyler, and Grant, too, if he is aligned with Tyler. Give me back yesterday if it's humanly possible."

"And if we can somehow make this all happen, and don't forget there undoubtedly are other people involved with Tyler, then what?"

"Then, my dear friend, I will resign from the Supreme Court. I am not one of those people who wants their cake and expects to eat it, too. I know what I have to do. What

I won't do is abandon all those women and children who need and depend on me. Isn't that how the vigilantes work?"

Nellie ignored the question. Pearl had given her the right answer, the answer the vigilantes could live with and work around. She nodded.

"How do you all do it? How do you stay sane? Look at me, I'm a basket case. Nellie, we have to get to those women and their kids and move them."

"Look at me, Pearl! Do I look like the picture of serenity to you?" Nellie knew she was finally admitting to Pearl what she already knew when she said, "We have an excellent network. In your case you had only Grant. I'm not faulting you. Money, and I assume money is at the root of his problem, can be one's downfall. The girls are here, Pearl, and ready to go to work. All I have to do is call Charles. Right now you need to tell me where that safe house is in Oregon so the girls can get your people to safety. I need to know *everything*, Pearl. And I do mean everything."

"What about Grant and Tyler?"

Nellie straightened her shoulders. "Well,

we'll just...What we'll do is...We'll just have to *take them out.*"

Pearl swallowed hard. "You mean like on those television shows when the gangsters say they're going to...to take someone out, as in...?"

It was Nellie's turn to swallow hard. "More or less," she said firmly. "We do not kill people, Pearl. We render them... What we do is..."

"Never mind, I get the picture. What about Elias Cummings? Is he going to be nosing around, too? How did Myra and the girls get here?"

"It might be a good idea to call Elias, too, and head him off at the pass. It certainly won't hurt to be preemptive now, will it? Are you game to going down into the tunnels? If so, I can show you how the girls got here. I think you might enjoy the coverage."

Justice Barnes stood up. "I want to see this. Lead the way, Nellie. Isn't it amazing how we've come full circle? Remember how we used to play here, sliding down the bannisters when we were little girls, playing dress-up in the attic? Riding our ponies out in the pasture? Remember the tea parties out under the old oak? We climbed trees, something girls weren't supposed to do back then. Oh, the skinned knees. Lemonade and those big fat sugar cookies we ate on the back porch. It was all so long ago. A lifetime, really. Look at us now. We're goddamn criminals, Nellie."

Nellie reached the bookcase, fumbled in the dark until the panel slid open. "Hold on to my shirt until the panel swings shut. Then I'll turn on the light. Just so you know, Pearl, there are rats down here. There's moss growing on the steps and they're slippery, so be careful. Once we get to Charles's command center, it's different, climate-controlled and modern. It's all so high-tech it boggles my mind."

"This is all so amazing. I had no idea you all had this kind of operation. Mine is in my head and on scraps of paper. Where did all the money come from to set this up?"

"Myra's fortune and then when Annie came aboard, she kicked in, too. Charles runs everything. The man is an absolute genius. Do you know he calls the queen 'Lizzie' and they talk on the phone in the middle of the night?"

Pearl shook her head. "No, I didn't know that. I think I might want to join you if you'll have me, once I resign. Do you think that's possible, Nellie?"

"You'll be a fugitive if you go with them. We're the second string, Pearl. It's me, Lizzie Fox—she's that flamboyant lawyer known for dazzling the courts—and Maggie Spritzer, a reporter from the *Post*. Then there is District Attorney Jack Emery and Harry Wong, the martial arts expert who also works for the police department."

"I'm impressed," Pearl said as she walked around looking at everything.

Pearl walked up to Charles's old station and turned on the three plasma screen television sets. She turned them all to the different 24-hour news channels. "I'm sure they'll show it all at the top of the hour. That's in four minutes. You ready, Pearl?"

Pearl focused on the big screen for the required four minutes. "It's those rock stars from South Africa. I read yesterday that they're putting on a sold-out benefit for AIDS."

"The G-String Girls!" Nellie said. "Look at that crowd. See, there's Jack Emery and there's Harry Wong. They had the security detail. With the Russian delegation in town they had to pull in every off-duty officer in town and from Virginia and Maryland, too. This is an event." She watched Pearl closely to see if there was any change of expression on her friend's face. She felt smug when she saw the perplexed look on Pearl's face.

"Those girls certainly have superb bodies. When is whatever you want me to see coming on? Oh, good Lord, that one is kissing Jack Emery! Well, that will certainly be a memory for that young man. Did we ever have bodies like that, Nellie?"

"I didn't. I was always kind of squat. You and the others were willowy."

"No, I can honestly say I never looked like any of them." Pearl looked at her watch to see how much time the station was devoting to theG-String Girls.

"See those two by the limo?"

"What about them?"

"That's Myra and Annie. Nikki Quinn is the one who kissed Jack Emery."

Pearl's jaw dropped. "No! How...?"

"Like Jack says, Charles is the go-to guy when you want something done. He choreographed this whole thing."

Pearl looked like she was in a daze. "Are you telling me they're going to give a *concert?* Myra and Annie don't know how to play a guitar. My God, they look *stunning!*"

"No, no. The real G-String Girls will be arriving incognito the day of the concert. Right now Myra and the others are at the Willard waiting for you to get off your duff and tell them where to go in Oregon to help your people. I need to call and tell them what you want done. Be sure you're okay with all of this, Pearl. I don't think I have to tell you what a chance those girls took coming here to help you. So be sure whatever it is you want, you can live with. Do we understand each other, Pearl?"

"I understand perfectly, Nellie. *I'm in.* Is that the right response?"

"It will do."

Chapter 15

His stint covering the Russian delegation over, Ted Robinson headed for the Willard hotel, hoping to get a glimpse of the G-String Girls. Who was he kidding? He was going to the Willard in the hopes of seeing Maggie. Even though he liked the G-String Girls, he didn't give a good rat's ass if he saw them or not. He'd pitched a fit when Liam Sullivan, his boss, told him he was to cover the Russian delegation and Maggie got the nudie gig. He'd protested hotly that there were other more qualified reporters who spoke a smattering of Russian who should get the assignment. Sullivan had merely blown cigar smoke in his face, fixed him with a steely gaze and asked him who his boss was. Somehow he'd managed to slink out of the *Post* with his tail between his legs.

With less than an hour of sleep under his belt, he was in a pissy mood and he knew it. He'd only had an overripe banana and half a cup of yesterday's coffee that was so bad his eyebrows had curled up. Maggie always made the best coffee, grinding the beans and making sure there was real cream in the fridge. A memory now.

"Hey, bud, the meter is ticking and I'm going to be stuck here unless you get out and walk the rest of the way. Them girls from Africa have tied up this city's traffic. Them Russkies just sailed through 'cause no one cares if they're here or not. You one of them reporters?"

"Tell me something I don't know." Remembering the question, Ted said, "Yeah, I'm one of them reporters." He dug around in his pocket for cab fare before he got out of the taxi. He looked around. Pennsylvania Avenue was a war zone. He listened to the curses from drivers, saw others shaking their fists at the cops, some on horseback, who were doing their best to keep things from exploding into a giant mess that would reflect badly on the administration, not to mention the law-and-order detail. He loped off, his backpack thumping against his shoulders. He wondered if the G-String Girls had arrived or if this unruly crowd had prevented their entry into the Willard.

The moment he saw the first satellite truck he knew he was in trouble. Every news outlet in the world looked to be in attendance. The Russians should only get this kind of coverage. He knew a single exclusive picture of the G-String Girls could go for as much as half a million dollars. He knew in his gut, just knew, *knew,* knew, that Maggie Spritzer was going to get one of those pictures. Maggie always had luck up her ass. He was getting crankier by the moment.

His press card around his neck, Ted elbowed his way through the crowds till he somehow managed to get to the front of the line where he spotted Jack Emery and Harry Wong trying to hold the excited crowd in check. He saw Maggie off to the side along with several colleagues from other papers. He recognized Jeff Josel from the *New York Post* and Tom Driscoll from the *New York Daily News*. Standing next to Josel was Rick Ferensic from the *Times*. All three of them were almost as good as he was but they weren't as sneaky, he thought smugly. He did his best to sidle up to Maggie without calling attention to himself. He didn't need a confrontation with Emery at this point.

Ted clapped Maggie on the back. "Hey, babe, how's it going? You get anything?"

"You!" Maggie screeched, but she was drowned out by all the noise surrounding her.

"Don't go getting pissy on me. I have as much right to be here as you do. I am a reporter. I was just trying to be nice. We did sleep together in case you forgot."

"No, you're a hack. And we are never going to sleep together again. *That* is not a memory, it's a nightmare. Get away from me, you crud."

"Stop being like that. Look, I'm sorry."

"Go tell that to someone who might care. Read my lips. I-do-not-care. Get away from me or I'm going to have you arrested."

Ted was saved from replying when a

shout went up that the G-String Girls' limousines were approaching. Things went from wild to wilder as law enforcement did their best to hold the rowdy crowds in check.

Cameras were aimed and ready. The news trucks blasted their horns to show they were the eight hundred-pound gorillas. Hotel security at the door looked panicked, the startled guests more panicked.

A cordon of private security for the G-String Girls exited the two limousines. The crowd went crazy, screaming and yelling to get the African stars' attention.

A megaphone in one of the guards' hands suddenly came to life. "I'm going to pick three reporters for *ONE* interview. Inside the lobby. The G-String Girls will pose for *ONE* picture." The guard walked to the rope line and pretended to be considering his choices. He zeroed in on Maggie, Ferensic and Josel. Stunned to be chosen, Maggie, in a daze, crawled under the rope. Her two colleagues followed suit. "Wait in the lobby by the concierge desk," the guard said tersely.

The limo doors opened and the G-String Girls stepped out. They waved, blew kisses and then disappeared. The media howled their outrage.

What followed for the staff of the Willard was a nightmare. The girls strutted their stuff as they made their way to the concierge desk. The burly guard was front and center. "*ONE* picture! Do it now." Cameras clicked. Maggie just knew she wasn't focusing. Sullivan would have her hide for getting personally involved.

"One question each," the guard said. "Make it quick!"

Ferensic went first. "How about a kiss?"

Isabelle, aka, Susy, leaned forward and kissed the reporter so soundly the assembled crowd gasped aloud.

Josel, not to be outdone, asked for the same thing. Kathryn stepped forward and stuck her tongue in the reporter's mouth. Maggie watched as Ferensic reached out to steady his colleague.

Maggie, her tongue thick in her mouth, finally got it to work. She didn't have a question. "I just want to thank you for doing this concert. I'm a huge fan."

"Okay, she's the one," the guard said, motioning for Ferensic and Josel to be escorted to the door.

"The one for what?" Maggie squeaked.

"Our one and only interview," Myra said in her new throaty voice. "We can give you five minutes."

"But I wasn't…I'm not prepared…Oh, damn, just my luck."

Annie stepped forward. "No problem, honey, we see this all the time. Here," she said holding out a sheet of paper. "These are the answers to the questions if you had asked. Chester, take a picture of all of us with this reporter. I like her."

Maggie thought she was going to pass out. She was a giddy teenager as she posed with the G-String Girls, a sappy look on her face.

Nikki stepped forward to whisper in Maggie's ear. "Look alive, Maggie, or you're going to blow our cover."

Maggie blinked, gasped and then slid to the floor, her digital camera in a death vise in her hand, the printed sheet in the other. The G-String Girls managed to get to the elevators whileothers attended to the intrepid reporter.

Within seconds, Maggie was being helped to her feet. "I've never fainted in my life," she mumbled.

The bearlike guard lowered his head. "The girls do have that effect on people. Act a little crazed when you get out there. You following me here?"

"Yeah. Yeah, I get it." She was still mumbling but she couldn't help it.

"You sure you're okay?"

"Hell no, I'm not okay. Don't worry, I know how to act crazy. Just give me a few minutes to get myself together." A second later she barreled through the door, screaming at the top of her lungs. "They gave me an interview. An honest-to-God interview! They *touched* me. Patty is the one who *touched* me!" she screamed again. "I have pictures!" she bellowed. "My God, I actually have pictures! Oh, my God, I can retire now!"

A reporter from NBC stuck a microphone in Maggie's face. "Tell us what it was like."

Maggie brushed him away. "I have an exclusive! Do you think I'm going to share it with you? Not." She looked over at Ted, whose expression was scary. She gave him her famous single-digit salute as she struggled to make her way through the phalanx of security and media. When she brushed past Jack Emery she hissed, "I don't like the look on Ted's face. I think he's putting two and two together. Do something and do it quick."

Jack looked over his shoulder to see Ted arguing with a fellow reporter as he tried to shove him out of the way so he could follow Maggie. Jack yanked at Harry's arm and jerked his head to the side. Harry turned, his eyebrows shooting upward. "Take him out, Harry. I don't want him doing any jukin' and jivin'. Stash him somewhere. I think he *thinks* he knows something. Don't hurt him but chop him off at the knees."

"No problem."

Jack watched. Ted's disappearance was so slick, he almost missed it. Good old Harry.

Inside the exquisite suite of rooms that were filled with fresh flowers in crystal vases and silver bowls filled with fresh fruit, the women shed their trench coats and started to peel away the latex that covered their bodies. They scattered in the direction of the bathrooms, calling out to one another, congratulating themselves on getting back into the country undetected.

Thirty minutes later they were back in the sitting room dressed in jeans, sneakers and T-shirts and munching on the fresh fruit. "That certainly was exciting," Annie gushed. "I think I could get used to all this . . . exposure."

Isabelle threw a banana at Annie, who caught it in midair. "Don't you mean scary?"

"Not at all, dear. I think it's obvious that we fooled everyone, even Maggie Spritzer. I wonder why Charles hasn't called us," Myra said as she reached for a kiwi. A second later her encrypted phone rang. The others grew silent as Myra listened to the voice on the other end of the line. When Myra's face turned beet red the others grinned from ear to ear.

As one they shouted, "What did he say? Did he like our performance? What are we waiting for? Come on, Myra, what did Charles say?" they teased, laughing uproariously at the discomfort Myra was showing.

She hung up and then cleared her throat several times before she finally spoke. "He said he was enamored of our performance and he taped it. We'll all receive a copy once this is all over. He...uh...He said he'd park his shoes under my bed any-time." In spite of herself, Myra burst out laughing when the others clapped her on the back. Suddenly they were a team again, all for one and one for all.

"Pearl is out at my farm. Jack Emery suspects that Ted was out at Nellie's farm spying. He can't prove it but that's what he thinks was going on. Pearl's live-in, Grant Conlon, showed up after midnight looking for Pearl. Earlier he went to the FBI to ask Elias Cummings to make discreet in-quiries as to Pearl's whereabouts. He lied to Nellie and said he hadn't spoken to the director. Pearl confided to Nellie that she thought Grant had been aligning himself with Tyler Hughes. By the way, Pearl wants to join up with us after she resigns."

"Wow!" Nikki said.

"There's more," Myra said. "Harry snatched Ted Robinson and has him stashed at his *dojo* with his people watch-ing him. It seems he was outside the Willard when we arrived and Maggie warned Jack that Ted was up to some-thing. He might have put it together some-how. Maggie returned to the paper to do

her article. She is going to set up a meeting if possible at the Watergate where Tyler
lives. We'll do a snatch and grab as soon
as Charles gives the go-ahead. The plan
at the moment is for Kathryn and Isabelle
to fly to Oregon, pick up a bus and drive to
the location where Pearl's people are
waiting to be taken to safety."

"What about Pearl's boyfriend?" Nikki
asked.

"Charles said he was working on that
end of it. That appears to be a little more
complicated. We're to wait for instructions
from Jack and Harry. That's all I know,
girls."

The phone on the desk shrilled to life.
Panic ensued as the women looked at
one another. "We said no calls were to be
put through," Alexis said in a strangled-
sounding voice. Already she was envi-
sioning something going wrong.

The phone kept ringing.

"Maybe we should answer it," Yoko said.

"Maybe we shouldn't," Isabelle said.

The phone continued to ring, the sound
so shrill it could be heard in the hallway.

Kathryn bounded to her feet. "Answer
the damn phone already! I can't stand to

hear a phone ringing. It might be Jack or maybe the front desk. It's probably important because I don't think this hotel wants to piss us off."

Annie reached out and snatched the phone. "Yes?"

The sudden silence was so deafening the others looked from one to the other, their eyes full of unasked questions.

"Who? I don't appreciate your humor and I thought we left orders that no calls were to be put through to our rooms. We've only been here a few hours and already you've broken the rules. What part of what I said don't you understand? We are not taking calls or accepting invitations. Period." However, she continued to listen to the voice on the other end of the phone.

The women collectively mouthed the words *"Who is it?"* Annie held up her hand for quiet and rolled her eyes. Their eyes popped when they heard Annie say, "Press secretary, my ass. If his boss can't call me direct, then I'm hanging up. Why should I wait? Time is money. Furthermore . . . All right, put him on."

"Who?" the women hissed.

Annie nestled the phone on her shoulder and flapped her arms. "The president! *Of the United States,*" she clarified. She yanked at the chair by the desk and flopped down when she heard a familiar voice. "Hello, Mr. President. Yes, we're liking this country just fine. You want us to come to the White House for lunch. We're flattered, Mr. President, but our schedule..."

Nikki stood in the center of the room hopping up and down as she hissed, "No, no, no! Get off the damn phone, Annie."

Annie stood up and squared her shoulders. "I think I speak for the G-String Girls when I say we cannot get involved in American politics. Our schedule is far too tight to fit in a luncheon *and* a performance." She listened for a few moments before saying, "I'll ask the promoters if there are any spare tickets for your daughters. I can't promise anything. Can I have one of my people get back to your people, Mr. President?" She tried to slam the phone back into the base and failed. Yoko had to pry the phone out of her hands to replace it.

"He... That was... He wanted us to

come for lunch tomorrow and give a performance for the staff of the White House. Oh, and his daughters. He wants tickets," Annie dithered. "Did I handle that okay?"

"Damn straight you did," Kathryn said, slapping Annie on the back. "I didn't vote for him. Guess he wasn't prepared for a turndown. How did he sound?"

"He tried to convince me to okay the luncheon. He did try to schmooze me. Oh, God, oh, God, I actually talked to the president of the United States! I was waiting for him to throw in a ride on Air Force One. He said his people tried to get tickets for his daughters but were told it was a sold-out performance. Hint, hint. You heard my end of the conversation."

Myra worked at the pearls around her neck. "I find this incredibly interesting. Charles is going to be so impressed," she said.

A knock sounded at the door. Yoko ran to the door and looked through the peephole. She threw open the door and jumped into Harry Wong's arms. Nikki flew past her to where Jack was standing and did the same thing. Bringing up the rear was Bert Navarro. He entered the room, zeroing in on Kathryn. Within seconds he swept her up into his arms and did a lip-lock that made Myra and Annie gasp.

"Oh, my!" Annie said.

Chapter 16

Maggie Spritzer knew she was strung as high as a kite as she settled herself to pound away at her computer. Any minute now she expected to go into orbit. She looked up when her boss approached her desk.

"Nice going, Spritzer! You got the by-line. We're going with the front page and you got the top of the fold even if you look like you're embalmed. Those women more than make up for your sappy expression. How the hell did you manage to pull it off?"

Sullivan's craggy features registered

such awe that Maggie laughed nervously. She thought she sounded like a frog in distress.

"Good reporting and perseverance, boss." *Oh, God, if you only knew.* Maggie thought she was being sly when she asked, "How'd Ted do with the Russians?"

Sullivan scratched at his gray hair with one hand, his other hand jerking at his glasses. "You ever watch paint dry or grass grow?" Not bothering to wait for a response he said, "That's how it went. He emailed in his report and I haven't heard from him since."

"I saw him at the Willard. I think the whole world was there, at least the media world. *They* gave me tickets. Two tickets. Do you believe that? I have two tickets!"

"My wife would kill you for a ticket and not think twice about it," Sullivan joked. "That was a hint, Spritzer. Since you and Teddy boy are on the outs, don't you need someone to take to the concert? Your job depends on your answer."

Maggie looked up at her boss towering over her as she tried to figure out if he was joking. She decided he wasn't. She fished around in her backpack and handed over the two tickets. "Your wife will need a partner. For sure you won't want to subject her to those mobs. Maybe you'll bust your eardrums. Enjoy," she said, clicking off her computer.

Sullivan hated the evil expression he was seeing on Maggie's face. "Smart-ass. Where you going? Don't you *ever* work a full day? Sometimes I think you're worse than Robinson, and yet I keep paying you two," he grumbled as he jammed the tickets into his shirt pocket.

"I'm going apartment hunting and then I'm going to rest on my laurels," Maggie said as she slid her chair up against the desk. "I figure those tickets bought me, let's say, two or three days of free time. See ya." Like she was really going apartment hunting.

As she waited for the elevator, the phone in her pocket chirped. Abner. "Whatcha got, Abby?"

The weird-sounding voice on the other end of the line squealed to life. "Meet me at Starbucks. The one around the corner from the *Post*. Get me a coffee, six sugars and light on the cream."

Still reeling with her success at the

Willard and seeing the vigilantes, Maggie had trouble downshifting to a neutral zone. "Huh?"

"I'm not sending stuff like this over the Net. Ten minutes. Don't forget the coffee."

"Yeah, yeah, okay." Maggie pressed the ground-floor button. Outside she raced around the corner to Starbucks where she ordered two coffees, laced Abner's with six sugars and a spurt of cream, gagged, and then carried the coffees to a table outside. The place was almost empty. How strange was that? Normally, at any hour of the day she had to stand in a line that wrapped all the way to the *Post.* Everyone must be at the Willard, she thought smugly. Well, she'd been there and done that.

Maggie sipped at the scalding coffee. She wished she'd thought to ask for some ice. She felt the breeze Abner created as he swooped close and then sat down. He reached for the coffee and took a mind-bending swallow without batting an eye. "How *do* you do that?"

"I can drink boiling water and it doesn't bother me. So, when are we sleeping together? I'm free this weekend," Abner said as he shoved a manila envelope across the table.

Maggie blew on the coffee in her cup. "I'm busy this weekend. Let's shoot for this time next year. Whatcha got in here, Abby?" she asked, pointing to the manila envelope.

Abner took the reporter's rejection with good grace. "Don't you remember what you asked for? Hey, if you're not going to drink that coffee, can I have it?" Maggie slid the cup across the table. "I got you everything you asked for plus a few extras. How come you didn't get me a muffin or something?"

"Because you didn't ask me to get you one. Just give me a summary, Abby."

"He travels a lot. He had some money in an offshore account but it's almost gone now. Ecuador, in case you want to know. He's a ladies' man. But only rich women. He appears to be overbearing. Women don't like that. Well, at first they do, but then they want to be boss. Like you, Maggie. He owes big bucks. He has an American Express Black Card. I think they call it Centurion or something like that. You have to spend $250,000 a year to get one of those babies. And this guy uses it. All his other cards, and he has six, are maxed out. Clothes, high-end dining, trips, cash advances. His bank account is about subzero. He has $22,000 in it. He's taken nine trips by plane to Vegas this year alone. This guy doesn't seem to work too much, he's off more than he's on. There were some whispers, and I want to stress the word 'whispers,' that some creative accounting might be going on. By one Tyler Hughes. I couldn't nail that down. Just know that the whispers are out there."

"Were you able to find out what his divorce buyout was?"

"Yeah, eight million. That's what went into the offshore account. It's all gone except for $40,000. That info took some doing to get so I hope you appreciate my abilities."

"I do, Abby, I do."

"He pays his rent late. Constantly gets late notices. He's got lousy credit. His FICO score is in the dumper. About the only thing he pays is that Black Card. In short, the guy needs money. Did I forget anything?"

"What about his emails? Did you get anything on that?"

"Well, yeah," Abby drawled. "That was a piece of cake. He's like most people who think if you delete them they're gone. Wrong. Nothing really interesting. He does everything on his computer, his reservations to restaurants, flight reservations. By the way, he flies on the cheap if he goes somewhere alone. If he takes a woman he goes first class. He does his tennis and golf times by email. No close friends that check in on each other. Just a few emails from women confirming a luncheon or tennis date. There were about a dozen emails to someone named Grant Conlon over the last eight months. They were deleted as soon as they were read. He didn't bother to delete his other emails. He'd do it every few weeks. I printed everything out. That's it, Maggie."

Maggie digested the information. "No emails to the ex-wife or the ex–mother-in-law? What about the daughter? Fathers usually stay in touch with their kids by email if they're too busy to make personal visits."

"Nope. Nothing like that. I saw you on

the news this morning. You looked spaced out. What was that like?"

"Awesome," Maggie said, her mind racing and twirling in all directions.

"How'd they look in person? Were they nice or snooty? You know—above all us little people."

Maggie stared across the table at her companion. She didn't know why but she thought Abner was acting a part for her benefit. Her stomach churned. "They were awesome," Maggie said once again, using her favorite word. "Really nice. They posed with me for a picture. I get the front page in tomorrow's paper. They weren't snooty at all. I liked them. You going to the concert?"

"I wish. They were sold out the moment they became available. I'll watch it on television."

Maggie was sorry she'd given up the two free tickets so easily to Liam Sullivan. Nothing she could do about it now. "Thanks, Abby. If I can get more tickets, I will. I'll let you know. What would I do without you?"

Abby flushed a bright red. "I like to help people. Not many people can do what I do even if it is breaking the law. I'm glad to help, Maggie, because you're one of the good guys. Call me if you need anything else. Thanks for the coffee. By the way, if you do get the tickets, will you go with me?"

Maggie smiled and nodded. She didn't see it happening, but you never knew what could happen at the eleventh hour. She realized at that moment she was genuinely fond of Abner. "Okay, how about we have sex over the Fourth of July? This way neither one of us will know if it's our rockets going off or the fireworks," she teased. She took a moment to wonder what sex would be like with the computer hacker. She burst out laughing when Abby winked at her. Suddenly she knew—and she didn't know how she knew—but she knew sex with Abner would be over-the-top. Oh, yeah. Ted who? she thought smugly.

Abby laughed as he hitched up his baggy pants. He offered up a sloppy salute as he sauntered away.

Maggie took a moment to think back to when she'd first met Abner. Even back then she hadn't shoved him off as a nerd. For some strange reason she thought what she was seeing today was a façade. She'd also bet a week's salary that his name wasn't really Abner Tookus, either. She'd once tried to track down a rumor that Abby had worked at the DOJ, the Department of Justice, and was an up-and-coming lawyer, and that something had gone awry and suddenly he was gone from the DOJ.

At one point she'd unearthed a picture of him dressed in a Brooks Brothers suit with a regulation haircut. She remembered how her heart had fluttered. Well, that was then and this was now. Whatever his reason for staying out of the limelight and wearing his sloppy disguise, not to mention the affected squeaky voice, who was she to blow his cover? In this business you needed all the allies you could muster up. One of these days she was going to go for the gusto and show up on his doorstep and whatever happened at that point would simply happen. First, though, she had to figure out where the hacker hung his hat. One of these days. She mentally put it on her To Do list. Yep, one of these days.

Maggie jammed the manila envelope into her backpack. She had to find Jack and turn it over to him. Then she needed to find a way to set up another meeting with Tyler Hughes.

Back in Virginia, Nellie Easter picked up her encrypted phone and held it up for Pearl to see. "The calls we make will be untraceable," she said. "It's almost nine o'clock. You should be able to get hold of everyone now. Give me Grant's cell phone number, I'll dial it and hand you the phone. You know what to say." Pearl rattled off a number and Nellie pressed it in. She handed the phone to Pearl, who licked at her dry lips before she spoke.

"Grant, it's Pearl. I understand you've been looking for me. Why? I don't go around asking your friends where you are when you go off. I don't appreciate the inquiries you've been making." She listened for a moment and then said, "Why does it matter where I am? To be blunt, Grant, it's none of your business. I have things to take care of." She listened again, rolling her eyes for Nellie's benefit. "You'll see me when you see me." Pearl chewed on her lower lip as a barrage of questions were put to her.

"Hurry up, you've been on long enough," Nellie whispered. Pearl nodded to show she understood.

"So what if I left my purse and cell phone home. Why are you snooping in my things, anyway, Grant? I just told you, you'll see me when you see me, at which point you and I will have a long-overdue talk. In the meantime, you might think about relocating. Good-bye, Grant."

Pearl handed the phone back to Nellie. "How'd I do?"

"Good. Now give me Elias Cummings's number." Pearl repeated it for Nellie's benefit and pressed in the numbers and then handed the phone back to Pearl. She listened as Pearl identified herself.

"Yes, Elias, it appears to be a fine spring morning. I understand Grant came to you because he thought I was...uh... missing. I'm not missing. I left the house because I needed to do some serious thinking in regard to Grant's and my relationship. I hardly see where my personal business is any business of the FBI. I do not appreciate Grant going to you to air my personal business. It's not important how I found out. I found out. Period. I'm alive. I'm well. I'm with friends whose wise counsel I sought. In other words, Elias, stay out of my business. Regards to your family."

Once again Pearl broke the connection and then handed the phone back to Nellie. "What now?"

"One more call, to your daughter. Smooth it over, be upbeat and natural. She's your daughter, she'll pick up on your anxiety if you let it show."

Five minutes later, that call ended.

"Now, we have to get you to the Willard where the others will take care of you. I'm not sure but I think that's what Charles is going to want you to do. Just give me a few minutes. I have to call him."

Pearl moved away toward the refrigerator and reached for a bottle of Green Tea, which she then guzzled. She looked into the depths of the refrigerator but there wasn't a scrap of food. She looked down at the expiration date on the bottle she was drinking from. She grimaced when she realized the Green Tea was two years past the expiration date. She shrugged and finished the bottle, capped it and set it back in the refrigerator, but not before she wiped off her fingerprints. She looked over at Nellie, who had completed her call. "What? You don't look happy, Nellie."

"I'm to get you to the Willard, just as I thought. Myra has a Jaguar here in the garage that she left behind. Who knows if it will start up. I ride over here every few weeks to check on things and start up the car. Charles was very explicit about keeping the golf cart charged and the Jaguar running. I'd turn on the Jaguar and then go for a ride. I think there's enough gas to get you into town. You'll have to park somewhere and take a taxi to the Willard. Jack Emery will be expecting you. Either he or one of his people will take you to Myra and the others. Can you handle that, Pearl?" Pearl's head bobbed up and down. "Let's go upstairs now and get you outfitted. All of Myra's clothes are still here and you two are pretty much the same size. I think a hat, a suit, heels and some sunglasses will do it. All eyes are on the G-String Girls and the hotel itself. You'll just be another rich guest staying at the Willard."

"What if someone is watching us from the woods?"

"That's been taken care of, Pearl. At the risk of repeating myself, this is not a Mickey Mouse operation. So get cracking and dude yourself up. I'll start up the Jaguar and bring it around. Hurry, Pearl."

Thirty minutes later, Chief Justice Pearl Barnes walked into the kitchen dressed like she was going to church, in a dove-gray Chanel suit with matching hat that shrieked money. Nellie nodded approvingly as she led Pearl out to the waiting Jaguar. "There's a lot of horsepower under that hood so be careful. You don't need a ticket at this juncture. And just to be on the safe side, check your rearview and side mirrors to see if anyone appears to be following you."

The two women embraced. "Thanks, Nellie. You have my word, I will not give up your secret. They can pull out my toenails and I won't give you all up."

"And we won't give you up, either, my friend. One last thing, Pearl. Are you certain Tyler had a meeting with Grant?"

"As sure as I'm standing here. I've made some bad choices, Nellie. If my mama was alive she'd say my chickens are coming home to roost."

Nellie forced a laugh she didn't feel. "Everyone knows a hen is smarter than a rooster. A hen isn't dumb enough to get up early and crow. She sleeps in."

Pearl offered up a weary smile. "And on that thought, I will leave you. Take care, Nellie. One more time, thanks."

"We're friends, Pearl. Enough said."

Chapter 17

Jack Emery paced the lobby of the Willard as he waited for Justice Barnes to make an appearance. His mind was ricocheting in every direction, his stomach in knots at the daring of the vigilantes and the possible outcome. Still, it wasn't up to him to do anything but follow orders. He'd signed on for the long haul and it was too late now to have second thoughts. He let his mind go to Harry Wong and Ted Robinson. Immediately his stomach turned sour. Robinson, razor-edge reporter that he was, had smelled a rat somewhere along the way. Just one more thing on his worry list.

He saw Pearl then and his first thought was she looked like Myra as she crossed the lobby. She also looked like a guest who knew exactly where she was going; a woman with a purpose. Jack met her at the elevator. She nodded slightly, the wide brim of the floppy hat she was wearing shading her face. Six other guests piled into the elevator, all of them mumbling about the inconvenience they were being put through because of the visiting celebrities.

The elevator door opened on the G-String Girls' floor. Immediately six men, shoulder holsters visible, formed a cordon. Jack held up his badge before he stepped out, nudging Justice Barnes to indicate she should follow him.

Jack's sigh was so loud, the security guards looked at him with suspicion. "It's okay, this lady is expected. Just do your job, okay?"

The guards nodded and moved off. Jack slid the key card into the lock and opened the door. "Anybody home?" he called out.

The women rushed forward to check out their new guest.

Jack moved off, Nikki at his side. They walked toward the bedroom where he kissed her soundly before they returned to the sitting room in time to see Pearl send her hat sailing across the room.

Things kicked into high gear as Alexis hauled out her Red Bag and started to work on a new look for Kathryn as Pearl shed her outfit. The moment Jack realized Pearl was in the middle of a striptease, he drew Nikki back to the bedroom. Out of the corner of his eye he saw Myra on the phone while Annie raced to the door. She opened it a crack and reached for a brown envelope one of the guards handed her.

Clutched in each other's arms, Jack could hear Annie babbling. The only words he heard that made sense were, "major problem." He and Nikki ran to the sitting room. "What?" he bellowed. He turned away so he wouldn't have to see Justice Barnes in her undies.

Startled, Annie swung around, an airline ticket in her hand. "It's Kathryn's plane ticket to Oregon. Charles just told Myra that there is a major problem in Germany."

"I don't want to hear about major problems in or out of Germany," Jack bellowed again. Unable to control himself he bellowed a third time, "What?"

The color drained from Myra's face as she fingered the pearls at her neck. She held out the phone in her hand. Somehow she managed to gasp, "Call Charles."

Kathryn bolted out of her chair. "I knew it! I knew it! I told you all something would go wrong. Will you call him already before my pores get more clogged up than they are already from all this damn latex? Damn, why am I always right?"

"If you shut up, I'll call him. I can't hear myself think around here." He was rewarded with instant silence. He punched in the numbers. The moment Charles said hello, Jack went into his wild spiel, ending with, "And this damn well better be good or I'm outta here and so is Harry. Well, Charles!"

"Calm down, Jack. It's not the end of the world, although Myra seems to think it is. Actually it's a *little* glitch."

"How little?" Jack demanded. He watched the women staring at him and knew they were more than capable of attacking him at any moment if they didn't like whatever it was he was about to say, even Nikki.

"I had a call from the *real* G-String Girls' promotion manager. It appears there's a *small* problem with their departure and of course their arrival in the States."

Jack clenched his teeth. "How small is small, Charles, and what the hell is the problem? I'm losing patience here in case you haven't already figured it out."

"Drugs," came the response. "We're doing our best to keep a lid on it, Jack. It's not the girls themselves but several of their handlers who are involved. For all intents and purposes the girls left for the airport yesterday in disguise. They're troopers, to say the least. To protect our girls they haven't given up a thing. There is going to be a delay, but I can't tell you how much of a delay. Our girls might have to . . . uh . . . they might have to perform on-stage. Right now there is nothing I can do until I get more information. You need to comfort the women. Understandably they are shy about giving a performance. Myra threatened to kill me. I believe her, so work some magic."

Jack's jaw dropped. For the first time in his life he was at a total loss for words. His stomach started to crunch up at the panicked looks on the women's faces. "Son of a bitch! Well, what does that do to Kathryn's departure for Oregon? What about Conlon and Hughes? Give me a little direction here, Charles."

"I'm working on it, Jack. I'll ring you back when I have more details."

Jack snapped the phone shut and then kicked out at the desk chair, sending it flying across the room. The women were on him then like a swarm of locusts as they screamed and yelled for information.

"Stop!" Myra shrilled. "Girls! Give Jack some air so he can tell us what's going on."

Myra's words were magic. The women dropped to the floor and as one, hugged their knees as Jack tried to come to terms with what he had to say. "Okay, okay, I'm just the messenger, so let's get that straight right now. Charles said the *real* G-String Girls have been delayed. Seems a few of their handlers had a problem with drugs at the airport. Everyone is in disguise so that's in our favor. Everyone is still safe, as is our secret. It's the time frame for their arrival here in the States that's a problem. You will probably have to perform in their place. Now you know as much as I know."

The silence was so deafening, Jack wanted to run for his life. At the very least he expected hysterics or the beating of his life. Instead the women stared at him like he'd sprouted a second head.

The eerie silence continued. The urge to run to the door was so strong, Jack dug his feet into the carpet. "Somebody needs to say something and that somebody needs to say it right now."

"It's not possible," Isabelle said.

"We really can't play guitars," Yoko said.

"The audience will know we're frauds within minutes," Kathryn said, an evil glint in her eye. "We'll be arrested, and all this," she said, waving her arms about, "is worth nothing. We risked our lives coming here."

"I think it's doable," Annie said. "We can use the G-String Girls' DVDs backstage. We can close the backstage off to everyone except our people. We can lip-sync. We can do it. Girls, we can do it!"

"I think you must be on drugs, Annie," Myra said. "We cannot do it. Read my lips, we cannot get up there and perform and fool the whole world."

Pearl chirped up for the first time as she looked from one to the other. "Oh, my dears, you *can* do it. You fooled me when I saw you on the news, and we've been friends all our lives. If you could fool me you can fool strangers. Have a little faith in yourselves. You're just experiencing stage fright. Once you get out there and your adoring public is cheering you on, you'll get over it. Mind over matter," she said matter-of-factly.

Jack gaped at Nikki, his heart thudding in his chest when she said, "Pearl is right, we can do it. It's a mindset. We didn't think we could get off the plane and play a part but we did. We did it again when we got here to the Willard. We pulled it off."

Jack weighed in. "Yeah, well, how do you explain Ted Robinson?"

"Easily. He's obsessed with the vigilantes. He sees vigilantes everywhere he looks," Nikki said. "As long as he's out of the picture I say we can pull it off. By the way, where is he?"

"Harry's got him locked up at his *dojo*,"

Jack said. "He's not going anywhere. At least for the time being."

"What about my people that are stranded?" Pearl asked.

Jack shrugged. "This is just a wild guess on my part but I'm thinking the second string is going to have to take over. Lizzie can go to Oregon. She can drive the bus with your people to my cabin in Montana that I supposedly own. I think that was the game plan for Kathryn, unless that's changed, too."

"I don't mean to sound selfish here, but what about Grant and Tyler and the people they're working for? What time is your scheduled departure?" Pearl asked, addressing Myra.

"I'm not sure. We were delayed getting here. Charles said he was allowing us some extra time but I'm not sure that option is still available to us. By my best calculations we have less than thirty-six hours to pull all of this off. By all of this, I mean the concert and getting Grant and Tyler to do what we want them to do. Don't pay attention to me," Myra dithered, "I don't know what I'm talking about."

"I want to see Harry," Yoko said firmly.

"Well, he's kind of busy right now, Yoko. I'll call him in a minute."

Jack was right, Harry Wong was so busy he didn't know if he was coming or going.

"How the hell did I get here?" Ted Robinson asked, looking around at Harry's *dojo* and the faces watching him.

"You walk in your sleep. Or if you don't like that answer, how about hocus-pocus, you got here by osmosis?"

"Smart-ass! I asked you a question. You damn well better answer it, too."

Harry looked around at his hired help. "Or...?"

"What the fuck did you do to me, Wong?"

Harry flexed his fingers and then waved them about. "You looked like you were getting ready to cause a disturbance. There was enough going on at the Willard without you acting out so I pressed on your neck and you went to sleep. End of story."

"My ass that's the end of the story. You damn well kidnapped me. Did Emery put you up to this?" Not bothering to wait for an answer, the reporter continued. "Damn straight he did and I'll have your ass for this and don't think I won't."

Harry shrugged just as his cell phone rang. He walked out of Robinson's earshot and spoke quietly before he dropped into a listening mode. His only comment was, "Now why doesn't all of this surprise me? Okay, okay, I'm on my way. Ted? He's fine, shooting off his mouth as usual. He's trying to figure out how he got here. He isn't exactly the sharpest tool in the shed." He continued to listen to Jack as he issued orders. "Yeah, yeah, I'll put him to sleep. My guys will watch over him. You sound like an old lady, Jack. My people are not *wusses*. Stop worrying."

Ted, who had been dumped unceremoniously onto one of the workout mats, did his best to scoot backward, only to come up against one of Harry's people. "Easy, sport," the man said.

"I'm not feeling any love here," Ted grumbled. "I know what you're up to, Wong. I knew it the minute I saw you and Emery on the security detail at the Willard. Yeah, Maggie, too. The vigilantes are back and don't try to con me. They're here for a reason and what better reason than Pearl Barnes. Yeah, yeah, I got it now. Those G-String Girls were just a diversion to get them back here. You son of a bitch! I'm going to ruin you when I get out of here. I'm going to plaster that ugly face of yours and Emery's, too, all over the front page of the *Post*."

Harry took a step forward and then took another step and looked down at Ted. "That doesn't quite compute. I'm standing here, you're sitting there ready to go night-night again and you're going to *what...?*"

"You heard me. If I figured it out so will someone else. Go ahead, stomp on my neck, put me to sleep. Unless you're a murderer, you have to let me go sometime. That's when I stomp on *your* neck, you son of a bitch. And you can tell good old Jack for me that when I'm outta here I'm gonna shove his balls up his ass. So, go ahead and do whatever the hell you have to do. I hope your ass rots in jail because they're gonna catch you. You can take that to the bank, too."

Harry didn't like what he was hearing. He didn't have a single doubt in his mind that he could kill Ted with one pinch to his nose or throat and get rid of him once and for all. Ted was right that he wasn't a murderer, though. He tilted his head to indicate his partner should put Harry to sleep. "Don't take your eyes off him, not even to take a whiz. We clear on that?" His partner nodded.

A moment later Harry was out of the *dojo*. He fired up his Ducati motorcycle and rode off at the speed of light.

Chapter 18

Charles Martin felt his left eye twitch. Then his right eye started to twitch. A sure sign that he wasn't his usual unflappable self. Maybe it was his new surroundings on this mountain, a mountain almost like the one he'd left fifteen hours earlier. He walked outside, Murphy and Grady at his side. They, too, seemed twitchy in their new surroundings. And they were probably picking up the scent from Havapopulas's wolf dog, Alpha. Everyone wanted to be top dog. Charles allowed a small grin to tug at the corners of his mouth at the thought.

He needed to think and he needed to

do it quickly. His girls were in a sticky wicket, and as everyone knew, sticky wickets could screw things up royally. Think, Charles, think! He'd always been good about thinking on his feet. Maybe a short stroll around this impressive compound would give him some fresh insight. He shifted his mind into a neutral zone as he walked, the dogs at his side.

A hundred million easy, he thought, to set up this compound. Maybe twice that much. Everything was man-made—all the buildings, the Olympic-size swimming pool, the tennis courts, the stables, the helicopter pad. The Black Hawk helicopter sitting on the pad like a giant black bird didn't surprise him in the least. He knew how much they cost. Maybe this whole operation was closer to a billion dollars. His own operation back in Spain simply couldn't compare to what he was seeing. He was impressed. He remembered when Lizzie had first told him about it. What was it she'd said? Oh, yes, "Sir Malcolm, it is right up your covert alley. I'll make all the arrangements." And she had. The proof was the fact that he was standing here on Big Pine Mountain.

Charles eyed the cable car. Unlike the mountain back in Spain, where if one were part mountain lion, one might be able to climb the mountain, this mountain could not be accessed by foot. And he knew for a fact that Havapopulas had the entire mountain booby-trapped. One either arrived by helicopter or by cable car. Safety-wise, this mountain was more secure, safer than the one back in Spain.

His eyes were still twitching. He needed to think about his immediate problem instead of his surroundings. The moment his eyes stopped twitching, Charles whistled for the two dogs, who were busy sniffing every bush in sight, and headed back to Kollar Havapopulas's command center.

Charles stopped at the bottom of the steps to look up at the 3,000-square-foot log cabin that had been Kollar's home for over ten years. State of the art. Rustically beautiful as well as comfortable. He looked to the left to see the huge satellite dishes that were camouflaged from the air. As Kollar said, even the CIA, the FBI and the White House didn't have anything near what was on this mountain, thanks to the billionaire industrialists that employed Havapopulas. The best part, though, was that the mountain was owned outright by Kollar and his father, Spiros, which was the reason why he and the women could reside here until such time as both he and Kollar deemed it time to move on.

Charles took a mighty breath and then exhaled as he approached Kollar's computer where dozens of emails waited to be read. He scanned them quickly and then pressed a button. The emails printed out faster than bullets. Twice his fist shot in the air at what he was reading. A moment later, his special phone was activated. Call after call was made at the speed of light. More emails flooded his screen and then printed out.

"All righttttt!" He looked down at the dogs, who were lying at his feet. "We're in business, boys." Murphy rose to his feet as he offered his paw to Charles, a sign that he understood what the big man was saying. Not to be outdone, Grady waved his tail and offered up his paw, too. Charles laughed, a rollicking sound of hilarity as he went back to his computer, his fingers flying over the keys.

* * *

Ted Robinson woke slowly, his eyelids fluttering. He knew instantly where he was and what had transpired. He let his gaze swing around the workout room in Harry Wong's *dojo*. He saw two skinny little guys with a thousand pounds of horsepower in their feet and hands playing a game with tiles. Only a fool would think he could take on either one of the men and he was no fool. What to do? Maybe if he pretended to be sick he could get away when they tried to help him. Stupid, stupid, stupid. He was smart enough to know he had no options. Pure and simple he was a prisoner. His brain clicked into high gear. Did they take the cell phone that was in his pocket? No, he could feel it pressing against his leg. If there was some way to get it out of his pocket maybe he could click it on and press in 911. Would his captors then whisk him away or would they put him to sleep again? He simply didn't know.

He had to get out of here and he had to do it fast. Maybe there was a way to trick them. The two one-hundred-ten-pound men might be physical powerhouses but they looked to him like they were lacking in the brain-power department. How could he do it? How could he trick them? His mind churned backward to his previous thought of pretending to be sick. He lay perfectly still even though he'd developed an itch in his leg. He wanted to scratch it so bad he thought he would scream out his frustration any second.

Two minutes passed, and then three. He could see the green numbers on his oversized watch. When five minutes passed, he rolled over and started to cough. Then he stuck his finger down his throat and gagged. Alarmed, the two martial experts stood and looked down at him. They jabbered between themselves and then at him. Ted rolled over the other way so they could see his face. They pointed to him and continued to jabber. He retched again, this time spewing forth the results of his earlier meal. One of the men ran toward what Ted assumed was a washroom while the other man bent lower to peer at him. Ted raised his head slightly and then with all the force in his body he slammed his head up into the man's groin. The little man emitted a howl of pain as he doubled over and dropped to the floor. A heartbeat later Ted was at the door that he slammed open and then he was running for his life. He looked over his shoulder once and lost his momentum but as far as he could see no one was following him.

Winded, Ted staggered out to the curb and hailed the first cab coming his way before he realized his backpack was back at the *dojo.* Son of a bitch! Now what was he supposed to do? Everything of any importance was in that damn bag, even his laptop with all his notes, his thoughts and the sappy letters he'd written to Maggie but didn't have the guts to send. Shit, shit, shit!

"Driver, drop me off at the *Post,* will you?" Thank God his wallet—with his money, his ATM card and his credit cards—was still in his back pocket.

Ted leaned back on the seat and closed his eyes. Would his boss Liam Sullivan believe him when he told him he'd been abducted on Jack Emery's orders? Probably not. If he told Sullivan what he suspected, he was giving up what he thought of as a possible scoop on the vigilantes. He remembered only too well how

Sullivan had chastised him for seeing vigilantes everywhere he looked. Sullivan had ended up by telling him he was obsessed and to get a life. Nah, he was keeping Sullivan out of the loop and going solo on his obsession.

"Driver, I changed my mind, take me home." Ted rattled off his address and then leaned back again and closed his eyes. He didn't open them again until the driver barked out their arrival.

Ted paid the driver and then took the steps three at a time to get to the lobby of the building he lived in. He rode the elevator to his floor, got out, looked around and then entered his apartment. Mickey and Minnie ran to the door. "Nope, it's just me, guys. Maggie isn't here." Mickey hissed and backed off. Minnie stalked him, nipping at his pants leg. He dumped some dry cat food into a bowl. Both cats looked up at him as though to say, *"We're not eating that crap, where's the salmon Maggie always feeds us?"* "So starve already," Ted muttered as he stomped his way into the spare bedroom he used as an office.

Ted clicked on the computer and while it booted up he raced out to the kitchen for a beer. He chugged from the bottle as he made his way back to his office. For the most part everything on his laptop was on this computer or the one at the *Post.* He transferred everything to a memory stick and then hid the stick in the toe of one of his smelly sneakers. Then he deleted everything on the computer.

The beer bottle was empty so he went back to the kitchen for a second one. He then decided to Google the G-String Girls. He printed out reams of information from a PR firm who, he decided, had nothing better to do in life but document every little tidbit on the red-hot women. Did he really care what brand of tooth-paste the one named Mandy used? Did he give a good rat's ass what size feet the one named Kelly had? Was his life in-complete because he didn't know how many piercings the one named Cindy had? No, he did not care. Not one damn bit. He did sit up a little straighter when he saw that all of the G-String Girls had tat-toos on their ankles. Aha, Claudia had a strawberry mark on the inside of her left thigh. Yesirree, the world really needed to know that.

The moment the computer finished printing, Ted stacked the papers into a neat pile. He'd used almost a ream of paper. Five hundred sheets to a ream. No one was *that* important.

The heavy reading ahead of him, Ted fortified himself with a third beer and a bag of stale chips that he scarfed down before he got to his desk.

Three hours later, Ted bolted off his chair and headed for the kitchen again. His throat was dry, parched, actually, from reading all about the G-String Girls, and his eyes were gritty from reading but now he had information he could use. He looked down at his watch. He'd lost track of time but Jack Emery never slept, or so he said, and who gave a shit if he woke him up or not. He'd ring his damn phone till the district attorney couldn't stand to hear it ring. Before he could change his mind, he punched in Emery's number. As the cell on the other end rang, Ted plopped down on one of the kitchen chairs, kicked off his shoes and propped his feet up on the table. If only Maggie could see him now. She'd give him a swat that would knock him off the chair and then Clorox the table.

Nine rings later, Ted knew Emery either had the phone off or he'd seen his name on the little screen. Ted redialed as he swigged from the bottle in his hand.

An hour later with no response, Ted dialed Harry Wong's number. He didn't answer, either. Next he dialed Maggie's number. She didn't answer, either. Batting zip, Ted decided to scramble some eggs when his stomach started to growl. He kept calling each of the three phones as he whipped and stirred. Finally, frustrated, he reached for the portable phone, dialed Emery's number again and then kept hitting redial when there was no answer. He cleaned his plate and dumped the dishes in the sink. He was walking away when he remembered Maggie wouldn't be doing the dishes. He retraced his steps, the phone cradled between his shoulder and ear, and washed his dishes.

Ted was tugging at his clothes to get ready for bed when he heard Jack Emery's angry voice. Ted stopped and leaned up against the wall, a smirk on his face. So it was true, persistence really did pay off, but then he already knew that.

"Well, hi there, Jack. Just wanted you to know I got away from those goons. I'm filing a police report on you, you son of a bitch. Goes to show how smart you and your goons are. I just wanted to give you a call to tell you I figured it all out. I know what's going on. *I know it all.*"

"Congratulations! You must have me confused with someone you think cares about your deductive skills. Stop calling me, you asshole."

Ted lowered his voice to a harsh whisper. "Hey, asshole, I know the G-String Girls are the vigilantes. How's that for my deductive skills?" Ted could hear laughter on the other end of the phone. His skin prickled at the sound. The laughter grew more robust.

Jack managed to control himself long enough to say, "Boy are you going to sound like a horse's ass when you spout that crap to anyone who cares to listen. The fans will damn well lynch you if I don't do it first. Go back to bed or crawl back under your rock. Whatever floats your boat. Just stop calling me."

"Okay, Jack, I'm going to call the FBI. They have more than a vested interest in catching your girlfriend and the others. Watch for the story tomorrow."

"Yeah, yeah, yeah. You finished?"

It suddenly dawned on Ted that Emery had been stalling for time. He knew it because Minnie and Mickey were racing for the front door. He stuck his head around the corner, one leg still in his pants, the other out. He tried to stare down the two goons from Harry Wong's *dojo.* "You bastards picked my lock. This is a home invasion. I'm going to screw your skinny asses to the wall. Do you hear me?"

One of the petite men crooked his finger, indicating Ted should come to them. His smile was almost as evil as Maggie's when she was pissed off.

Ted narrowed his eyes as he tried to figure out which one of the guys he'd plunked in the nuts. He didn't have long to wait when he saw the high-flying kick. He went down, excruciating pain rivering up through his entire body. The pain was so bad he wanted to cry. He did cry when the little man butted him a second time and the world went black.

"Night-night," the little man sing-songed. His partner reached down and picked up the lanky reporter like he was a sack of rice. He slung him over his shoulder and together the two men left the apartment, careful to make sure the cats stayed behind.

Chapter 19

Jack Emery paced the lobby of the Willard hotel, his gaze sweeping to the doorway every few seconds. Where the hell was Maggie? More to the point, where the hell was Harry Wong? He didn't want to be down here in the lobby. He wanted to be upstairs with Nikki. On top of all that he wanted to kill Charles Martin. Nothing would give him more pleasure than to put his hands around the Brit's neck so he could squeeze the life out of him.

He saw Maggie then, frazzled as always, bounding through the door. He held up his hand and waved. He led her across the lobby to two empty chairs where they couldn't be overheard. "Well?"

"I need two more tickets," Maggie said breathlessly.

Jack's face went totally blank as he tried to figure out what the reporter was talking about. "Huh?"

"Tickets. I need two more and I need them right away. That's as in immediately."

Jack smacked his forehead. "Maggie, what the hell are you talking about?"

"Tickets for the G-String Girls concert. I need two more tickets. I had to give mine to my boss so he'd get off my back. Two, Jack, and I need them right away. By the way, you look like shit."

Jack ignored her. "We had to snatch Ted. He figured it out."

"Well, don't look at me. I haven't talked to him. If you recall, it was me who told you he was acting a little weird when the girls first arrived. That was the last time I saw him. That means I gave you a heads-up. If Ted figured it out, you're on shaky ground, Jack. What do you want me to do? Listen, I really need those tickets."

Jack shook his head. This woman was all over the map. "Things are moving at the speed of light. According to Charles, it looks like the real G-String Girls are going to be late arriving here in the States. There was a problem with some of their handlers at the airport. Drugs," he said succinctly. "That means our girls are going to have to perform. There's a revolt going on upstairs. Charles has been on the horn every two minutes. Kathryn was supposed to leave for Oregon to take Justice Barnes's people to a safe location. Now Lizzie is the designated traveler. I have no idea how she's going to drive a goddamn bus but she's going to have to do it. Justice Barnes is acting up. Myra is in a tizzy. Annie is having the time of her life and I haven't had any time with Nikki."

Maggie did her best to absorb all Jack was telling her. She, like Jack, shook her head to clear away her thoughts of Abner and the tickets so she could concentrate. "Like I said, what do you want me to do?" was the best she could come up with.

"Not me. Charles. He wants you to arrange another meeting with Tyler Hughes and somehow get Grant Conlon to that same meeting. The girls will take it from there. Can you do it, Maggie?"

Maggie's mind raced, her shoulders slumping as she recalled her last meeting with Hughes. "It's not going to be easy but I'll give it a try. Where and when do you want this meeting to take place?"

"Nikki's house in Georgetown, where I now live, and we need that meeting immediately. This way the girls can get in and out without too much trouble. Personally, I don't like it but no one seems to care what I think at the moment. Charles thinks the Georgetown address will work in our favor. We need to do this quickly. As to Conlon, I think if you call him to set up the meeting and tell him Justice Barnes will be there, he'll show up. Then your job is done."

Maggie worked at a strand of hair, twirling it between her fingers. "What if I can't entice them to the meeting? Hughes flipped me the bird at our last meeting. I don't even know Grant Conlon and couldn't pick him out of a crowd of two. Don't look at me like that, Jack. I'll try and do my best. I can't force them to a meeting."

"Then threaten them. You're a reporter, aren't you? They're not going to want to see themselves in print. Call me as soon as you have the meet set up."

"Just like that you want me to threaten two high-profile people. I could end up in jail. I need those tickets first. I'm serious, Jack."

"All right, all right!" Jack motioned to one of the police officers stationed next to the door. He held a whispered conversation with the officer as he dialed Nikki's number.

Ten minutes later the officer handed over two tickets to Jack.

Maggie literally snatched the tickets from Jack's hands. She ran over to the concierge's desk, asked for an envelope, slipped in the tickets and scribbled a note from a sticky pad that said, *Pick me up at the paper an hour before the concert.* "Can you messenger this to the address on the envelope?" she asked the concierge. She handed over twenty-five dollars and walked away, her heart kicking up a beat at what she'd just done. She wondered what Abner would think when he opened the envelope and saw the tickets and her note.

One wet dream coming up. She wasn't sure if it would be Abner's or hers.

"You got any insight on Ted?" Jack asked when she returned to his side.

"Ted who?" she asked breezily.

"That bad, huh?"

"Yeah, it's that bad. Okay, I'll get back to you. Any other instructions?"

"That's it for now. Good luck, Maggie."

Jack moved off to walk the lobby again before coming to rest near the elevators. He wanted nothing more than to go upstairs but that was out of the question. He looked down at his watch and grimaced. The countdown was on. He closed his eyes for a moment as he wondered if Nikki was upstairs thinking of him just the way he was thinking of her. How in the damn hell, he wondered, did it ever come to this? He jerked back to reality when he felt a light touch to his arm. Jack whirled, his hand going inside his jacket to the gun in the holster under his arm. "Damn, Harry, you're like a spook. You need to cough or something before you come up on me. I could have killed you."

Harry snorted. "You and what army? What's going on?"

Jack briefed him. "Where's Ted?"

Harry laughed. "Our intrepid reporter is

trussed up like a turkey and sleeping like a baby. That guy can really cuss. That means he was pissed big-time. He figured it out, Jack. What are we going to do with him when this is over? It is going to be over, right?"

Jack sighed. "You need to ask me an important question like that when I'm bright-eyed and bushy-tailed. Right now I'm about dead on my feet. I'd kill for an hour of sleep."

"It's quiet. Go on upstairs and crash. I can handle things here. Navarro just got here. I saw him outside a few minutes ago. We got it covered."

"You sure, Harry?"

"Kiss my girl for me, okay? But only on the cheek."

"You must be kidding. That little lady would wipe up the floor with me if I came within a foot of her, kiss or no kiss."

Harry laughed as he pushed the elevator button and moved off to where Special Agent Bert Navarro was holding court with two other special agents.

Jack stepped out of the elevator and knew if he leaned up against the wall he'd fall asleep. He didn't think even Nikki's lips on his could keep him wide-awake. He did blink, not once, not twice, but three times when he entered the suite of rooms to see all the women sitting on the floor in a circle.

"I just came up to see if I could get an hour's sleep. Will one of you wake me in an hour?"

Nikki scrambled to her feet to lead Jack into one of the bedrooms, where he fell onto the bed. He murmured something she could barely hear as she leaned over and kissed him lightly on the lips. A small smile tugged at the corners of her mouth when she realized he was already asleep. She pulled at a light blanket at the foot of the bed and covered him. The smile left her face when she walked out of the room.

Nikki shrugged when she sat back down. She looked over at Yoko and said, "Jack said Harry wanted him to give you a kiss but he was afraid you'd deck him."

Yoko broke into a fit of giggles.

"Where were we?" Nikki asked.

"We were bitching about how we can't possibly take on Conlon and Hughes and still do a performance. We're good but I don't think we're *that* good," Kathryn said.

"Is there anything I can do?" Pearl Barnes asked.

"For now not much, Pearl. If Maggie runs into problems you might have to call Grant. I see him as the one who will give her a hard time. If Hughes digs in you might have to call him, too. In fact, one of us should call Maggie and have her toss in your name if either one of the men balk at the meeting," Myra said.

Pearl nodded as she withdrew slightly from the circle, aware that she didn't quite belong.

"Twenty-four hours is all the time Charles is allowing," Nikki said. "It takes about eight hours to get us made up to look like the G-String Girls. We don't know what kind of problems we'll run into with Conlon and Hughes. Even with Jack and Harry covering our backs, we all know what can go wrong will go wrong. On top of that, Alexis's supplies haven't been delivered yet."

"Charles assured me that everything on Alexis's list will be delivered momentarily.

Right now, girls, time is our enemy," Myra said.

"If Maggie is successful in enticing both men to Nikki's house, how are we to get there? In what disguise this time?" Isabelle asked.

"I'm working on it," Alexis said. "I do think, though, you're going to have to leave one at a time so as not to draw attention. I can make you up to look however you want to look. I won't know for certain until my supplies arrive."

The dark moment lightened when the women pondered who they wanted to look like. They grew quiet when Myra's cell phone rang and a sharp knock on the door could be heard. Nikki raced to the door and opened it. Four huge boxes were carried into the sitting room by one of the police officers. Nikki thanked him and closed the door. "Your stuff is here, Alexis," she called out.

Before she joined the circle of women she tiptoed into the bedroom to check on Jack, who was sleeping peacefully. She leaned over to kiss his cheek. "Only God knows how much I love you and only God

knows how sorry I am that I got you involved in all of this." She kissed him again
as tears puddled in her eyes. She didn't
see the lone tear that dropped onto
Jack's hand.

When the door closed behind Nikki,
Jack wiped at his own wet eyes as he
kissed the wet spot on his hand before he
fell back into his fitful sleep.

Back in the sitting room, Myra snapped
her cell phone shut and looked around at
the expectant faces staring at her. Her
hands went to her neck as she searched
for the pearls she was never without and
then remembered they were in the pocket
of her trench coat. She struggled to clear
her throat before she spoke. "The good
news is the G-String Girls' band was allowed to depart. They are in the air as we
speak. The girls themselves and their handlers weren't so lucky. So far there has
been a ban on all publicity, thanks to people Charles has on the scene. If it gets
leaked that the real girls are in Germany,
we're going to have a problem. Right now it
looks like, perhaps, the real girls will have
wheels down an hour into the concert. That

means we have to...We have to...per-
form for an hour." Her tone was so desperate sounding the others smiled. "Perhaps a
question-and-answer kind of thing at the
onset."

The others hooted with laughter at the
preposterous suggestion. Myra deflated
like a pricked balloon.

Nikki's cell rang. She looked down at
the name of the caller before she clicked it
on. "What's up, Maggie?" She listened
and nodded. "Okay, we'll take it from
here." She shoved the cell into the pocket
of her sweats. "Conlon and Hughes told
Maggie to hit the road. Neither one wants
to talk to a reporter." She turned to Pearl
Barnes. "I guess it's up to you to turn the
screws, Pearl. If you want us to help you,
it's the only way to get to the name or
names of the people who want to ensure
your decision at the Supreme Court.
Hughes is almost secondary to this problem. Getting the names from him, or from
Conlon if he knows, is going to be the big
problem."

Kathryn snapped her fingers and then
pointed to one of the boxes in the sitting
room. "Piece of cake." The others giggled,

knowing the contents of the box with the big red letters that said, FRAGILE. HANDLE WITH CARE.

Alexis looked at her watch. "Okay, I can have you made up within three hours. You'll need another hour and a half to leave here, travel to Nikki's house, convince Conlon and Hughes to give up the names of their people, wait for said people, do the deed and get back here, at which point I will start to transform you into the G-String Girls. Again. This time the transformation will go quicker since I had a little practice the first time. We can do it but just barely, so you're going to be on a very tight schedule. You'll all need to stay aware of the time. Who wants to go first?"

Yoko bounced to her feet. "Just make me look different."

"Oh, you will look different," Alexis said as she pawed through one of the boxes. "You're all going to be cops. Complete with real guns." Alexis laughed at the expression on the women's faces.

The women shrugged and then grinned as they drifted off to gather in one of the bedrooms to allow Pearl Barnes privacy to make her two phone calls. When she walked into the bedroom minutes later she looked so stricken Myra and Annie rushed to put their arms around her. Her voice was shaky when she said, "I'm just having a little trouble that Grant would betray me after all these years. Tyler I can understand, he's a greedy man who hungers for power and wealth. Grant was . . . Grant was like me, he just wanted to help. Maybe I was blind and I just wanted to believe that. If there were signs that he wasn't what I thought he was, I totally missed them. I just can't believe he would betray me like this. Both of them agreed to meet me at noon. Tyler said he would give up his lunch hour, if you can believe that."

"Don't you worry, Pearl. We'll make him pay for his involvement," Annie said cheerfully.

"What's in the box marked FRAGILE?" Pearl asked as she dabbed at her eyes.

"You don't want to know," Kathryn said.

"She's right, dear, you don't want to know," Myra said. "Now, tell us what the situation is with your people in Oregon."

"My runner is holding up. She managed to get some supplies from friends without tipping anyone off. It wasn't much. My pro-

gram is not designed for any one to stay
for more than twenty-four hours. It's been
weeks. Each stop on the railroad is just
temporary. There are no accommodations
for more. That's why everything has always worked so smoothly. What's happening now is a disaster. The people that
are stranded are frightened out of their
wits. It's hard to keep the children happy
and content with their mothers so frazzled. It's just not a good situation."

"Where will they go once Lizzie takes
them to Montana? Have you made provisions for them, planned a route, what?"
Nikki asked.

"I wish I could tell you but I can't. I've
been afraid to make any calls for fear
Grant might have penetrated some of my
security. It's better that I alone am held responsible for everyone's safety. I'm working on a plan and if you can take care of
Grant and Tyler and the other people who
are blackmailing me, I think I can bring the
plan to fruition. In addition to the eighteen
people in Oregon, I have nine mothers
and their children waiting to be taken to
safety via the first stop on the underground,
but I can't take a chance on moving them

until I know I can keep them safe. I am so fearful some of them will go back to their situations where harm will come to them if I don't act quickly."

"If there is one thing in this world I can't stand it's an abusive husband. We'll take care of your problem, Pearl, and you can get back to doing what you do best, saving the lives of all those women and children," Kathryn said vehemently.

Jack Emery rubbed the sleep from his eyes as he rode down in the elevator. In the lobby he searched out Bert Navarro. "Here is the plan, Bert. You go out to Nikki's house in Georgetown with Justice Barnes. She'll be down in a minute. Here's the key. Open up and then split via the back door but don't lock it. Stay outside so your people can take Justice Barnes wherever she wants to go after Conlon and Hughes arrive. Barnes will just stay until the others get there. Harry will be outside the house also. You okay with this?"

"Well, yeah, Jack," Special Agent Navarro drawled. "You sure you can arrange something with Kathryn?"

"Well, yeah, Bert," District Attorney Emery drawled in return. "Either a front row seat for the concert or you stand in the wings. Your call."

"I'll take the wings. I want to get up close and personal with her. She's my kind of girl. The kind I've dreamed of all my life."

"Even knowing what you know about her and the others?" Jack asked. It was important for him to hear the agent's response.

"Yeah, Jack, even knowing what I know. And, yeah, it's tough playing both sides of the fence but the end justifies the means in my eyes. Right or wrong, I made the decision even before Kathryn came on my radar."

Jack smiled. It was exactly what he wanted to hear. "Go on, get out of here. Justice Barnes just stepped out of the elevator. Watch your back, Bert."

Bert adjusted his government-issue sunglasses. He clapped Jack on the arm. "Always, buddy."

One by one the newly appointed police officers made their way to the house in

Georgetown, three of them entering by the front door, the other three entering from the alley and then the kitchen door.

Nikki felt her throat constrict at how neat and tidy Jack kept her house. It even smelled like Jack. She fought the tears that burned behind her eyelids. Another life, she thought sadly. "I'll make some coffee. We have ten minutes. All of you, check out the house. The minute Pearl admits Conlon and Hughes, one of you has to go out the back door to alert Bert to take up his position by the front door in case either guest makes a run for it. That will be you, Kathryn. Harry will be at the back door. We all clear on that?"

"Where's our stuff?" Isabelle asked.

"Right here, dear," Annie said as she carried in the box with the big red letters.

Myra had two duffel bags in her hands.

"Looks like we're good to go," Yoko said as she turned to wave at Harry, who was peering into the back door.

Nikki busied herself by getting a tray and cups and saucers out of the cabinet. She looked at the others and said, "The smell of fresh-brewed coffee will lull those two asses into believing Pearl is here to talk. A good hostess always serves refreshments. She'll excuse herself to get the coffee and we move in. Watch the time. Annie, be *very* careful with that box."

"Yes, dear."

The front doorbell rang at one minute past twelve. Nikki pointed to the clock on the kitchen range.

"Showtime," Kathryn said.

Chapter 20

Pearl Barnes licked at her lips and then smoothed back her unruly gray hair. She took a huge breath and then exhaled slowly before she opened the door. She thought her guests looked wary.

"For God's sake, Pearl, I've been worried sick," Grant Conlon bellowed. "What's going on? Whose house is this? What are you doing here? Why are you hiding? You damn well owe me an explanation."

Pearl ignored Conlon's questions. She looked at her handsome ex–son-in-law but didn't say anything. Instead she turned and motioned the two men to follow her

into the living room. Just as she was turning around she noticed a shadow by the
front window next to the door. That was
good, one of the vigilantes' people had
taken up his position.

"Damn it, Pearl, will you say something? This is like . . . like cloak and dagger
stuff. Why is he here?" Conlon asked, jab-
bing a finger in Hughes's direction.

"You're both here because I invited you
here. The time for pretending is over. I will
not allow you to blackmail me, Tyler. And
you, Grant, how could you betray me after
all these years? I know the two of you are
in this together. This little get-together is
so we can talk it out. I'm going to leave the
two of you for a few minutes. I'm going to
get us all some coffee. Sitting around
drinking coffee is so civilized and right
now that's exactly the kind of feeling I
need. Please," Pearl said, holding up her
hands, "don't insult my intelligence by trying to protest. Shame on both of you for
taking me for a fool."

The women clustered around the
kitchen door but while they could hear
voices they couldn't distinguish the words.
They jumped back as one the moment

they heard Pearl's footsteps on the hardwood floors.

Myra led Pearl to the back door. "Your job is done. You have to go now. Bert's people will take you to your home. Stay there until you hear from one of us. If we don't call you, Charles will." She stared into Pearl's glazed eyes. "Pearl, get a handle on yourself. We're going to make everything all right but you need to leave. Tell me you understand."

"I do, Myra. I do. Thank you. Thank you so much."

The back door opened and then closed.

Nikki looked down at the pretty lacquered tray on the table. She'd poured the coffee from the pot into a saucepan, brought it to a full boil and then poured it into a silver coffee pot.

Nikki was through the door first, followed by Isabelle carrying the tray, which she set down on the coffee table between the two men, both of whom jumped to their feet at the sight of six police officers standing in a tight circle.

"Pearl had to leave to keep a previous appointment," Yoko said. "She asked us to stand in for her. Coffee? Cream? Sugar?"

Both men stood up, the color draining from their faces. Hughes was the first to speak. "What's going on here? Who are you? What has that woman said to you?"

"Tsk, tsk," Kathryn said, clicking her tongue. She pointed to her badge and the gun at her waist. "We're cops. What's going on here? We're serving coffee. I believe my fellow officer asked you if you'd like cream or sugar. Quick now, make a decision. By *that* woman, I assume you mean Justice Barnes. You need to show a little respect here." To show she meant business, she pulled her nightstick out of her belt and whacked Hughes across the knees. The man howled in pain.

"Shut up!" Annie said, pouring him a cup of coffee. She looked into the cup and thought the dark brew was still boiling.

Hughes, doubled over in agony, cursed ripely. "This is police brutality. I'll see you in jail for this. I know important people."

"Yeah, yeah, yeah," Annie said. "I know people, too. So, do you want this coffee or not?"

"No, I do not want your fucking damn coffee!"

"Too bad, too sad, oh, boo hoo!" Kathryn

said, reaching for the cup on the delicate saucer. She took a dead aim and tossed the hot liquid into Hughes groin. His bellow of pain and outrage could be heard all through the house.

Grant Conlon took that moment to sit down, his hands clasped seven inches below the belt holding up his trousers. He was no fool. "Who are you? What do you want?" he managed to whisper.

"We did not give you permission to speak, Mr. Conlon," Myra said.

The man immediately clamped his lips shut.

Nikki looked around at her sisters. "He wants to know who we are. I think we should tell him. What do you all think?" She sounded like she was asking directions to a gas station.

The six women removed their visored caps. It was Conlon who said, "Oh, sweet Jesus, you're the *vigilantes!* Hughes, you son of a bitch, these women are the ... the ..."

"Vigilantes!" Isabelle said, triumphantly finishing Conlon's sentence. "Would you care for some coffee?"

"No thank you." Conlon pushed himself

so far back into the couch the women thought he'd come out on the other side.

"Enough with the socializing," Kathryn said as she whipped around the room, her nightstick tapping the furniture as she went along. "We're going to ask you this question only once. Look alive here, Mr. Hughes!" she said, giving him a good crack on the shoulder. "And...the question is... What are the names of the people who hired you to blackmail Justice Barnes? The people who are worried about her Supreme Court decision that's due soon."

"I don't know what the hell you're talking about," Hughes said through clenched teeth. "Come on, Conlon, we're outta here. They aren't cops, they're just a bunch of women who are PMSing."

"Just a bunch of women who are PMSing, is that what you said?" Kathryn demanded in a voice so dangerous sounding Conlon turned bone white. "Do you by any chance remember what happened to the national security advisor? He's sort of, kind of, a vegetable. Well, almost. His wife that he beat senseless has to feed him and change his diaper. Well, she does that sometimes. Most of the time she forgets. The man drools."

Conlon started to babble. "He came to me! I didn't seek him out. I don't even like the bastard. Please don't hurt me."

"Well, that sure doesn't say much for you, Mr. Conlon. You betrayed Pearl's trust in you for money. You have to pay for that."

"For God's sake, I don't have any money. Money is the reason I'm sitting here right now. I have a gambling problem and I admit it. But he," Conlon said, jerking his head in Hughes's direction, "has a *big* gambling problem. I never laid a hand on Pearl. I love her. That guy Woodley, he got what he deserved for harming his wife. I tried to get out from under but the son of a bitch wouldn't let me. He said *his people,* that's what he said, his people, would take care of me. He scared the crap out of me. Look, let me go and I'll make it up to Pearl. I'll explain the whole thing. She's a kind woman, she'll forgive me once she understands."

As one the women hooted with laughter.

"Pearl is the reason you're here," Nikki told him. "She's the one who contacted us. She knows all about your visit to your brother-in-law, you know, the one who is the new director of the FBI. She wants us to take you both out," Nikki said in a voice so low the men had to strain to hear her. "No holds barred."

Conlon's hand flapped in the air. He tried to get his mouth to work but couldn't quite get the words out. "What... What are you... What are you going to do to us?"

"Depends on your buddy here. If you know the names, now would be a good time to spit them out," Nikki said.

"Oh, Jesus, I don't know. He just said they were paying him millions. I think there are two of them, partners in some business. That's all I know. I swear it."

"Shut the hell up, Conlon. You don't know what you're talking about. You can't prove a thing," Hughes sneered.

Annie approached the two men. She loved the feel of the gun on her hip. She flipped it out and almost dropped it. She'd forgotten how heavy it was. "I'm not very good at this. I wish it wasn't so heavy. My hand shakes when I hold it. Oh, that's right, the left hand is supposed to cup the right hand. Well, shoot, it's still heavy. Don't worry, I might not hit your heart but I'll hit *something.* Give us the names. Now!"

"Screw you!"

Nikki looked down at her watch. "We don't have time for this bullshit. Strip! Now! Both of you! What? You're shy! Girls, help them out here. No need to be gentle. Myra, get the camera ready."

"It's ready, dear."

Kathryn and Isabelle jerked both men to their feet. "Take them off or we'll burn them off. Now!" Kathryn bellowed. She almost burst out laughing when she noticed out of the corner of her eye that Yoko was doing high-flying pirouettes in the far corner of the room. From time to time her tiny fists shot outward as she screamed something that sounded like *"Eyow!"*

Conlon was shaking so badly he could barely open the buttons on his shirt. Myra leaned forward and ripped it loose. Hughes glared at them defiantly.

Yoko stepped forward, did a little dance backward, the air moving before she stepped forward, her foot shooting out, striking Hughes in the throat. "The next time, I'll crush your windpipe."

Tears rolled down the man's face.

"The names please. Gambler that you are, I'm sure you know there's a time to hold and a time to fold. This is definitely a time to fold in my opinion," Kathryn said.

"Will you give them the damn names already?" Conlon whimpered. "I saw pictures of Woodley. It was the talk of this town for months. I know what these women can do."

"If I give you the names, what do I get out of it?" Hughes asked.

Annie advanced a step, stuck the wavering gun in his chest and said, "You get to *live*."

Kathryn and Isabelle were busy ripping at Hughes's clothes. Conlon was naked and sitting on the sofa, his hands covering his private parts. He was crying at his humiliation. The women ignored him, their sights on Hughes.

Kathryn held up a pair of silk skivvies that were so minuscule the women went into fits of laughter. "Kind of fits what it was covering. You know, s-m-a-l-l!"

"Bitch!" Hughes seethed.

"The names. This is the last time I'm going to ask you," Kathryn said, waving her nightstick wildly.

"All right! Two lawyers contacted me. I don't think their clients know what they're doing. That's just my opinion. I don't know who they are. They promised me a lot of money but I haven't seen a penny of it yet. They said they have offices on Connecticut Avenue. There, I told you all I know. Can we go now? I think you broke my kneecaps. Please," he whined, "I'm in a lot of pain."

"You aren't going anywhere, you piece of crap. I told you, I want names. A man like you, well, you would have checked them out someway, somehow. You aren't going anywhere either, Conlon. Your life as you knew it no longer exists. Now, shut up and sit there and don't say another word unless you're prepared to give me names," Kathryn said.

Nikki moved then to the box with the big red letters. She ripped at the tape, opened the sides and looked inside. The women started to laugh. The two men on the sofa squirmed.

"Last chance," Kathryn said, pulling on a pair of latex gloves. She gave an extra pull so that they snapped against her wrists.

"I told you, I don't know their names."

"Liar, liar pants on fire. Ooops, that so doesn't work because you aren't wearing pants. Okay, stand up, bend over and assume the position. I sure hope those guys who promised you all that money find out how loyal you are to them."

Conlon started to squeal and whine when he saw the other women pulling on latex gloves.

"I thought I told you to get up and assume the position."

The two men dug themselves deeper into the sofa. Annie and Isabel pulled a protesting Conlon to his feet. Myra and Kathryn pulled Hughes to his feet.

"This might be a good time to show these two fine gentlemen what's in that box, Nikki."

"My pleasure," Nikki said. All eyes were on her as she rooted through the box, finally pulling out two long sticks. She stuck two more in each of her pockets.

It was all Kathryn could do to keep a straight face. "Dynamite, boys. We're going to stick it up your ass and light the fuse. Not to worry, we coated them with Vaseline. Now, assume the position! That's a goddamn order!" she screamed to show she was finally out of patience.

Conlon slipped to the floor in a dead faint as Kathryn approached Hughes with the firecracker that looked exactly like a stick of dynamite, with a long red fuse. "Spread those cheeks, dude." She turned to the others and said, "Oooh, I so don't want to do this!"

"Oh, it will be such fun. Get Conlon on his feet. We don't want him missing a minute of this," Nikki said as she handed another firecracker to Annie, who looked so gleeful, Hughes lost his water. Myra had the camera posed and ready.

"No, no, no, you're clenching your cheeks." Kathryn eyed Hughes's rectum, fixing it in her mind as she squeezed her eyes shut and jammed the firecracker as far up his butt as she could. "I think some-one else should light the fuse. I had my fun. You all deserve to have some fun now."

The front door burst open and Jack and Bert Navarro arrived in the living room just as Kathryn ripped off the latex gloves.

Navarro's eyes almost popped out of his head. Jack turned around and walked

back out the front door. Navarro ran behind him.

"*Wusses,*" Yoko giggled. "Your turn,
Annie."

An evil look on her face, Annie jammed
her firecracker into Conlon and then
stepped back. "Okay, who wants to light
the fuses?"

Nikki, Yoko and Isabelle volunteered.

"Draw straws," Myra said.

"Oh, sweet Jesus, don't do this. If I knew
who it was, I'd tell you but Hughes never
told me. He knows. I know he knows," Conlon cried.

"Is that true?" Nikki asked as she pulled
a box of long fireplace matches out of the
cardboard box. "We're going to light these
fuses on the count of three. Think of the
reconstructive surgery. You could end up
a eunuch if the blast doesn't kill you."

"For Christ's sake, will you tell her the
name, you turd!" Conlon screamed as
Nikki approached with the long matches
and a bright red lighter.

Sweat rolled down Hughes's face. He
was terrified. "All right, all right! I told you
the truth, two lawyers came to see me.
They have an office on Connecticut Av-

enue. They never told me who their clients were but it's some big case that went to the Supreme Court. Huge guys, brothers. They're big on class action suits. McGregor and McGregor. Attorneys to just about every politician in the city. Now, take that damn thing out of my ass."

"Shut up," Nikki snarled as she snapped a set of flexi cuffs on each man's wrists and another set on their feet. "Don't move! If you expel that stick, I'll shove it up to your tonsils, so use some control," she ordered.

A nanosecond later Myra was on the phone to Charles. When she hung up she motioned for the others to follow her to the kitchen. All eyes went to the clock on the stove. "Charles said he'd have the men here in thirty minutes."

"What if they're in court?" Nikki asked.

Myra shrugged. "When the FBI goes after someone they can go into court and do a snatch. At least that's what Charles said. If he said they'll be here in thirty minutes, they will be here in thirty minutes."

"Then what?"

"Then we leave, but first we have to torment them a little. Hey, what would you think if you saw someone with a stick of dynamite up his ass? I think they might talk and tell the boys everything they want to know. At that point, it's their show. We're almost out of time, ladies."

"Aren't we going to light the fuses?" Annie asked. "I want to see the shower of confetti when the fuse burns down."

"I'm afraid we're going to miss that, dear," Myra said. "You need to put that gun away, you're making me nervous."

"Myra, I think you should call Pearl so she can get back to her...uh...vocation. I'm sure she's a nervous wreck," Nikki said.

"What's going to happen to those guys?" Kathryn asked.

"This is just a guess on my part, but I think they might all be on the same flight back to Africa with the G-String Girls. Never to be seen or heard from again."

"That'll work," the women said in unison.

All eyes went to the clock on the stove. If Charles's promise was to be kept they had one minute to go.

The front door opened. Jack called out, "Company!"

"Well, our work here is done," Annie said.

The women donned their visored caps, saluted one another and one by one they left by the kitchen door.

Nikki looked back once and thought she saw Jack at the kitchen door. She waved as tears gathered in her eyes. Then she waved again.

Chapter 21

Charles Martin stood at his computer, scanning the emails as they blitzed through the printers. He raised his eyes once to stare at the bank of clocks that told him the time the world over.

For hours now he'd been in touch with fellow retired operatives who were only too glad to offer up their expertise and get back into the clandestine world where Charles still operated. In the end he'd had to place a second call to his friend on the other side of the pond to pull it all together. At the moment the ground he was standing on was a little less shaky, and that was a good thing.

Now, with things stabilized for the moment, he had to concentrate all his efforts on getting the Sisters safely to this mountain in North Carolina. He let his mind wander for a brief second to Myra and her last phone call. He didn't want to dwell on her whispered threats because he knew she meant every word and yet he couldn't seem to concentrate, the words hanging over his head like a sword. He could feel his insides curdling at her strong language, something Myra had never before resorted to. In all fairness, was it his fault that the German authorities were holding the real G-String Girls hostage for their handlers' peccadilloes? No, it was not, but Myra didn't want to hear that.

At least the real G-String girls were in the air now. The best he could hope for was that they would have good tailwinds and would arrive sooner rather than later. The curdling in his stomach increased, making him aware of the seriousness of what was going on.

"Stop fretting, Daddy. Mom is busting your chops. She's having the time of her life!"

Charles whirled around. "Barbara!" He

felt so light-headed he had to lean against the shelf holding his computer. This was only the third time his daughter's spirit had come to him. He wondered if he was dreaming. He pinched himself.

"It's me. You need to stop worrying. Germany was beyond your control. What's happening in Washington is way beyond your control, too. The Sisters will make it come out right. You do trust them, don't you? Jack will make it come out right."

"What a silly question, darling child. Of course I trust them. It's the variables I don't trust. Murphy's Law, you know. I also know your mother never says anything she doesn't mean."

A chill washed over Charles when he heard the tinkling laugh he loved and remembered so well. He was still new to talking to a spirit and wasn't sure what he should say or do. "Are . . . Are you okay? Have you . . . uh . . . *talked* to your mother?"

"I did. Right now she's a little busy but she's fine but worried about you. Are there any problems with getting them to the mountain?"

"So far, so good. But again, things can

go wrong at the last second. I hate to admit it, but my stomach is tied up in knots. That concert is making me bloody crazy. I'm not sure my girls can pull it off."

Charles heard the tinkling laugh again. *"Not to worry, they can pull it off."*

The encrypted phone in Charles's pocket chirped to life. He didn't want to answer it but knew he had to. He wanted nothing more than to stand here and talk to his darling daughter.

"Take the call, Daddy. I'll be back."

A second later Charles felt a whisper of warm air on his cheek. He touched the spot and it felt warm and tingly. He had to shake himself back to reality when the special cell chirped again. The sound was alarming for some reason.

"Charles, Jack here. A monster problem just presented itself and I don't know if a phone call can take care of it."

Ted Robinson opened his eyes and knew instantly that he was alone in the semidarkness. Where the hell was he? Within seconds he remembered what had happened to him. He tried to move but whatever was tying him down had little slack. He wiggled his toes and fingers. At least he had feeling. Was he in Wong's *dojo?* He sniffed the air. He smelled sour sweat (probably his own), disinfectant and something that smelled like cedar. Maybe cedar chips were in the green plants outside, wherever the hell outside was. Yeah, yeah, he was probably in the *dojo.* Where the hell was everyone? It was way too quiet. Were the classes cancelled? Was the building empty? He thought about calling out but decided it was a bad idea.

What time was it? Was it day or night? How long had he been here? He struggled to see the watch on his wrist but the way his arms were trussed up, it was impossible. He took a deep breath and rolled over. The smell on the floor was so terrible he gagged. He rolled over onto his back and lay quiet, his mind racing. If there was a way to get to the key chain in his pocket he might be able to work the little pocket knife that Maggie had given him. Was it still in his pocket? There was no way to tell because he really couldn't feel the chain pressing into his leg. At the time he'd thought it a useless gift, but Maggie had seemed so pleased with her little gift he'd made a big deal out of it and hooked it onto his key chain. His eyes burned when he remembered how she'd kissed him when he'd thanked her. Maggie was big on giving little gifts, most of them useless, more whimsical than anything else. Maggie was a giver.

His hands groped and searched, but he couldn't work either of his bound hands into the pocket of his jeans. He tried rolling on his side and bringing his knees up, hoping if the key chain was in his pocket, the movement of his legs might push it upward. He thought he felt something press against the outside of his upper thigh. He wiggled and squirmed. Maybe if he could find a way to stand on his head the chain would fall out.

Never athletically inclined, Ted struggled to get on his knees and then on his head. Three tries left him exhausted as he vented, making up curses as he went along. Plus, he was making noise but so far no one had come to check on him. When his breathing was more or less normal, he tried again. And again. And then again. Right before he collapsed he thought he heard the tinkle of the key chain hitting the floor. His breathing was so shallow he thought he was going to black out.

Ted tried to calm himself by thinking of Maggie. She was the athletic one. She ran, she jogged regularly, and she worked out three or four times a week. She also did yoga from time to time. He'd always marveled at how she could literally twist herself into a pretzel. Now, he wished he'd joined her in her quest to keep her body in shape.

He grappled with his arms and face, hoping to come in contact with the key that opened the door to his apartment. He rolled over and over, his face and tied hands searching the hard floor. He moved slowly, back and forth, then slid his bound body up and down. For all he knew he might be lying on the damn thing. Then he felt something under his cheek. He almost whooped for joy but the pain in his face and hands that he knew were rubbed raw made him suck in his breath instead. He smashed his cheek into the floor so that the key chain wouldn't move. If, indeed, it was the key chain. That was when he realized his hands were numb and tingly. He cursed under his breath as he tried to flex his fingers to bring back some semblance of feeling.

Ted moved his face gingerly as he tried to feel the key chain with his bruised and bloody lips. He knew he was bleeding because he could taste his own blood. There definitely was a God, not that he had ever doubted it. The key chain felt wet and slippery. His teeth clenched tightly over it.

Ted tried rubbing his hands up and down on his pants legs, hoping to restore some feeling to his numb hands. His left hand seemed to be coming back to life, but what good was that going to do him? He was right handed. He started to rub his right hand with a vengeance. The moment he felt the feeling return to his hand he dropped the key chain into the palm of his bloody hand. He sucked in his breath again as he tried to pry the little knife out of the sleeve it was in. Then he remembered how tiny the blade was. It would take him forever to saw through the nylon cord that bound his hands and legs.

Forever turned out to be ten minutes, give or take a few seconds—because while the blade was tiny it was razor sharp. "Thank you, Maggie, thank you, Maggie," he muttered over and over as he sawed through the nylon rope. He wanted to scream his joy when his hands were finally free. Instead, he gulped another breath and sawed away with renewed determination. And then he was free! At the same time he saw a sliver of light under the door. He heard voices from behind the door. Two voices. No, three voices. Panic rivered through him as he tried to get into the same position he'd been in before he freed himself. He wound the ropes over his hands and feet, hoping he was getting it right. If the men on the other side of the door decided to check on him he hoped they wouldn't notice how raw his face was. He prayed then. He closed his eyes and clenched his teeth.

Ted knew light had spilled into the room even though his eyes were squeezed shut. He listened for footsteps. The voices babbled in a language he didn't understand. Obviously they could see his still form and were reassured that he was still unconscious. The door closed. He didn't hear a lock snick into place. Thank you, God. Thank you, God. He waited to see if the light outside the door would disappear.

It did, a good ten minutes later when the high-pitched jabbering stopped. He shucked off the ropes and sat up, the blood rushing to his head. He looked down at his watch with the glow-in-the-dark numerals and waited another ten minutes before he got to his feet. He had another head rush before he was able to take the steps that would carry him to the door. He opened it gingerly. He could see out into the training room and he could see neon lighting coming through the top half of the plate glass windows.

Was the *dojo* empty? Were there guards outside? He tried to remember all the things Jack had told him about Harry Wong and his people. He vaguely recalled him saying some of the instructors stayed in one of the three apartments on the second floor. Harry, he knew, had his own apartment on the other side of town. Jack said Harry owned the building and was an astute businessman. Like he gave a good rat's ass about Harry Wong.

The moment Ted's eyes became accustomed to the dark he inched his way toward the back door. He looked around to see if there was any kind of alarm system in place but he didn't see one. The door, however, had three different locks. His heart started to pound as he worked quietly to slide the three bolts back. He turned the old-fashioned door handle, hoping and praying that the babbling voices weren't waiting for him outside. He stepped outside into pitch-blackness. Again, he waited. He strained to see in the darkness. He didn't want to bump into a trash can or anything else that might create a noise.

Ted looked upward and could see dim lighting on the second floor. Unfortunately the light was so dim it didn't light up the alley. He made his way slowly, his arms out at his sides in case there was something he could bump into. His steps were small, first one foot going to the left, then the other foot going to the right to see if anything was on the path. Then he was on the street. He wanted to run but he knew that would be a mistake. He forced himself to saunter down the street. He took a minute to stare into a shop that sold electronics and was so well lighted he could see himself in the window. What he saw horrified him. He looked like some alien creature. If he wasn't careful he was going to get picked up for vagrancy because he looked like a derelict.

Ted looked down at his watch again. In a while the concert was going to be under way. Staying in the shadows he tried to figure out what he should do. Should he try to make it to the *Post* or should he go home? No, to both. He looked up at one of the street signs. He was closer to the *Post* apartment where Maggie was currently living. What did he do with the key? He couldn't remember. Maybe he could use the little knife to pick the lock. If not, he'd just have to break down the damn door. After he rang the bell of course. Shit!

He damn well needed a plan and he needed it right now.

Thirty minutes later he was standing in front of the door to the *Post's* apartment. He rang the bell and waited. He rang it a second time. Satisfied Maggie wasn't home, he tried the doorknob. Locked. What a surprise. He groped in his pocket for the little knife on his key chain. It took a full fifteen minutes of gouging, digging and body slamming the door before he could get it open. He was light-headed with relief. He blasted into the apartment and headed straight for the bathroom where he tried not to look at himself in the mirror as he stripped down. He stepped into the shower and almost screamed in pain when the warm water washed over his head and down his face that was scraped raw. He looked down at his hands where the skin on the palms of his hands and wrists was raw and oozing blood. He wanted to cry.

He stepped from the shower and awkwardly wrapped a towel around his middle as he walked out to the kitchen. He used the phone on the counter to call his colleague. "It's me, Espinosa. I need your help. We're pretty much the same size. I need you to bring me some clothes, from the skin out. And some medical supplies. Ointments, peroxide, some gauze. I got kidnapped and I'm in bad shape." He listened a minute and said, "Jack Emery and that goon Wong had his people snatch me right in broad daylight at the Willard. Now, Espinosa. Like in immediately, and bring some food with you." He listened again and said, "I'm in the *Post* apartment." He rattled off the address. "Make it snappy, Espinosa. I'm counting on you. Yeah, yeah, you get half the byline."

Seething with rage, Ted pressed the numbers that would block the phone number he was dialing from and then pressed in the numbers to Jack Emery's cell phone. Jack clicked on after three rings, sounding frazzled and angry.

"Hey, asshole! Guess who? I'm calling you an asshole because you couldn't find your ass if I gave you a mirror on a stick. I'm free! That means I got away from those cruds of Wong's. Bet you don't have a clue as to where I am! I'm on my way to the Hoover Building! You and that evil little man of yours are going to pay for what you've put me through. I'm going to charge you both with kidnapping. How do you like them apples, hotshot?"

Jack's voice was so dangerous sounding, Ted flinched. "I *don't* like it. Now I'm going to have to kill you. You know that, right?"

Ted tried to bluster. "Yeah, right, you and what army?"

"No army, Teddy. Just me." Ted choked on his own saliva when he realized Jack had hung up on him.

Chapter 22

Jack Emery snapped his cell phone shut. He couldn't help but notice how his hand was shaking. His guts were churning, too. That was new. Usually he was cool under fire. The proverbial cool cucumber. That must have been in his other life before he became a member of the Sisterhood. Harry Wong, who was standing next to him, noticed his shaky hands, too. He looked up at Jack's eyes and then he, too, started to twitch.

"You gonna tell me what that was all about or are you going to let me stand here and guess that we're in some kind of deep shit, which is par for the course when I'm around you?"

Jack whirled around, his gaze raking the lobby of the hotel. All seemed busy but normal. Six people were in line to check in. Two guests were checking out. Two bellmen were pulling a dolly with luggage piled to the top. The concierge looked harried with a knee-deep line of gray-haired ladies waiting for an audience with him. Normal.

Ignoring Harry he whirled around and asked, "Where's Navarro?"

"I haven't seen him in the past fifteen minutes. He was here but he might have stepped outside. What's going on?"

"Find him, Harry. Then we'll talk."

Harry rolled his eyes. A second later his Blackberry was in his hand. Three minutes later Bert Navarro raced across the lobby.

"Bert, call some of your friends at the Hoover Building. Have them stake out every exit. Ted Robinson is on the loose. *Again,*" he said angrily, eyeballing Harry. "This time, lock him in a cage and throw away the key. Just make sure you remember where you threw it when it's time, if that time ever comes, when we have to let him loose.

"Now, Harry, we can talk. You heard what I just said. That bastard is going to charge us both with kidnapping. He's on his way to the Hoover Building. I'm not sure I believe that. Ted is smart as hell. He might have just said that to spook us. But one thing I am sure of and that's that he knows the girls are here. I just want you to tell me how the hell he got away from your guys."

The Whippet-thin martial expert winced at Jack's words. Like he didn't want to know the same thing. His shoulders stiffened as he worked his Blackberry. A second later his cell phone came to life.

Jack had no idea what Harry was saying to the person on the other end of the line. If facial features were any indication of what was going on, the person he was talking to was going to have a hard time of it when Harry got his hands on him. He'd never really seen Harry pissed off but he was pissed off now. Big-time.

The cell phone clicked off. "I hate you, Jack."

"Oh, yeah? Well, guess what, you took

responsibility for Robinson and your guys were asleep at the switch. He got away from you *twice,* Harry. Twice! Just tell me how the hell that happened."

"He had a knife in his pocket, that's how. Must have been one of those mini things because my guys searched him. The guy had deep pockets, I'm thinking. Sometimes things get jammed in the corner of your pockets. It's happened to me and you're a damn liar if you say it never happened to you. Look, it happened, okay? We can't un-ring the bell. Tell me what it means. Tell me what you want me to do."

Jack's gaze swept the lobby again. Things still looked normal—nothing differ-ent other than a florist who was switching out the wilted flowers for fresh ones. The gray-haired ladies were walking out the door, brochures in their hands.

"Finding Robinson is going to be like looking for a needle in a haystack. He could be on his way to several different places, mainly the armory, where the con-cert is being held. I don't think he's been in touch with Maggie yet or she would have called. Hell, he could be on his way here for all I know. What I know for certain is it's not wise to underestimate Ted Robinson. Shit, he might be at the *Post* convincing his editor the women are here. I can't pull anyone off this detail. You got any guys stashed someplace we can use? What that means, Harry, is we're operating blind."

"Six guys, tops. They're not detectives, not into this spook shit. I can call them and have them available but where?"

"Put all of them at the armory. I have to go upstairs now and alert the girls. We need to switch to Plan B. Call Maggie and tell her to get her tail over here ASAP." Without another word, Jack turned on his heel and headed for the elevator.

Harry flipped him the bird, his eyes just as angry as Jack's. He worked the Black-berry with his left hand while his right hand worked his cell phone.

The Sisters stopped what they were doing the minute Jack walked through the door. He knew they were already aware that there was a problem. Good old Charles.

"Change of plans, ladies. Robinson is on the loose again." He saw no reason to sugarcoat anything. "He called me and said he's on his way to the FBI. I sent Navarro to check it out. I'm not sure I believe Robinson. I think it's a red herring to throw us off his tracks. Seems Harry's people didn't check his pockets because he sawed through the ropes they tied him up with, so I guess he had one of those key chain mini-pocket knives in his pocket. He's loose, that's what matters at the moment. He's going to charge Harry and me with kidnapping. Right now that's not important, either. What's important is you need to get back into your police attire. You can't travel in your G-String... uh...costumes to the armory. Is that going to be a problem, Alexis?"

Alexis looked around at her sisters who were in various stages of transformation. "I need at least another ninety minutes to turn them into the G-String Girls. If I get them fully made up the police uniforms shouldn't be a problem. That's just a matter of the uniforms and wigs. We can do the stage makeup at the armory. It will be tight but I think we can do it."

Jack almost fainted in relief. "Okay. I need to make alternate transportation plans. I think what we'll do is you each walk down a floor or two, don't take the elevators. Wear sunglasses. I'll commandeer a van of some sort and a few police cruisers if possible. I'll get back to you on the specifics. Do any of you have any questions?"

Yoko stepped forward. "Where is Harry? You cannot hold him responsible for what his people did or didn't do. He's helping us the best way he can. If you didn't trust him you should have done it yourself. That is all I have to say."

Chagrined, Jack turned to Nikki, who simply glared at him. Then she smiled and Jack's whole world turned right side up. "We don't deal in blame, Jack. We've been under the gun in every mission we've undertaken to date. It's a ripple, a bump in the road. We'll be fine. We can't worry about Ted. Right now we have enough on our plates."

The others shouted their agreement as Isabelle shooed Jack toward the door. He turned and looked over his shoulder at the love of his life in her G-String Girl attire. She looked like a goddess. She wiggled her fingers and winked at him. His heart felt a little lighter as he rode the elevator to the lobby.

Jack barked questions at Harry the minute he saw him.

"We got it covered, Jack. Maggie was at the *Post* but she's on her way here. Ted has not made an appearance. Yet. He doesn't have his cell phone because my guys took it. But, Maggie did say Joe Espinosa, a colleague of hers and Robinson's, has been calling her. She didn't answer any of the calls and the guy didn't leave messages. It's possible Robinson hooked up with him. She said Espinosa is his flunky, whatever the hell that means. I didn't know reporters had flunkies."

"They do if they want bylines. Robinson knows how to network. As does Maggie. She might have some information we can use. Keep your eyes open. I have to make arrangements to get the girls to the armory. If Maggie shows up before I get back, tell her to stay because I need to talk to her. Look, Harry, I'm sorry about... I meant it but I didn't mean it, okay? I feel like a train wreck right now so cut me a little slack. I swear to God those women are so damn cocky they make my head spin. For whatever it's worth, your girl defended you. She was ready to deck me, I could tell. I don't mind telling you I think my heart stopped beating for about five seconds. She loves you, you . . . you . . ."

"Enough with the sweet words. Get the hell out of here. I'll hold the fort. When I don't hate you, I love you."

"Aw, gee whiz, you're making me go all mushy."

Harry discreetly flipped him the bird a second time. Jack grinned as he sprinted to the back of the lobby and the exit door.

The Sisters' suite was a beehive of activity as the women rushed about trying desperately to help Alexis in their transformation, aware of the problems and the time constraints. The police uniforms were unpacked, the holsters and guns checked. ID was scrutinized. Alexis worked feverishly as she manipulated the yards and yards of latex required for the Sisters' transformation.

"This is so exciting, isn't it, Myra?" Annie asked as she checked the safety on the gun that was in its holster. "I actually feel like I belong in law enforcement. I just can't believe we're doing all this. It's like one of those edge-of-your-seat movies where you're chewing your nails down to the quick."

"What's the latest on the girls' arrivals? What time is wheels down?" Kathryn asked as she buckled the gun belt around her slim waist.

"If all goes well, we'll only be onstage twenty minutes," Myra responded. "If there's a glitch, it could be an hour onstage." She searched for the pearls that always adorned her neck. She wanted her pearls. No, she *needed* those pearls.

"Easy does it, Mom. You need to stay cool and calm. Remember, you're in control."

Myra whirled around when she felt a light touch to her arm. She walked away in the direction of the bathroom. "Darling girl, you always come to me when I need you the most. I...I don't think I can do this. I'm too old. I'm frightened, Barbara," she whispered.

"I know, Mom. Daddy is just as frightened. I was with him a little while ago. He's worried about you and trying

to pretend he isn't. It's going to be okay. It really is. You're just frightened of going onstage. And another thing, age is just a number. You can do this. You're my mom. Remember how you used to tell me and Nikki that moms could do anything? Are you telling me that was a lie?"

"No, dear. No, no, no. This is just un-charted territory for me. I've never been comfortable in the public eye. You know that. Wearing virtually no clothes in front of thousands and thousands of people... at my age... I'm afraid I might freeze on the stage and ruin everything. I know it's not really bothering the others but I'm..."

"Mom, I'll be right there with you. I promise. Another thing, Mummie, you aren't really going to be naked. You're going to be plastered with latex. That means your own skin is not going to be showing. Think of it as a nude cos-tume. Can you do that?"

It was the old childhood endearment term of *Mummie* that made Myra square her shoulders. If her darling daughter's spirit had such faith in her how could she disappoint her? She nodded.

"Now, don't you feel better, Mummie?"

"You know what, I really do, darling. Is Charles all right?"

"More or less. He was kind of frazzled but when I left he seemed to be getting it all under control. It's you he's worried about. He doesn't know what to expect when you get back."

Myra forced a laugh. "And, well he should. Always keep them guessing, right? That's what you used to tell me about your various beaus when you were a teenager."

"You got it. Okay, I'll see you onstage. Make me proud, Mummie, okay?"

"I will darling girl, I promise. Even if it fractures me."

Eyes sparkling with happiness, Myra whirled around. "Chop-chop, ladies, let's get a move on. Charles is counting on us. We need to make him proud of us. We can do it!"

"Rah! Rah!" Kathryn said as she danced across the room in her cop uniform. "You heard the lady, chop-chop!"

Nikki looked over to the far corner of the room and smiled. "Thanks, Barb," she whispered.

"No problem, Nik."

Forty-five minutes later the Sisters were ready to exit the suite. A flurry of phone calls went over the cyber network to alert those on the ground level. They left, two by two, each group walking down to a different floor.

Three police cruisers and one battered green van were lined up in a neat row. Looking like they knew what they were doing, the Sisters climbed into their assigned vehicles and they peeled out of the parking lot, sirens wailing, blue lights flashing.

Jack Emery heaved a huge sigh of relief. "I wish I could say our job here is done, Harry, but we still have to wait to make sure Alexis gets to the armory. The minute she steps into the taxi in whatever getup she's wearing this time, then we have to head for the armory. I got the last cruisers for the girls so we're going to have to take a cab, too."

"See! See! You don't think ahead, Jack. I have our transportation parked on the street. While you were running around like a chicken without a head I was taking care of our transportation. Translated . . . I was thinking ahead. We're going on two wheels. Play your cards right and I promise not to buck you off when I take the corners. Who is going to sanitize the suite once Alexis leaves?"

Jack shrugged. "Some of Charles's people, I'm sure. Fortunately for us that doesn't come under our purview."

Jack's cell phone chirped. He had it open in a nanosecond. It was Navarro calling in. "No sign of him, Jack. I have the lobby and all entrances covered. What do you want me to do now?"

"Head to the armory. I'd bet my next paycheck Robinson is either there or on his way. We'll be leaving in a few minutes ourselves. Stay alert." Jack craned his neck to take in his surroundings. "Where the hell is Maggie? She should have been here by now."

"I don't know, Jack. My guess would be traffic," Harry said.

They were back in the lobby when they saw Alexis step out of the elevator. She was dressed in a maid's uniform, complete with apron and carrying a string bag. She paused a moment as if she was looking for something or someone. She made eye contact with Jack before she made her way to the door where she disappeared.

"Okay, we're good to go."

"What about Maggie?"

"Give her another call. I have a call coming in." Jack clicked on his cell phone. "Lizzie! Jesus, don't tell me you already have a problem. All hell is breaking loose here. I can't handle anymore so whatever is wrong, take care of it."

"Shut up, Jack, and listen to me. I'm on my way to your cabin in Montana. My bus is almost full. I'm calling to... I think I'm calling to thank you for allowing me... No, that's not right, not *allowing* me, I mean, to *trusting* me with all these women and children. They're a bit of a ragtag group right now. I understand now what Justice Barnes has been doing. I understand why each person only knows his or her job. Anything more would screw it up. These people who are helping aren't rich. In fact most of them are on the poor side and yet they've pooled the food, the clothing, the toys for the kids and don't ask anything in return. When I got here they were down to their last box of crackers. That was it, Jack, crackers. The good news is the bus was loaded with fresh fruit, sandwiches and milk. I guess Charles's people took care of that.

"I've never driven a bus before. The last time I was even in a bus was in grade school. I need to know these people are going to be okay. I'm not coming back until I know that for sure. Are you listening to me, Jack?"

"You can't stay there. You don't belong to the underground. Charles and Pearl know what they're doing. There will be another runner who will pick up once you're gone. Everything is fine on this end. The girls got Conlon and Hughes and they're under Charles's wing as we speak. Time is still crucial but it's not quite so urgent right now. Just follow your orders."

"Jack . . . I . . ."

"I know, Lizzie, I know. Suddenly those Armani suits and the three-hundred-dollar designer sunglasses don't seem to matter anymore. You're seeing some of the real world now. I felt the same way when I . . . Look, I gotta go. You did good, Lizzie. I'm proud of you. I'll tell the others. See you when I see you."

Lizzie's voice sounded choked up when she said, "Jack, tell Justice Barnes I'm at her disposal, anytime, day or night, 24/7. I mean it, Jack."

"I'll pass it on, Lizzie. Take care of those women and children. Hey, maybe you can get a bus driver's license." Jack could hear nervous laughter on the other end of the phone when he clicked off.

"Let's get this show on the road. That was Lizzie. Everyone is alive and well. That was the good news. Where the hell is Maggie?"

"Like I said, stuck in traffic. Told her to back up and head for the armory. She'll probably get there before we do. Okay, buddy, hop on and don't go screaming in my ear when you get excited," Harry said.

"You couldn't get me excited if you tried, Harry."

"Wanna bet?" Harry asked, peeling away from the curb.

Jack just knew he would be suffering from whiplash in the days to come. He clenched his teeth and gripped the seat with both hands.

Chapter 23

Ted Espinosa was a handsome, dark-eyed Latino. Normally he had a smile on his face, showing off perfectly aligned white teeth that gleamed like beacons. Now, though, he was scowling, his hand gestures wild and furious. "Either you're crazy or you're a couple of hardboiled eggs short of a picnic. If what you're saying is true, you need to go to the FBI. I'm not hanging my ass out to dry even for you. I thought you were smart. This is not a smart thing you're doing, Robinson."

"They're not going to listen to me, Joe. I was right the last time and they screwed it up. Those women got away. I know they involved Justice Barnes. Do you have any idea how powerful that woman is? Her long-standing live-in of twenty or so years is the brother-in-law of Elias Cummings who heads up the FBI. I'm telling you, those goddamn vigilantes are standing in for the G-String Girls. Maggie gave it away. She's one of *them* now, Joe." Ted's mouth turned into a grimace, like he'd just bitten into the sourest lemon on the tree.

"The only thing I don't know is why and what Barnes has to do with the vigilantes. Something, for sure. Something that could destroy her career. Nothing else makes sense. I think they came back to help her. But why? I can't reach Conlon. Before Wong's people snatched me, I called the think tank where the ex–son-in-law works and he's gone. Like in *gone.* Just walked out and didn't come back."

Espinosa was still scowling. He knew and respected Ted Robinson. He was a real newshound and he was usually right. Yeah, the guy was hung up on Maggie Spritzer, who he hated with a passion, but it was no skin off his ass if Robinson wanted to noodle around with her. "Proof. Facts. Two sources. You have zip! Intuition is not going to cut it."

Ted looked at his newly appointed partner. He could see Espinosa slipping away from him. He couldn't let that happen. He needed the guy. "Means. Motive. Opportunity. The holy trinity of law enforcement. That British guy who controls the vigilantes has help blowing out his ass. That's the means. The motive is Barnes needs them for a reason. She's of an age with Rutledge and de Silva. All of them are rich as hell. Rich people stick together. Opportunity...the G-String Girls. Those goddamn vigilantes have more guts than brains. Who the hell is going to question something like that? Front and center with millions of people watching them. They're bold and brazen. And Maggie is part of it. That's why I want to get hold of her. I need to sweat her. She'll cave and tell me what I want to know."

Joe Espinosa laughed until he choked. "I'll pay to see that! If Maggie is one of them, she's not going to tell you anything. My paycheck against yours."

Ted actually thought about taking the bet for a second. "I always know when she's lying," he said lamely.

Espinosa looked disgusted. "All you have right now is a theory. You need proof, facts and two sources. You're wasting my time, Ted. And here is the clunker: How are those two old broads going to pass for two of the G-String Girls? They have to be at least seventy years old. Don't you think someone might notice something like that? You know, drooping tits and asses. Blue veins. Yellow toenails. Wrinkles. Maybe even false teeth. You did *not* have an epiphany, my friend."

"I never said I did. Emery, Wong and that sexpot Lizzie Fox joined forces with the vigilantes. I think Judge Easter did, too. I just can't nail it down. I'm telling you, I'm right."

"No, Ted, what you're telling me is they're smarter than you if your suspicions are right. We are not Woodward and Bernstein."

"You're right but *we* could be if you'd get your head out of your ass and help me. Believe in me because I'm right. I feel it in every bone in my body. Call Maggie again."

Espinosa rolled his eyes. "She's on my speed dial and she isn't going to answer, the same way she didn't answer for my last nine calls. Doesn't that tell you she's avoiding you? Knowing you'd get to me and that's why I'm calling her. I've never, ever called her so why all of a sudden am I calling her? Two plus two equals four. You need to get with the program here."

"Yeah, right." Ted looked around at the snarled traffic heading toward the armory. They were jogging, and he was already out of breath.

"What, Ted? What are we going to do when we get to the armory? That's assuming we can actually get within a mile of the damn place."

"Something will come to me when we get there. Keep your eye out for Maggie. I'm sure she's going to be there, right out in the open."

Horns blared, drivers stuck their hands out the window with salutes to the drivers ahead of them. Curses could be heard up and down the street. More horns blared and not a cop in sight. Ted shrugged as he loped along, Espinosa at his side.

Suddenly the cacophony of sound was shattered by even more noise. Ted stopped in his tracks and looked toward Joe, who was yanking at his cell phone. A chorus of "Yankee Doodle" erupted.

Joe looked up at his jogging partner. "I'm from the South. What do you expect? It's Maggie. At least she's calling you back." Ted snatched the cell phone out of Joe's hand before he could blink, and clicked it on.

"Maggie, it's Ted. Thanks for calling us back. Please don't hang up on me. If you do, I'm turning you over to the FBI. I'll do it and you damn well know it. All I want you to do is listen to me. Will you do that? Please," he said as an afterthought.

"You threaten me and then you expect me to listen to you! I don't think so!"

"Then think again, Miss Hotshot. I'm giving you a heads-up because...well, just because we have a history. Jack Emery had Harry Wong kidnap me, but then you probably know all about that. I'm not making this up, either. I'm going to the FBI. I know it all, Maggie. I even know you're one of them. I know the vigilantes are impersonating the real G-String Girls. I might not know what's going on with Justice Barnes but I'm going to find out. This is your chance to get out from under. Once I talk to the FBI, there's no taking it back. By the way, Espinosa agrees with me."

Maggie felt her stomach crunch into hard knots. "You know what, Ted, you're crazy. You'll do anything to get back at me because I dumped you. You never did a thing for me except make me miserable." It was a lie and she knew it but she said it anyway. "Well, get over it. Another thing, stop calling me."

Ted was stunned at his former lover's response. "You'd risk going to a federal prison to protect those . . . those vigilantes? My God, Maggie, you're more stupid than I thought. Okay, I gave you a heads-up. You're on your own now. My conscience is clear where you're concerned," Ted said, anger ringing in his voice.

"I've always been on my own, Ted. Sullivan is going to fire you. There, that's a heads-up for you. Tell Espinosa he's just as big a jerk as you are."

Ted snapped the phone shut and handed

it back to Espinosa. He threw his hands in the air. "I gave her a chance. You're my witness."

Espinosa moved away from a gaggle of people who were trying to cross the busy road. Breathless with all his jogging, he turned to Ted. "Now what? Are you going to call the FBI and the cops?"

Ted's eyes narrowed. "Yeah. Yeah, that's exactly what I'm going to do. For all of ten minutes I had Maggie's cell phone. Not the regular Sprint one but a special one. I think that's how those damn women stay in contact with each other. I couldn't even figure out how to turn the crazy-looking thing on. I know in my gut it was one of those encrypted things that no one but another spook can decipher. I heisted it from her backpack at the apartment. Then those cruds took *my* backpack and they've got it now."

Ted's eyes narrowed even more until they were mere slits. He squinted down at the cell phone Espinosa handed him. He dialed, said his name was Tyler Hughes and went into his spiel. Then he did the same thing with the police department, one of the local news channels, and then, disguising his voice, he called his own newspaper and said the exact same thing all over again but said his name was Grant Conlon. In every call he was careful and precise when he fingered Maggie Spritzer, Jack Emery, Harry Wong, Lizzie Fox and Judge Easter. He patiently spelled out each name for accuracy. He was blunt and to the point when he said the vigilantes were here to help Justice Barnes in some illegal activity and impersonating the G-String Girls. He stayed as vague as he could so he wouldn't be blamed for crying "wolf" one too many times to be taken seriously.

Ted handed the phone back to Espinosa, who stuck it in his pocket. "How come you didn't call Emery or Wong?"

"Because I want the both of them to be slammed from all sides. Five will get you ten right now they're fielding calls like crazy. Serves them right," he said petulantly. "Son of a bitch, my face feels like I shaved with sandpaper and I look like some wild creature from another planet. It hurts like hell. I don't have any feeling in my left hand."

Espinosa didn't bother to offer sympathy.

Instead, he agreed with his partner's assessment. "Now what?"

"Now we stand back and watch the fireworks as we write the story. The minute they close in on the vigilantes, we hit SEND and the *Post* gets the scoop of a lifetime. But, we need to get as close to the action as possible. You know what, I think *you* should call Emery. Tell him you're in on it. Tell him to check with the Fibbies and the media to show you're on the level. You say you want to be part of this team and get half the byline, then you have to perform. This story will be front page. *Above the fold.* We both know it doesn't get any better than that. That's it, Espinosa. Your call."

"What if you're wrong, Ted?"

"I'm not wrong, goddamn it. Just do it."

"If we get our asses in a sling, I'm going to kill you. You know that, right?"

"Yeah, yeah, yeah."

Maggie Spritzer whizzed through the door of the *Post.* She felt like she'd been run over by a train and then ground to a pulp. How could Ted Robinson do this to her? Eyes glazed, she rushed across the lobby, paying attention to nothing. She did turn when she heard her name being called. She whirled around. Her eyes almost bugged out of their sockets when she saw her snitch, Abner Tookus. He was dressed in creased khakis and a white button-down shirt, open at the throat, the sleeves rolled up. His hair was freshly trimmed and fashionable. He smiled. Maggie's heart skipped a beat when he said in a voice she'd never heard from him, "I know I'm early. I didn't want to get caught up in that mess out there," he said, jerking his arm backward to indicate the snarled traffic and frantic drivers.

Maggie was so stunned she had to grapple for words. "What time is it?" He told her. "I have...Listen...Do you mind going alone and I'll meet up with you there? I have a meeting with my boss. It... It's a last-minute thing. I can't get out of it. I still have to change."

"No, I don't mind. You look great just the way you are." His voice was so low and husky, Maggie felt shivers run up and down her arms.

"You...You look great yourself." She blushed with the words. It was no lie. In a million years she could never have imagined the Abner Tookus standing in front of her as the squealing-voiced snitch she had been working with for years. "Okay, I'll see you later."

"Oh, be still my heart," she muttered over and over as she took the elevator to the newsroom. She pulled up short when she saw Liam Sullivan standing by her workstation. Her stomach started to churn at the look on his face. She did take a second to wonder why he wasn't home with his wife getting ready to go to the concert. When his scowl deepened she thought better of asking.

Maggie took a deep breath and exhaled slowly. "What's up, boss?"

The EOC handed her a sheet of paper. "This just came in a few minutes ago. Do you care to comment, Spritzer?"

Her heart fluttering, her stomach churning, her eyes twitching, the best she could come up with was, "Tell me you aren't taking this seriously?"

"The caller was very serious. Everyone in this town knows Grant Conlon is Justice Barnes's live in...whatever they call it these days...boyfriend, for lack of a better term. He's also the brother-in-law of the director of the FBI. You're damn right I have to pay attention. There's something here. I can smell it, Spritzer. And if this guy is right, you're up to your eyeballs in it. It would certainly explain that exclusive you got and those magical tickets you gave me, now wouldn't it? I am paying attention. All the media got the same call and so did the FBI. If you have anything to say, this would be a good time to get it off your chest. Well?"

Maggie cleared her throat. "Ever hear of brownie points? I was trying to be nice by giving you the tickets. End of story."

"There's nice and then there's *nice.* I'm putting you on unpaid leave as of this minute. If nothing comes of this, you have a job. If I find out otherwise, you're outta here, Spritzer."

Maggie's back stiffened. "Since when do you pay attention to anonymous tips? Don't I have rights?"

"Right now, no. Get your gear and don't come back here until I call you."

"What about Ted? He's behind this. I know it. We have issues. He's trying to get back at me. This isn't fair, Liam."

"Maybe not but that's the way it's going to be. Thanks again for the tickets."

Maggie turned on her heel but not before she said, "I hope you rupture your eardrums tonight."

Back in the lobby, Maggie looked around. Abner was gone. She couldn't decide if that was a good thing or a bad thing. Whatever it was, she'd have to think about it later. She yanked at her cell phone. She needed to call Jack and warn him. She should call Nikki or Myra, too. She walked over to a bench and sat down. She closed her eyes and tried to make sense out of what was going on all around her. She'd had no idea Ted could be so vindictive. How could he just up and ruin her life like this? How?

Memories of their time together flooded through her. At times they were like a matched pair of socks, like a set of salt and pepper shakers, him and her. Other times they fought like tigers and made up like wild animals. Ted called it imperfect love. And he did love her. Past tense, *had* loved her. Of that she was sure. She'd loved him, too. They were good together and they did respect one another. For the most part there was total trust in their relationship, except when it came to work and in that respect they were competitive. Then it all went wrong with that Sunday brunch. She should have handled that a little better. But a girl did have her pride. At the time it had seemed like a bump in the road, but it had turned into a mountain road.

A lone tear trickled down her cheek. Ted must really hate her. *Really* hate her. The thought left her sad. All her empty tomorrows flashed in front of her. Abner Tookus was no Ted Robinson. No challenge there. Shame on you, Maggie, for even thinking there might be something there to hang your hat on. Maybe she was a one-man woman. She'd go through life without a man, she'd get cranky and curmudgeonly and become a spinster in an old, creaky rocking chair living off her memories.

Maggie flipped open her cell phone. She debated all of one full minute before she hit her speed dial. Maggie didn't think it was possible for one person to say so little to convey anger, disappointment and then even more anger in so few words. She bristled not only at Jack's tone but at his words. She defended herself. "Is it my fault this town is a zoo? Traffic is not moving. Do I need to remind you I have a job?" She was about to tell him what had just transpired but decided to wait until Emery was done railing her out.

Finally, when she had had enough, she shouted to be heard over Jack's tirade. "What, Jack? What do you want me to do? Even if I can get to the armory, what am I supposed to do? I'm the press. My colleagues have been there for hours. They've got it covered. Unless you have something specific you want me to do, I'm staying put. Make up your damn mind." Right now, right this second was when she was supposed to tell Jack about Ted's phone call. She should be telling him about Sullivan putting her on unpaid leave, too. She should be telling him that law enforcement was hot on her trail. Yeah, that's what she should be doing.

An unbidden memory floated to the surface. She'd had the flu and Ted had taken care of her. Much better than her mother had ever taken care of her when she was sick as a child. He'd made her chicken soup that was so bad it probably made her better. He fussed and fussed, setting the alarm to make sure she got her meds on time. He'd rubbed her down with alcohol when her fever spiked at 104. He'd held her hand and read her fairy tales from one of his old treasured schoolboy books. He'd spoon-fed her, held her hand and head when she gave up the soup. He'd been there for her. More times than she cared to admit. They were supposed to get married and grow old together.

"Maggie, are you still there or am I talking to myself? Did you hear what I just said?"

Maggie shook her head to clear her thoughts. "You said you have Ted's backpack and my encrypted phone was in it and it hasn't been damaged." *I should tell him. Maybe he already knows. If he knows, he'd be rattling my cage. I really should tell him.*

"Do you know where Ted is? Have you heard from him, Maggie?"

Tell him now or forever hold your peace. Maggie knew she was probably making the biggest mistake of her life when she said, "No, I don't know where Ted is. No, I haven't heard from Ted." It was true in a sense. She really didn't know where Ted was. It was Espinosa who had called her.

"Stay available in case I need you."

"And how likely is that, Jack? You've pretty much kept me on the outside all along. I'm not turning my life upside down for you for no reason." Maybe she could still make the concert if she didn't go back to the apartment to shower and change. Abner said she looked good just the way she was.

She waited for a response. What she got was a dead tone in her ear. "Screw you, Jack Emery, and the horse you rode in on."

Maggie looked down at her watch. If she ran all the way, she could make it back to the apartment, take a quick shower, spruce up a little, put on sneakers, carry her heels, and if she ran all the way back to the armory she just might make the concert. Well, she'd never know unless she gave it her best shot.

Maggie barreled through the lobby door at a hundred miles an hour, shoving people out of her way. Tears blurring her vision she ran like she was in a marathon.

Fourteen minutes later she blitzed

through the door of the apartment building and took the stairs two at a time.

It registered, but barely, that the apartment door was unlocked. With all that was going on in her life, did it really make a difference? She did slide the dead bolt home when she closed the door behind her. She started to remove her clothes as she walked toward the bathroom where she came up short in the doorway. All she could see were the bloody gauze and cotton balls. The peroxide bottle had no cap on it. Two tubes of ointment were squeezed dry. The wet towels had blood all over them, and Ted's filthy clothes were in the bathtub.

Maggie sat down on the edge of the bathtub and cried.

Chapter 24

Judge Cornelia Easter looked down at the caller ID and wished the little compact phone would disintegrate in her hand. This definitely was a call she didn't want to take. She looked at her watch, noted the time and then closed her eyes as panic engulfed her. She took a great gulping breath and expelled it in a loud swish. *I can do this. I know I can do this. He's probably taping this conversation.* "Hello, Elias." Her voice came out flat and even. That was a good thing.

"Nellie, hello. Listen, I'm going to get right to the point. This is too important to beat around the bush and right now time is of the essence. The Bureau received a very disturbing phone call and it involves you to a certain extent. Bearing in mind there are a lot of crazies out there, we still have to pay attention to calls like this. A man calling himself Grant Conlon called and said that you, Elizabeth Fox, Jack Emery, Harry Wong and Maggie Spritzer, the reporter, are all sympathizers or out-right members of the vigilante group. The caller said the vigilantes are right here impersonating theG-String Girls. The man went so far as to say you're all new members of that little organization. Are you, Nellie?"

Nellie struggled to work indignation into her voice. "Shame on you, Elias. I refuse to dignify that ridiculous question with an answer."

"Well, you better think twice, Nellie. Justice Barnes's ex–son-in-law has been calling around to the media saying the exact same thing. We can't seem to locate either man. They appear to have dropped off the face of the Earth. This same caller implied that Justice Pearl Barnes has been included in all this...

this . . . conspiracy. Now, if you were me, what would you do?"

Nellie sucked in her breath. "If I were you, I'd get a new phone number and then I'd go home and take two aspirins and go to bed. I think you and everyone in the District are obsessed with the vigilantes because they made fools of all of you. You know I'm right, Elias. I think it's hilarious that you think the vigilantes are posing as those scantily clad singers. Have you considered their ages and how they could do something like that? This is beyond ludicrous, Elias. Shame, shame on you. Now, if you have nothing else to say, let me get back to being miserable with this stomach virus that has attacked me. You can apologize to me later."

"Don't leave town, Nellie. I'm posting an agent near your compound. For your information, the Bureau and I will never ignore a phone tip. We depend on concerned citizens. Like I said, don't leave town."

"I suppose the next thing you're going to tell me is you're going to tap my phone."

"No, I won't tell you that. It's already been done. By the way, where is Elizabeth Fox? She seems to have disappeared."

Nellie sighed for Cummings's benefit. "Now, how would I know Elizabeth Fox's whereabouts?"

"Doesn't she belong to that little poker group of yours? Grant told me all about it the night he came out to inquire as to Pearl's whereabouts."

"As a matter of fact she does belong to our little poker group. She's a real card shark, I can tell you that. I seem to recall hearing her telling Maggie Spritzer she was going out West but I am unaware of a time frame. Lizzie said she always wanted to take a road trip. Bear in mind I just overheard her telling Maggie this. Check with her. She does have a cell phone, Elias. I can give you her number if you like."

"I have her number. She doesn't answer. It goes straight to voice mail."

"Smart girl. I'm going to turn mine off, too, when I hang up."

"I hope you're taking this call seriously, Nellie."

A black furry cat leaped onto Nellie's lap and then clawed her way to her shoulder. She purred so loud Elias Cummings asked her what the strange sound was.

"Are you recording this conversation, Nellie?"

Nellie forced a laugh she didn't feel. "What a ridiculous question, Elias. What you're hearing is my cat, Baby Girl. She's purring on my shoulder. I think this conversation is finished. I'm going to hang up now and forget this insulting phone call. Good-bye, Elias."

Baby Girl squirmed when her mistress threw the cell phone across the room. She jumped to the floor and started to hiss as the other four tabbies investigated the thrown object, their backs arched in the air. Satisfied that nothing further was going to happen, the cats scattered as Nellie fumbled for her encrypted phone. Her old gnarled hands were shaking as she punched in the number three that would connect her with Jack Emery. Her gaze dropped to the watch on her wrist. She almost swooned when she saw the time.

Nellie wasted no time. "Elias Cummings just called me. He told me he was taking a phone call that came into the Bureau seriously. Someone calling themselves Grant

Conlon said you and I and the others are either vigilante sympathizers or actual members. He told me not to leave town and he asked about Lizzie. I said she was on vacation. Obviously she has her cell turned off because she didn't answer. What's going on, Jack?" Nellie heard the harried district attorney suck in his breath on the other end of the line.

"Well, Judge, the rubber is meeting the road as we speak or if you don't like that explanation, then the shit is going to hit the fan very shortly. I'm just winging it from here on in. The girls are here and are *suiting up* as we speak. The atmosphere here has changed. I've never seen so many cops and agents in one place. The media has it going on with coverage that would make the president jealous. That's all I can tell you, Judge. Before you can ask me, yes, I am nervous. Hell, that's the understatement of the year. I'm scared out of my wits. Charles just called and the real G-String Girls are ten minutes out. They should be landing soon. I just hope they can get here before anything goes down. This is just a little too damn close for comfort. There's just so much Harry,

Bert and I can do. Oh, shit! I gotta go, Judge, I think I'm about to get arrested. Call Charles right now."

Nellie dropped her head between her knees so she wouldn't pass out. Deep breaths, she told herself. Inhale, exhale. Inhale, exhale. She had to call Charles. But she couldn't do that until she got herself under control. A minute later she was bellowing at Charles. "Do something! Jack said he was about to get arrested!"

"Yes, I know. I have it under control, Nellie. Calm down, take a deep breath. Listen to me. Call Maggie and talk to her. She's our weak link right now. Can you do that, Nellie?"

"I'm not an idiot, Charles. Of course I can do it. Elias Cummings just called me and he's been trying to call Lizzie. She's not answering her phone. That's not good, Charles."

"I know, Nellie. I've got it under control. Who do you think told her to turn off her cell phone? Call Maggie. Something isn't quite computing there."

"Oh," was all Nellie could think of to say before she realized she was talking to dead air. How *did* the man do it? How could he be up on every little detail? She was certain he had an entire army at his disposal. She had no clue how he made it all work but was glad he was doing whatever it was he was doing.

Well, she had her marching orders so she better hop to it or Charles would come down off his mountain and take her to task. She realized as she dialed Maggie's number that she'd never really been comfortable around the reporter. It wasn't that she didn't trust her, she did, but only to a point. Once a reporter, always a reporter. She pressed the cell phone hard against her ear. She wasn't surprised when the call went straight to Maggie's voice mail. Her message was blunt and frosty. "Charles asked me to call you. Please return my phone call ASAP."

In her gut Nellie knew Myra and the others were walking into a trap. She started to wring her hands until they painfully protested. She looked down at her cats who were swarming around her ankles. "I'm too old for this," she mumbled. "Nonsense," she responded to herself. "Age is just a number." Her other self retaliated. "Bullshit!"

Nellie settled herself, the cats on her lap and on the back of her recliner. All she could do was wait and watch the news coverage. She clicked her remote to one of the 24-hour news channels. Her jaw dropping, she could only gape at what she was seeing on the big plasma screen.

Jack Emery looked around at the pandemonium that surrounded him. He heard the shout that went up from the crowd and saw Special Agent Daniel Saxon bearing down on him, flexi cuffs in his hands. "Vigilantes! The vigilantes are here!" It was a roar that drowned out everything else. Where the hell was Harry Wong? He whirled around but the crowd was so thick there was nowhere to go. Panic set in. He yanked at the gun in his shoulder holster, double-checking to make sure the safety was on. "Move, goddamn it!" he roared. The sea of people nearest him screamed and parted and then closed ranks again. At best he had a minute, maybe two, before Saxon got his hands on him. Everyone who was anyone in law enforcement knew Saxon was the FBI's eight hundred pound gorilla.

Another roar of sound split the early-evening air, this one different. "There they are! There they are! Look!" More roars shrieked in the air just as the skies opened up and a river of rain drenched the screaming crowd.

Jack wanted to look over his shoulder but knew that would lose him precious seconds. "Harry, where the hell are you?" he bellowed at the top of his lungs.

"Covering your ass, where else do you think I'd be? I took care of your little problem. Put the damn gun away. Saxon's out for the count. He might wake up around midnight. The girls made an emergency appearance at the entrance. That's why the crowd is going nuts. They threw out some stuff to the crowd. Underwear, I think. Lacy panties! *Thongs!* All colors. Animal prints."

"Jesus Christ!"

"Yeah, that's pretty much what I said. Hey, it worked. Thirty minutes to showtime. Bert just weighed in before you got yourself between a rock and a hard place. The G-String Girls just landed. They have to go through Customs and should be here within the hour. Right now that could be iffy with the rain that's coming down.

Charles has people who will bring them here. In police uniforms. They step in, our girls step out. Simple. *If* it works."

"We have to get out of here, Harry. We need to get inside to make sure the girls get away safe and sound. Tell me how the hell we're going to do that?"

Harry's shoulders slumped. "We aren't. Charles assigned others to that little task."

"Screw that! I don't trust anyone but us. Come on, think of something!"

"You keep telling me you're the one with the brains so act like you have one. I'm just your muscle. C'mon, c'mon, I'm getting soaked here. You know what, desperate times call for desperate measures. Fire the fucking gun in the air and run like hell. On the count of three. I guarantee a path will open up for us. I'll scream a sighting of the vigilantes at the same time. You ready, fearless leader?" Not waiting for a reply, Harry started to count. "One! Two!"

Jack took a deep breath and released the safety.

"Three!"

Jack held up the gun and fired as Harry let loose with a bellow of, "There they are, the *vigilantes!*"

Chapter 25

Backstage at the armory it was a zoo, a circus, a carnival, all rolled into one. Outside law enforcement struggled to control the frantic fans as the rain came down in torrents. Inside, Jack and Harry, drenched to the skin, fought their way through the gantlet of security, their badges held high in one hand, their guns high in their other to show they were the ultimate authority. The crowds stepped aside as music blared throughout the armory. The mind-bending music was merely preliminary enticement for the appearance of the G-String Girls to soothe the impatient crowds.

"Okay, we're in," Jack bellowed to be heard over the ear-splitting music. His gaze raked over the girls, who were clustered together in their G-String attire, loose robes covering them until it was time to go onstage. He thought they looked excited. *Excited?*

Jack and Harry both kept their guns high in the air so everyone would see them. The backstage chatter came to an abrupt halt. Even so, you still couldn't hear yourself think with the thunder outside the armory.

The cell phone in Jack's pocket started to vibrate. He'd turned off the ringer earlier, because with all the noise he couldn't hear it, but he could feel the vibration. "What?" he barked, his eyes staying on the girls and the security surrounding them. He heaved a sigh when he spotted Bert Navarro, who had eyes only for Kathryn.

"The girls are twenty minutes out," Charles said. "You're running thirty minutes late. Get those girls onstage before you get blown out of the water."

Jack didn't bother to answer. He clicked the phone shut, jammed it in his pocket and yelled, "Showtime!" at the top of his lungs.

As one, the robes dropped to the floor. For one wild moment Jack thought he had swallowed his tongue as the girls did a little shimmy and shake, and then pranced out onto the stage to a drumroll so loud he couldn't focus his eyeballs. He thought he heard Myra say, "Oh, God, oh, God!" as she strutted past him.

When Jack realized he hadn't swallowed his tongue he yelled, "Look alive here! *Twenty minutes out!* No one gets backstage. Shoot anyone who tries and make sure you don't miss. We clear on that?" he bellowed to security.

Jack turned to Harry and said, "Best-case scenario, after the intro, maybe one number and they're outta here. That doesn't mean it's going to happen. Murphy's Law! The techs got it going on. Cross your fingers, Harry. You see any Fibbies out there?"

"Like I can see past those klieg lights! Get real! We're going to be damn lucky if the power doesn't go out."

"The techs got it covered. I heard them talking about it earlier. Two of those big trucks out there by the rear entrance are backup generators with a hundred miles of cable. They have enough juice to light up Shea Stadium for two years running. This goddamn concert is going on no matter what."

Harry leaned closer so he could shout in Jack's ear. "I'd feel a whole lot better if I knew where Robinson was."

The sudden silence made Jack look toward the stage. All he could see was delicious-looking latex skin. He gulped, as did Harry. The women onstage were holding up their hands for silence. It was time to perform. Even from where he was standing Jack could see the ripple of excitement on the women's faces. Annie looked like she was about to explode right out of her latex skin. He knew she was having the time of her life. Hell, all of them looked like they were having the time of their lives. He shuddered at what could happen in the blink of an eye.

Jack continued to watch, his eyes straining to see past the stage as the women separated, brought up their guitars, their fingers poised to hit the first chords. He looked toward the tech guys and saw one of them bring up his hand. Sound, so powerful it almost took the roof off the armory, began. The girls separated, pranced and danced, and then shimmied, every ounce of flesh on their bodies jiggling as they plucked at the strings of their guitars to the shouts of, "Shake it, baby, and bring it on!" The girls obliged with megawatt smiles. The crowd turned wild, some of the more adventuresome fans trying to climb on-stage. Within seconds, big burly men appeared and the fans were hauled away. The girls didn't miss a beat and kept per-forming, their smiles in place.

Harry bellowed in his ear again. "It's the bodies, not the music."

Jack nodded as Kathryn stepped up to the microphone and began to lip-sync lyrics about a gold digger. The crowd whistled, hooted and stomped their feet. Jack decided Harry was right because whatever the words were about the gold digger were drowned out by the enthusi-astic crowd and the blaring music.

Annie had the first inkling that some-thing was wrong when she jiggled to the right and her left leg stayed in place. *Oh, God, I'm melting!* she thought. She swung her arm wide so that she could touch Myra's shoulder. Myra reacted to the panic in her eyes and looked down at her legs when she felt the first sensation. She swallowed hard.

"Aw, shit!" Bert exploded. "Look at Isabelle. She's right under the lights. Her face is starting to melt. It's the lights, they're too damn hot! Yoko's arms are softening up. The tattoos are running together. Look, for Christ's sake!" Harry and Jack both gasped. "Annie's ass is starting to droop. Two more minutes and she's toast. Myra's knees look like she's wearing long underwear. We have to do something and we need to do it right *now!*"

Jack raced back deep into the wings. "Dim the fucking lights! Right now!" The tech looked at him but didn't move. Jack yanked at his gun. "Now, goddamn it!" The tech yanked at a lever and the stage lights came down. "Now put some blue and red in there!" He waved his gun again, this time wildly. The tech turned white just as the stage was bathed in a rainbow of color. Jack moved over to the music techs. "How much longer for this number?"

"Five minutes!"

"Okay, blast some other kind of crap, I need to get those girls off the stage. Didn't

I see a box of panties somewhere?" The tech pointed to a box.

"You know what to do, Navarro. Signal the girls as soon as the number ends. We can't patch them up. The lights are just too damn hot. Why the hell didn't someone think about that?" Knowing he wasn't going to get an answer, he kept on shouting orders until the music crashed to an ear-splitting finale.

Nikki looked toward the wings where Jack was standing. He did his best to pantomime a problem. She raced toward him, leaving the others standing and talking to the crowd. The moment she realized the problem she grabbed a handful of the panties and raced back, held a whispered conversation with the others who beelined for the box. At best it was a few-minute reprieve.

The crowd went wild as thong panties flew through the air.

Harry slammed Jack on the back when the rear entrance to the armory opened and six cops walked through. The moment the door closed behind the newly arrived cops the real G-String Girls started to rip at the Velcro police uniforms.

Jack gaped. Harry's jaw dropped. Bert slapped his thigh and reeled backward. This was synchronization down to the last sync.

Nikki looked toward Jack as she pitched the last pair of panties to the crowd. She saw the real G-String Girls at the same time, stripping off their police uniforms. She gave a signal to the others who bounded off the stage. Within seconds the real G-String Girls were center stage and the blinding bright lights were back up.

"What happened?" the women asked as one.

"You're melting is what's happening. Look at Isabelle and Yoko!" Jack cried.

"Oh, my God!" Myra groaned as she looked down at her knees.

Annie was trying to see her rear end but had to give up. She yanked at the latex and cursed at the same time.

"That was the best my rear end ever looked. I think I might get a lift if I can find a plastic surgeon willing to take me on. This is too thrilling for words!" she gushed as she looked down at the pasties with the swinging tassels. "I feel like Cinderella at the ball!"

"Annie, put a cork in it," Jack said. "We don't have time to talk about this. Put those uniforms on and let's get all of you out of here."

The girls ripped at the latex covering them as they raced to their dressing room to struggle into the police uniforms they had arrived in.

Jack pointed to his watch as he grabbed Nikki's arm. "Five minutes!" he roared.

She nodded and blew him a breathless kiss.

Onstage the real G-String Girls gyrated, danced and pranced as they, too, blew kisses to the roaring audience. From time to time they remembered to pluck at the strings of their guitars. The raging crowd didn't seem to mind one way or the other. The visual was all that was important and the girls were happy to oblige.

Jack felt the phone in his pocket start to vibrate. He plucked it out and clicked it on. "They're almost out of here. Two minutes and counting. What? I don't want to hear any bad news, Charles." He listened, the color draining from his face. He clicked off.

"That was Charles. Ted Robinson is at the back door with the feds. They're getting ready to bust it down. Bert, do you outrank them? Stall them until the girls get out!" Not bothering to wait for a response, he said, "They're interested in the girls on-stage, not female cops. Harry, go to the dressing room, alert the girls. Maybe we can work around this. You're both still standing here! Go!"

Bert raced to the door. He called over his shoulder, "How come I always get the shit detail?"

"Because you have one of the special gold shields! Just do it, Bert. I promise you a date, a real date with Kathryn, with wine, flowers and a good-night kiss if you pull this off. C'mon, c'mon, make it look real!"

Jack forced himself to look as noncha-lant as possible by leaning against a wall and tapping his foot to the sound of the mind-numbing music. His heart pounded in his chest at what was to come.

The back door opened. A crowd of peo-ple and a flood of rain poured into the nar-row area. "Guess Bert doesn't outrank the director of the FBI," he mumbled under his breath.

His back stiff, his face a mask of worry, Bert led the small group to where Jack was standing. Introductions were made. Jack held out his hand. The director shook it. Ted Robinson smirked.

"You gonna let the girls finish their set? If you don't, the fans will stampede the stage and someone is going to get hurt. They have one more number to this set before they take a break."

Elias Cummings looked at Jack and then at the girls on the stage. He dispersed two of his men to the far end of the left wing. Two agents remained at his side along with Robinson and Espinosa.

"You're under arrest, Mr. Emery. I'm going to read you your rights." He Mirandized Jack and then asked, "Do you understand these rights as I've read them to you?"

"I do," Jack replied.

"Since you're an officer of the court, I'm not going to cuff you. I want your word as an officer of the court that you won't hinder this arrest."

"Well, yeah, but what arrest is that?" Jack drawled, his eyes on Ted and Espinosa.

The director jerked his head toward the stage. "The vigilantes. Aiding and abetting."

Jack offered up a great belly laugh. "That guy," he said, tilting his head in Ted's direction, "is obsessed with the vigilantes. I'm telling you, those women on the stage are not the vigilantes. Therefore, I have not aided and abetted them." Out of the corner of his eye he saw two figures in police uniforms walking slowly down the dim hallway. Both of them were swinging their nightsticks. Five seconds later, two more cops walked toward one of the EXIT signs.

Jack decided it was in his best interest to pretend outrage. "I'm gonna get you for this, Robinson. You've been a pimple on my ass from the minute I got this assignment. I can't wait to see the egg on your face when those women walk off the stage." He was pleased to see the sudden worry in the reporter's eyes. Two more cops walked toward the EXIT sign. Jack thought he would black out with relief when the emergency door closed behind the last two cops. Almost home free. The key word being, "almost."

Onstage the real G-String Girls continued with their wild antics. The crowd was loving them. Jack looked toward the stage aware that all eyes backstage were on him. It would always be a mystery to him as to how the real G-String Girls could stay onstage for hours under the bright lights and not tire out. They all looked fresh as daisies. Maybe it had something to do with the adoration from the screaming crowd. He was getting tired just watching them perform.

Where the hell was Harry? No sooner had the thought popped into his mind when he felt a hand on his shoulder.

"We're under arrest," Jack told him.

"No shit! Can I ask why? Does our arrest have something to do with that crud Robinson?"

Jack shrugged. "It surely does, my friend. Just ask him," he said, pointing to Director Cummings. "Or him," he said, pointing to Ted Robinson. "In case you don't know it, Director, he's fucking nuts, okay? I'm going to be filing law suits out the kazoo, but before I do that, I'm going on Fox 5 and telling them all about this whack job." He pointed to Ted again and jabbed his finger right between his eyes. "I'm going to tell them loud and clear how you at the Bureau are wasting taxpayer dollars, mine in particular, so that asshole can get a byline. I'm naming names, too."

At the end of Jack's tirade, the director was the one who looked wary.

The set finished and the G-String Girls scampered off the stage. They were immediately surrounded by the director and the four special agents. Jack and Harry inched their way backward, their eyes never leaving Ted, who suddenly looked like the Devil was coming after him.

One of the girls snapped her fingers and one of her handlers was front and center. "Fetch our passports, Simon. There seems to be a question as to who we are."

Minutes later the director was perusing the passports, one after the other. He nodded and apologized profusely to the young women, who returned to the stage and the clamoring audience awaiting them.

"You'll be coming with us, Mr. Robinson. We also desire your company, Mr. Espinosa."

Jack let loose with an evil smile.

The director turned toward Jack and addressed him quietly. "There is the allegation that you and Wong here have joined forces with the vigilantes. I'm going to need to speak with you both also. The minute this concert is over, make your way to the Hoover Building, gentlemen. Don't make me send someone for you."

Jack simply shrugged but he did nod to show he understood.

Jack turned to Bert. "I thought that gold shield gave you carte blanche."

Bert rolled his eyes. "It does. I was told to cooperate and there wouldn't be any fall-out. I just do what I'm told. Are *they* okay?"

"Are they, Harry?"

"They got away clean. That storm is still going on. I don't know if they got off the ground or not. I haven't heard a thing in that regard."

Jack yanked out his phone and hit speed dial. Charles's voice came through, sweet and clear. "They're taxiing down the runway as we speak. They'll be airborne in five more seconds." Five seconds later, his voice boomed over optic cables. "And we have liftoff!"

Music drummed in Jack's ears. He felt like he was floating in space as he sagged against the wall. Harry reached out to grab one arm, Bert took the other. "They're airborne. We did it!" He closed his eyes and came back to Earth. "I'm getting way too old for this shit, boys."

Bert leaned back against the wall on Jack's left. Harry took up his position on the right. "Let's enjoy the concert, gentlemen. You want my opinion, the first group had it going on. These girls are slugs compared to the first crew."

The three of them high-fived each other as they roared with laughter.

The cell phone in Jack's pocket vibrated. He walked farther into the wings to take the call. Maggie Spritzer. "Yeah," he shouted.

"Jack...I..."

"What?"

"Jack...Jack..."

Jack's blood ran cold. Once before he'd had a phone call like this one. Only that time it had been Nikki, when she was going through her own personal meltdown.

"Yes, it's me, Jack. Where are you, Maggie?"

"Jack...I..."

"Maggie, where are you? Talk to me. I can make it right. Just tell me where you are."

"I'm...sitting on the side of the bathtub. I am so...Jack..."

"Are you at the *Post* apartment? Is that

where you are, Maggie? C'mon, c'mon, tell me where you are."

"I . . . Yes. Oh, Jack, I'm sorry."

"It's okay, Maggie. I'm coming to get you. Will you stay there till I get there?"

All Jack could hear on the other end of the phone were Maggie's sobs. "Keep the line open. I'm coming for you now. Just stay put."

Jack raced back to where Bert and Harry were standing. He shouted as loud as he could to be heard over the thunderous music. "Bert, you have to hold the fort. Harry and I have to get Maggie. I think she's in some serious trouble. You okay with that?"

"As long as you keep that promise you made to me."

"You got it."

Outside in the pouring rain, Jack explained Maggie's call. "It happened to Nikki when things got out of hand. We have to get to her before Ted and the Fibbies do."

Both men slid onto the motorcycle and roared their way past the drenched crowd.

"C'mon, is this as fast as you can go? Give it some juice, Harry!"

"Is she going to be okay?" Harry bellowed over his shoulder.

Jack thought about Nikki's ninety-day recovery. "Yeah, I think so. But you know Murphy's Law! What can go wrong, will go wrong. Goose this thing already, Harry. Don't forget we have an appointment with the Fibbies before this night is over."

Epilogue

Five days later
Big Pine Mountain

It was a beautiful, warm summer day with blue sky, a scattering of puffy white clouds and tubs of colorful flowers all about the rustic terrace, a picture postcard kind of day on top of Big Pine Mountain. Murphy and Grady played with tennis balls on the spiky green grass to the left of the terrace where the Ladies of Pinewood were having late-afternoon cocktails.

"It really is beautiful here," Kathryn said. "And it's not lost on me that this is Big Pine Mountain and we came from Pinewood in Virginia. I bet that means something but I'm not sure what it is. Of course, the states are different but it doesn't matter. We're back in the good old U.S. of A."

The women whooped and hollered as they clinked their glasses to toast their new residence, the beautiful surroundings and their safety.

"And we're getting company shortly," Nikki said happily. Meaning, of course, that Jack, Harry and Bert Navarro were going to come calling.

The women clinked their glasses again.

"Oh, here comes Charles and look what he has...newspapers! I can't wait to see our write-ups," Alexis said, her eyes on one of the gardeners whose muscles rippled as he circled the dogs on the power mower.

The girls poked one another at the way their sister was staring at the newest addition to the staff.

"He's hot!" Annie said. "I mean *hot!* I wish I was thirty years younger!"

"You know it. Know this, though. I would fight you for him," Alexis hissed. "Charles said he's ex-CIA. Something went awry and he was almost caught doing something covert. This is just a reprieve for him until his people can get him safely away. Maybe he'll stay."

"Ladies! Ladies! Time for business. I see you've all been celebrating and that's a good thing. You did well. So, let's get down to business before our guests come up on the cable car. It's all rather like Annie's sanctuary in Spain, is it not?" Charles asked, waving his arms about.

"We voted and we like this place better," Isabelle said as she poured a cocktail for Charles. "So what are the papers saying about us? I like seeing a paper as opposed to watching the news on television. But before you tell us that, is there any news on Maggie and Lizzie?"

"I have good news and I have sad news. The good news is that there has been no fallout from your visit to the nation's capital. Ted Robinson and his partner, Joseph Espinosa, are on unpaid leave from the *Post*. Jack told me after the meeting in Director Cummings's office that he, Jack, whispered in Ted's ear that you walked away right under his nose dressed as police officers. Jack said he could see the wheels turning in Ted's head, visualizing just how it all happened.

Not that he could do anything about it. But he is now more determined than ever to bring you all to justice. Jack said he needed to do that but vehemently denied saying it when Ted felt duty bound to announce that message to the director. Jack said the whole thing was quite amusing.

"The sad news is yesterday Justice Barnes tendered her resignation to the Supreme Court. She gave one interview to Maggie Spritzer. She said she wants to spend more time with her daughter and granddaughter. She said she's relocating back to her father's roots at the old Alabama homestead. She refused to discuss the breakup of her longtime relationship with Grant Conlon. She will have two helpers from here on in. Can anyone guess who those two helpers are? No? Maggie and Lizzie.

"So what that means to all of us is we've lost our second string back in McLean. Judge Easter can't operate on her own and Jack and Harry have to keep a low profile. Lizzie is giving up the practice of law to help Pearl. Pearl tells me that Lizzie said she's sick of defending criminals and wants to help women and children. You can't argue with that. She'll be a huge asset to Pearl, since Conlon is no longer in the picture, and, no, you don't need to know where he and Hughes are. All you need to know is neither man will ever bother Pearl again nor will either besmirch her reputation. She said to tell you she will be forever grateful for your intervention.

"Maggie had a bit of a meltdown but Jack got to her in time. A small matter of conflicting loyalties, which is understandable. Jack says she has her head on straight now. Any questions?"

"Well, I have one," Annie said. "What do the papers say about the first part of the concert?"

"The terms 'outrageous,' 'classy,' 'over-the-top' and 'awesome' were used freely in all the papers. There wasn't one word about melting latex. The girls raised a boatload of money for AIDS Relief."

Myra clapped her hands. "Then our mission was successful. What's on our agenda, darling?"

Charles straightened his shoulders, his expression serious. "A very frightening one, ladies. That's if you're up to it. It will

take at least six weeks of preparation on
my part if..."...

"What? What?" the women chorused
as one.

"The World Bank!"

"Oh, dear God," Myra said, fingering
her pearls. "Are we supposed to rob it?"

"Now, that's a caper if I ever heard one.
Count me in," Annie said exuberantly.

"No, not at all. It seems there's some
funny business going on with the funds.
Those funds are not being dispersed the
way they should be. You'll be special in-
vestigators. And then, of course, you'll do
what you do best, bring the culprits to justice. In your own way, of course."

The sound of the cable car rising from
the foot of the mountain sounded loud
and clear. Yoko, Kathryn and Nikki ran to
the platform but managed to call over their
shoulders. "Count me in!"

"I guess that's my cue to get to work.
Remember, Myra, we have a date later to
view the video."

Myra blushed a rosy hue. "I haven't forgotten, dear. I think perhaps you might re-
gret it later."

"On that note, I think I'm going to coax

the gardener to let me ride on his mower. See you all for dinner," Alexis said.

"Whatever shall we three do now?" Annie asked as she pointed to Isabelle and Myra.

"What we always do when we complete a successful mission, rest on our laurels," Myra said happily.